FERN
MICHAELS

EXCLUSIVE

KENSINGTON PUBLISHING CORP.
http://www.kensingtonbooks.com

KENSINGTON BOOKS are published by

Kensington Publishing Corp.
119 West 40th Street
New York, NY 10018

All Kensington titles, imprints and distributed lines are available at special quantity discounts for bulk purchases for sales promotion, premiums, fund-raising, educational or institutional use.

Special book excerpts or customized printings can also be created to fit specific needs. For details, write or phone the office of the Kensington Special Sales Manager: Kensington Publishing Corp., 119 West 40th Street, New York, NY, 10018. Attn. Special Sales Department. Phone: 1-800-221-2647.

ISBN-13: 978-0-7582-2720-1
ISBN-10: 0-7582-2720-5

First Hardcover Printing: April 2010
First Trade Paperback Printing: September 2010

10 9 8 7 6 5 4 3 2 1

Printed in the United States of America

EXCLUSIVE

Books by Fern Michaels:

Sins of the Flesh
Sins of Omission
Return to Sender
Mr. and Miss Anonymous
Up Close and Personal
Fool Me Once
Picture Perfect
About Face
The Future Scrolls
Kentucky Sunrise
Kentucky Heat
Kentucky Rich
Plain Jane
Charming Lily
What You Wish For
The Guest List
Listen to Your Heart
Celebration
Yesterday
Finders Keepers
Annie's Rainbow
Sara's Song
Vegas Sunrise
Vegas Heat
Vegas Rich
Whitefire
Wish List
Dear Emily

The Godmothers Series:

Exclusive
The Scoop

The Sisterhood Novels:

Game Over
Deadly Deals
Vanishing Act
Razor Sharp
Under the Radar
Final Justice
Collateral Damage
Fast Track
Hokus Pokus
Hide and Seek
Free Fall
Lethal Justice
Sweet Revenge
The Jury
Vendetta
Payback
Weekend Warriors

Anthologies:

Snow Angels
Silver Bells
Comfort and Joy
Sugar and Spice
Let it Snow
A Gift of Joy
Five Golden Rings
Deck the Halls
Jingle All the Way

EXCLUSIVE

Prologue

Teresa Amelia Loudenberry, "Toots" to her dearest friends, clutched the Egyptian bedsheets as though they were a life preserver. So tight was her grasp, her knuckles were as white as the sheet she was holding in a death grip. Bluish green veins stood out like small canals against her otherwise unblemished hands. Tiny beads of perspiration formed on her pearly forehead before forming rivulets around the contours of her face and settling in a pool of auburn hair splayed across the pillow.

Toots bolted upright in her bed, startled awake by what felt like a flock of wild geese trapped inside her chest. Taking several deep breaths meant to calm her pounding heart, she ran a hand along the unfamiliar sheets, touched the heap of silken covers tossed aside, then opened her eyes as wide as she could, trying to familiarize herself with her surroundings. As she looked around her, she detected several shadowlike images skirting the edge of the bed, cloudlike puffs colored an eerie, translucent blue. Toots counted four. Four clouds clustered around her bed. She could swear that inside each cloud were faces, faces she seemed to recognize but to which she couldn't quite put names. Her heart hammered faster, and her hands trembled like the last dry leaves on a barren winter limb. Feeling light-headed and disoriented, Toots squeezed her eyes shut, trying to assure herself that she was in the grip of a crazy dream.

But her skin still felt clammy, her heart continued to beat at a faster-than-normal pace, and she knew she was forcing her eyes to remain shut. No, this definitely was not a dream.

Slowly, she opened one eye, then the other. The mist, or fog, or whatever the hell she'd seen, was gone, but she could feel a coolness lingering around the bed. Toots snapped the bedside light on and looked at the clock.

Three o'clock in the morning. Hadn't she heard somewhere this was the witching hour? Probably one of those silly ghost programs Sophie had recently become obsessed with. Whatever, Toots knew enough to know that something supernatural had awakened her from a sound sleep. A ghost, an apparition, something not of this world lingered in the room, sending a prickling sensation up her spine. Frightened and shaky, she climbed out of bed, remaining alert and uneasy as she paced the unfamiliar room.

Walking back and forth while trying to ease her nerves, Toots allowed her eyes to dart around the garishly decorated room she now called her own. When she thought of all the remodeling ahead, she almost wished she'd kept her bungalow at the Beverly Hills Hotel until the work was completed. Who in their right mind could live, let alone sleep, in this purple-and-hot-pink hooker haven? Toots glanced at the ceiling, expecting mirrors, black lights, the whole kit and caboodle, and was surprised once again when there was just a ceiling. She wondered what the original owners, Lucille Ball and Desi Arnaz, would think of their former home? No doubt they were spinning in their graves. The Realtor had explained that a former pop star had rented the house from the Ball/Arnaz estate and decided she would make the house her own while living there. Years ago, when Toots had toured Graceland, Elvis's home in Memphis, Tennessee, she had thought it tacky. Compared to this, however, Toots had to say that the King's old digs were sufficiently tasteful to be featured in *Architectural Digest*.

To be sure, the exterior of the Malibu beach house was in decent enough condition. The three-story house, each level of which had floor-to-ceiling windows giving access to magnificent views and jutted out toward the Pacific Ocean, had its attractions. White stucco, brick-red tile roof, several small balconies and decks scattered about each level; one was never without the extraordinary view. Mountaintop and beachfront, the best of both worlds, the Realtor had said. It was the interior design that turned Toots inside out. Hot pink and purple. Garish blues and greens in six bedrooms made it a disaster.

Toots had almost backed out of the purchase. However, she wasn't stupid. Three point eight million for mountaintop beachfront property, in Malibu no less, was a steal. She wrote out a check for the full amount, knowing it would probably cost her that much or more to remodel the inside.

And now here she was, scared half out of her mind. At the Beverly Hills Hotel, she'd had Elizabeth Taylor's bungalow. She left that for this nightmare? Maybe she really was out of her mind.

Taking a deep breath, Toots scanned the perimeter of the bed. Nothing unusual, nothing out of place. Maybe those puffs of clouds had been a crazy dream. Maybe, but something told her it was much more.

Toots had always believed in an afterlife, knew spirits or souls didn't always make it to the other side, but this? Transparent clouds floating around her room with faces inside them? Mouths forming words, but no sound? No, this definitely wasn't her image of lost spirits and souls; this was more like something right out of *The Twilight Zone*.

Having lived in Charleston, South Carolina, for more than twenty years, Toots was perfectly familiar with tales of hauntings and sightings of those long since passed. When she had first moved to Charleston, she'd actually gone on several ghost-walking tours and heard all the stories about hauntings that had supposedly taken place over the years. However, Toots had never had anything even resembling a supernatural experience.

Until now.

Upon her arrival in Los Angeles, she'd paid little attention to the tales of old theaters, movie studios, and historic homes being haunted by some of Hollywood's greatest actors and actresses. This was Hollywood, the land of dreams, not nightmares!

When Toots decided to purchase a home in order to be close to Abby and run *The Informer*, the tabloid paper she had recently acquired, she hadn't intended on sharing her space with a spirit—or spirits.

"Go back to wherever the hell you came from!" Toots shouted in the dimly lit room. She heard the false bravado in her words and hoped that Sophie, who was sleeping in the room across the hall, hadn't heard her. Thank goodness Ida and Mavis were upstairs. Toots could only imagine what her old friends would say if she thought something otherworldly had entered her room.

Hell, what was she thinking? Sophie's newfound interest in paranormal activity, Toots decided, had just earned her the master suite.

Deciding that a room change was in order first thing in the morning, Toots climbed back into bed, wondering how she was going to convince Sophie to switch rooms without alerting her of her suspicions, then decided she couldn't. This was too scary to keep to herself.

Toots almost wished she'd gone ahead with the purchase of Aaron Spelling's mansion. Wanting and actually purchasing the 56,000-square-foot mansion had been an ordeal she hadn't anticipated. The widow of the former television mogul made it very clear to the Realtor that she must be present to examine any prospective buyer. Of course, not just anyone was allowed to bid. First requirement was an income check. Then came the real fun.

Toots simply could not believe what she was doing. Never in a zillion years had she stooped so low just to become eligible to view a piece of real estate. So what if it had belonged to former television mogul Aaron Spelling? A house was a house as far as she was concerned, or in this case a mansion was a mansion was a palace. Anything could be had for the right price, Toots believed, but this?

She looked at the three other prospective buyers seated in the Realtor's office. Two women and one man. Toots was positive the man was gay. He wore a silk leopard-print shirt with tight black slacks. Gold rings encircled all the fingers on both hands. Toots guessed that his ears had at least eight piercings. Gold hoop earrings sized according to position, from small to large, hung from his ears. More gold bangles around his wrists and an ankle bracelet wrapped around a pale, skinny ankle. His face was all but hidden behind a giant pair of sunglasses. Toots wondered who he was but decided she really didn't give a good shit.

Then she scanned the woman to her right. Though she was not 100 percent sure, she thought it might've been Joan Collins, minus the mountain of makeup. She sneaked another peek when the woman wasn't looking. Yes, it was her all right, and Toots saw recent scarring by her ears. Plastic surgery, no doubt, possibly the reason she wore no makeup. She'd mention this to Abby; maybe she could use this information for some tidbit of gossip in *The Informer*.

The woman seated to her left was staring straight ahead. She hadn't moved a muscle since arriving. Toots had the sudden urge to poke her in the side just to see if she would get a reaction but decided against it simply because it wouldn't seem very ladylike. Just the visual was enough to make her smile.

The real estate agent, a slim brunette who looked as though she could be anywhere between thirty and fifty, finally opened the door to her office. "Ms. Loudenberry, Mrs. Spelling and Madison will see you now."

Toots stood, smoothed her black pencil skirt. "Madison?"

"Mrs. Spelling's dog."

"I see," Toots said as she trailed behind the Realtor, even though she didn't see at all. What the hell did a dog have to do with selling one's home?

The real estate agent stopped and turned to Toots. "Mrs. Spelling prides herself on Madison's reaction to people. I might as well explain this to you now before you meet Mrs. Spelling. If her dog doesn't approve of you, then you won't be allowed to view her property."

Toots had the sudden urge to run, forget the whole thing, but she was so intrigued now that she couldn't force herself to walk away. A dog, huh? She gazed down at her black pencil skirt, black open-toed sandals, and cream-colored blouse, hoping Madison would approve. She laughed at the thought.

"If you will follow me," the real estate agent insisted.

Whatever happened to secretaries, Toots wondered?

She followed the woman down a long hallway, where she was greeted by a closed door. A low growl emanated from behind the door. "Please stand aside," the woman said. Toots did as instructed, expecting Madison to attack her any moment.

The woman opened the door to a plush modern office. Seated on a long white sofa to the left of the desk was the one and only Candy Spelling, widow of Aaron Spelling. Toots was instantly reminded of a guppy—plumped lips and bulging eyes. Toots wondered if the overly made-up widow had a thyroid problem. The mound of fur in her lap must be the infamous Madison.

The widow didn't bother to stand or offer a word of greeting. When Candy gave a hand command, Madison leaped from the widow's lap and stopped when he or she, Toots hadn't got that far as of yet, reached her feet. Toots was about to reach down and pet the dog when a "Stop!" came from the blonde on the sofa. "She can't be bribed!"

"Don't touch Madison," offered the real estate lady. "This is a quick process. If you'll just give her a few minutes."

So the cute little pooch was a female, a true honest-to-goodness bitch in every sense of the word. Toots knew how persnickety some females could be. Human females anyway.

The dog, a cute little bundle of white-and-tan fur, circled Toots three times, stopped at the position where she'd started, barked three times, squatted, then proceeded to leave a puddle of urine directly in front of Toots's shiny black sandals.

"You've just been given permission to enter the Spelling mansion," said the Realtor.

Among the amenities of the mansion were a bowling alley, a wine cellar, a beauty salon, and a humidity-controlled silver storage room. There was a rooftop rose garden, a library, tennis courts, and a theater. Anything one wanted, one could find at the Spelling mansion.

When Toots saw the conveyer belt in the main master bedroom, she'd immediately withdrawn her offer. The change of mind had cost her fifty thousand bucks, and for that she'd been pissed, but she refused to live in a house with a conveyer belt. It reminded her of that old *I Love Lucy* episode in which Lucy and Ethel worked in a chocolate factory, wrapping candy as it traveled down a conveyer belt. The enterprise turned out disastrously as the conveyer belt kept moving faster and faster, and the pair kept stuffing chocolates in their mouths, hats, and blouses in order to keep up. Toots visualized her bags and shoes flying through the air, then herself getting stabbed in the eye by a sharp stiletto as it flew off the conveyer belt, and decided that her eyeball was worth the fifty grand she'd lost.

Leaving the light on, she wiggled beneath the pile of covers, squeezing her eyes shut. Sensing that whatever had awakened her was no longer sharing the room with her, she relaxed, drifting into a state of half sleep, where dreams shifted so quickly that recalling them would be almost impossible.

Tomorrow was another day.

Chapter 1

"What the hell were you screaming about in the wee hours this morning? You just about scared the hell out of me," Sophie said, while Toots made coffee. "It was all I could do to get back to sleep. I thought you were being attacked."

Toots debated telling her what had happened but remembered Sophie's new enthusiasm for anything in the realm of the occult. She sniffed. "So much for rushing to my aid. I'd hate to depend on you for protection, but luckily for you it was . . ." Toots turned away from the counter and gave Sophie the evil eye, unsure whether or not to tell her about last night. When she saw no sign of amusement or mockery, she continued. "Don't laugh, but I swear I saw a . . . a ghost, or at least something ghostlike, hovering around my bed. It was like a cloud. Woke me out of a deep sleep. And the cold." Toots shivered at the memory. "I felt such a strange, cold sensation in my room—like I'd opened a window on a frosty morning. You know that instant gush of freezing air that smacks you square in the face?"

She let her words settle, waiting for Sophie to make some smart-ass remark. Or tell her she'd lost her mind. Or worse, that she needed to visit Dr. Sameer, whom Sophie had recently deemed a whack job since he'd started sending Ida prayer rugs after Ida's miracle cure from her obsessive-compulsive disorder.

Toots had been meaning to sit Ida down and have a real heart-to-heart talk, but ever since their move to Los Angeles, neither seemed to have a free minute for that kind of discussion. Toots added that to her lengthy shit-to-do list.

"Interesting." Sophie took a slow pull from the mug of coffee Toots placed in front of her. Toots kept both hands securely wrapped around her own cup as though it were a lifeline of sorts.

Toots made a big pretense of searching inside the tacky hot-pink cabinets. Using her thumbnail, she traced the purple grout that surrounded the lavender tiles on the countertops. She even went so far as to mutter a few jumbled words that she knew Sophie could barely hear, much less identify. She opened and closed drawers, pretending to search for something. She also added another item on her shit-to-do list. Never, ever, no matter what, buy the music of her new home's former tenant. Though she was lucky to have purchased the former estate of Lucille Ball and Desi Arnaz for what amounted to a song in California terms, it was costing her much more than a song to restore the estate to its former glory. However, with its endless view of the Pacific, the beach just steps away from her deck, and the convenience of living close to Abby, it was worth the aggravation and the remodeling expense.

"Cut the crap, Toots. I'm thinking, okay? And you know I can't think clearly when you're banging around drawers and doing all that mumbo-jumbo stuff."

Toots smiled. She liked it when Sophie had to think. "Don't think too hard, you might scare me," she added, just to have the last word.

Coffee spewed from Sophie's mouth, showering the table-top of white Formica with cream-colored dots. "Isn't that what this is all about? You're being such a wuss. I'm not even sure I believe you."

Toots turned around and reached for the pot of coffee. "Give me one good reason why I would lie about something so . . . crazy."

Sophie used her napkin to mop up the coffee she had splattered across the table. "You wouldn't; I was just saying that to get a rise out of you, which I did. Now I need to think, Toots. Seriously. I know you and the others consider my fascination with the supernatural abnormal. It's not, and I'm not the only one on the planet who believes that spirits, ghosts, whatever you want to call them, linger on in this world. There's a new television show about ghosts. You call them up, and they come to your house. Want me to give them a call?"

"Hell no! I don't need TV ghostbusters, Sophie. I just need to know that I'm not completely off my rocker. I could have Alzheimer's or a brain tumor! This isn't funny to me."

Just then Toots finally realized just how terrified she'd been last night. She hoped she wasn't losing her grip on reality, not now, when she was just starting to have some ass-kicking fun in her old age.

Sophie had the grace to appear remorseful. "I don't think it's funny either, Toots. Really. I've read a lot of stuff on the subject. It's scary, if you don't know what to expect or what to do. I've even read that some people resort to suicide while experiencing a haunting. There are a number of procedures you can do to remove a spirit. I need to decide which one is most appropriate. Come here." Sophie motioned for Toots to take the chair next to her. "Now tell me every single detail from start to finish, and don't leave anything out. You never know how important it may be."

Toots went into great detail as she retold the events that had left her shaken and so uncertain. She had always been solid, all nuts and bolts, hammer and nails, not prone to seeing whispery puffs of clouds and faces of the unknown. She'd always told herself she could deal with anything. Hell, she'd buried eight husbands. With that track record, she should've been able to fight off Satan himself. Fearful, she was not.

"So did you recognize their faces, could you make out what they were trying to tell you?"

Toots rolled her eyes. She couldn't quite believe she was having this conversation. "You know, I didn't think about total recall as I lay there scared half out of my mind. I guess I should've taken notes, maybe a picture or two. Seriously, Sophie, I was frightened. I know it sounds crazy. I know you're into this type of thing, but it's not something you want to experience, trust me on that. Why don't we change rooms? You can sleep with the spirits and fill me in on all the gory details."

Sophie lit a cigarette, handed it to Toots, then lit another for herself. "Yes, that's a good idea. I'll take notes, too. Something else. When a house is disturbed"—Sophie made finger quotes when she said the word *disturbed*—"it's possible, hell it's more than possible, it's highly probable that you've riled a few spirits who were content to live in this dump as is. You can thank that pop tart's overzealous publicist for the tip she gave you telling you this house was about to go on the market. I wonder if there is some kind of haunting clause, something along the lines of buyer's remorse."

Toots glanced over her shoulder to make sure Ida and Mavis weren't up and about. "I'm sure there isn't, and whatever you do, don't tell the girls. Or Abby. They'll insist I've lost my marbles. I want to keep this between the two of us. At least for now."

Sophie inhaled deeply. "I won't say anything. I wouldn't want to be responsible for causing Ida to get whacked out again. And Mavis, well, she's so full of herself now since she's lost all that weight, I'm not even sure I like her anymore."

Right after burying her eighth husband, Leland, who'd been a pompous, self-righteous ass, Toots had strictly adhered to her usual ten days of mourning, then tossed out her widow's garb for good. Wanting to add some excitement to her golden years, she'd immediately sent e-mails to Abby's godmothers, Sophie, Ida, and Mavis, her dearest friends of more than fifty years, inviting them to Charleston, where she'd lived for the past twenty years. They had all instantly accepted her invitation.

Ida lived in New York City, where she'd spent most of her adult life in three or four serial marriages. Toots had lost count. After her last husband, Thomas, had died from E. coli, she became obsessed with germs, rarely venturing into the world outside her penthouse apartment. Ida and her traveling circus of germ-fighting paraphernalia made the trip South. When Toots realized just how dire the situation was, she cajoled and threatened until Ida agreed that it was time to do something about her obsessive-compulsive disorder. It hadn't hurt that Toots had threatened Ida with following her to New York City and forcing her to ride in the dirtiest taxicab she could find. She'd also made a few other germ-related threats before Ida succumbed to the lure of being able to lead a normal life, or as normal a life as anyone associated with Teresa Amelia Loudenberry could lead.

Mavis, a retired English teacher living on the coast of Maine with her dog Coco and barely surviving on a small pension, had been thrilled when Toots invited her for a visit. Toots had been shocked when she saw her friend emerge from the plane. Mavis had gained more than a hundred pounds since their last visit at Abby's college graduation. Fearful for her friend's health, Toots knew immediately that she had her work cut out for her.

And then there was Sophie. Toots had been closer to Sophie than any of the others, but she'd never tell them that. Sophie was tough, strong, and street-smart. Or so she wanted the world to believe. But Toots knew better. She'd seen Sophie at her lowest point in life. Living with her husband, Walter, whom she'd married when he was an up-and-coming Manhattan banker, Sophie had endured years of abuse at his hands while he spent life with bottles of booze as his only friends. He'd finally died while Sophie was in California. Toots helped arrange a quick funeral, or *event,* as she now called funerals, and Sophie was happier than she'd ever been.

Making no bones about how she felt about it, Toots assured Sophie that she fully agreed with her that Walter's dying alone was well deserved. Toots prayed that he was roasting in the fires of hell for all that he'd put Sophie through.

Sophie had, in fact, been looking forward to Walter's dying for a long time. Since her Catholic upbringing made it impossible to walk out on Walter, however badly he treated her, she had spent more than thirty years working as a pediatric nurse to support a man who did nothing but drink and smack her around whenever he chose. Poor Sophie.

Well, actually, rich Sophie. Knowing she couldn't plan on spending her golden years with a loving and caring husband, she was not at all unhappy when the nonfunctional, alcoholic partner she had married years before was diagnosed with cirrhosis of the liver. Luckily, she'd had the foresight to continue to pay the monthly premiums on a five-million-dollar life insurance policy. Now that Walter had finally departed for wherever he would land, Sophie was a rich woman, finally able to enjoy life without fear of getting the snot beaten out of her. And her passion just happened to be anything paranormal.

"For shame, Sophie. Mavis has worked her tail off, quite literally I might add, and you should support and encourage her."

Sophie stubbed out one cigarette and immediately fired up another. She took a deep drag before she said, "I *am* proud of her, Toots. You of all people should know that. I'm just tired of watching her admiring what's left of her ass when she walks past a window, a mirror, anything that shows a reflection."

Toots laughed. "Lately I've noticed her doing that, too, but you have to realize how hard she's worked to lose all that weight. Six months ago, I feared she was nothing more than a heart attack waiting to happen. Now I suddenly find myself wanting to ask her for fashion advice."

Sophie grinned. "Yeah, that stylist you hired for her didn't hurt either. Mavis is a quick one; it's no wonder she's advising the rest of us on what not to wear."

Toots eyed Sophie up and down. "You might want to take her advice."

Sophie wore a pair of fading purple baggy sweatpants with what once had been a bright pink UCLA sweatshirt. "What's wrong with my outfit? It's the thing to wear out here. I found these in the back of the closet in my room."

"And I'm sure they belonged to that pop star who lived here, too. So what does that tell you?"

Sophie looked down at her baggy, fading sweats. "Pink and purple aren't my colors?"

Toots couldn't help but laugh. "Seriously, I don't care what you wear, but I would change into something else before I went out in public."

Sophie chuckled. "Probably a good idea. Now let's get back to the problem at hand. You think you're seeing ghosts or spirits in your room. I want to spend a few nights alone in the room before I make my decision on what ceremony I want to perform."

Chapter 2

If Toots rolled her eyes any more, she felt sure they would get stuck in a cross-eyed position or worse, one eye viewing east and the other west. She forced herself to stare straight ahead at the horrific pink wall. The remodeling couldn't begin soon enough. If she had to look at these walls much longer, she would go bonkers.

"You haven't heard a word I've said," Sophie said, loudly enough to break through Toots's preoccupation with things ocular.

"Yes, I have. I'm just mesmerized by these walls. They need to go, and the sooner the better. Remind me to toss everything I own that's pink, or even close. Purple, too."

Sophie grabbed the pot of coffee and refilled both of their cups. Toots dumped at least a quarter of a cup of sugar in hers before taking a sip.

"That's disgusting, Toots."

Before she could roll her eyes upward, Toots stopped as a mental image of her wearing inch-thick glasses flashed before her. She glared at Sophie. "I like sugar, so what? It could be worse. I could smoke cigars." Toots reached for her pack of Marlboros. She planned to quit someday. Maybe. At her age, she wasn't sure it mattered. Even with her sugar addiction and chain-smoking, she'd suffered no ill effects.

So far, she'd been lucky. No diabetes, no lung cancer, no emphysema. Maybe she should write a book about the virtues of living a life filled with bad habits and rich husbands.

Sophie offered up her usual smirk. "Someday we're gonna be old, or at least feel old. Then we'll both wish we'd lived healthier lives."

Toots examined her friend closely. To be so morose wasn't like her. "What is it with you this morning?"

Sophie pushed her chair away from Toots. "You don't have to get in my face. For Pete's sake, there is nothing wrong with *me*! You're the one who's seeing ghosts floating around in your bedroom. And I will never understand in a million years why you bought this dump. It's beyond ugly. Hell, it was ugly when it was new. I pity the poor jerk who has to make this place livable."

"I would be 'that poor jerk,' I'll have you know. You don't have to live here, smart-ass. Last time I heard, you had a few million tucked away. Go buy your own damned house." Toots smiled wickedly when she saw that Sophie was about to bust a gut at her outburst.

"You're a real bitch, Toots, you know it?"

"You'd best remember it, too," Toots added affectionately. "And for your information, this *dump* cost me three-point-eight million dollars, and that was a bargain-basement price."

"Then I say someone got screwed."

Toots eyed the pink-and-purple kitchen, the white Formica kitchen furniture, and knew she and whatever contractor she hired were facing an uphill battle. If she'd been really smart, she would have consulted with the HGTV crew. It was going to take time and more money than she'd originally planned, but when she looked out at the view, she decided that it would be worth every penny.

Today the beach was empty of the usual crowds, the view

of the Pacific endless, the sky a clear robin's-egg blue, and the smog a distant memory. This view and being close to Abby was worth every single penny of the $3.8 million and a lot more, which it was obviously going to take to make the house inhabitable by ordinary humans, not pop tarts.

"So what's your suggestion?"

"Sell it and buy a condo?" Sophie replied in the blink of an eye.

"You know I won't do that. I don't mind the remodeling, it's the other that I'm . . . not so comfortable with."

Sophie took a deep breath, crushed out her cigarette, and lit another. "Yeah, okay. We'll start by switching rooms. Tell Ida and Mavis the mattress hurts your back if they ask, though I doubt they'll even question it. They're too involved in their own lives right now to notice either of us."

Toots considered this. "I agree. Ida and our good Dr. Sameer can't seem to get enough of each other's company. When she's not on the phone with him, she has an appointment at his office. Something is going on between the two of them, I'm sure. He sent another prayer rug yesterday, too. And Mavis is either jogging with Coco or designing her next outfit. It's hard to believe how much the two of them have grown in the past six months."

"Mavis has shrunk, remember? Okay, okay, I know what you mean. It's Ida who worries me, though. She and that doctor spend too much time together, if you ask me. I know they're more than just friends. Ida keeps telling me that, but I don't believe it for one minute." Lowering her voice and looking around, Sophie continued, "She simply cannot be without a man."

Since the fire at *The Informer*, Toots had been so involved in its cleanup and rebuilding, getting the paper ready for production without revealing to Abby that it was she who'd purchased the failing rag—not to mention the time she'd spent searching for the perfect home—that she'd hardly given much thought to Mavis's and Ida's activities. "I think we all need to have a sit-down to catch up with one another before something happens."

"What do you suppose will happen, Toots? Think one of us might get laid? I'd bet my last dollar Ida and the good doctor are doing the dirty." Sophie laughed when she saw the look of disgust on Toots's face.

"Your mind is always in the gutter, Sophie. I swear, you haven't changed since seventh grade. I can't recall a single conversation in which sex didn't pop up at some point."

"*Pop up?* Is that a Freudian slip, Toots? Or sheer coincidence?" Sophie teased.

Toots huffed. "See? You find a sex connection in everything I say. Seriously, what are we going to do about my . . . *visitors?* I want them, it, whatever, out of here. Or I'm going to commit myself to the nearest nuthouse. Tell me what one does, Sophie. How do you go about ridding your home of a ghostly presence?"

Toots poured the rest of the brown sludge in her cup, then added a large splash of milk and more sugar. "Want more? I'll make another pot real quick."

Sophie shook her head. "Let's go sit out on the deck, in case the girls come downstairs and creep up on us. I just don't trust Ida, although I don't quite know why." She fretted. "She's always been such a damn sneak. I wouldn't put it past her to try and sell your ghost story to *The Enquirer* or *The Globe.*"

Grabbing her cup, Toots laughed and followed Sophie onto the deck. Even though it was summer in Southern California, the early-morning air held a chill. Sophie motioned her over to a pair of weathered deck chairs. Toots saw an old iron table with a glass top jammed in the corner of the deck, dragged it over by the two chairs, and placed it between them. Sophie snatched the shell they'd been using as an ashtray and set it on the small table before removing her cigarettes and lighter from the pocket of her sweats. As was becoming the norm, she lit up for the both of them.

"Okay, you want to know about ghosts," Sophie said matter-of-factly, as though they were discussing what they would have for breakfast. "I've been interested in the paranormal for as far back as I can remember."

Toots cast her an odd look.

"It wasn't something I talked about. Back in our day we would've been tarred and feathered for even thinking about this stuff, let alone believing it. I used to visit a lady in Queens, she called herself Madam Butterfly, if you can believe that. Everything was butterflies with her. Jewelry, clothes, even her damned wallpaper was butterflies all over. She read tarot cards for me once a week after I married Walter. She warned me about him, too. Said he was bad for me, but I was young and in lust and wouldn't listen to her." Sophie paused. "I wonder how my life would've turned out had I taken her advice? Oh well, too late for that."

Toots interrupted. "Get to the point, Soph."

"I'm explaining how I became interested in this stuff. I started reading astrology charts and doing my own little tarot readings on the side. Oh, nothing for the public, just for myself and a couple of girls at the hospital. Never made much of a big deal out of it. It was all in fun anyway. Sure helped me get through some rough times with that son of a bitch I married. I just want you to know that this isn't a new hobby, in case you're wondering."

Toots couldn't help but roll her eyes. "I think we've discussed your interest enough. Just tell me what I need to do, Soph. You can't imagine just how weird I feel in that room. When I put my robe on this morning, I kept looking around to see if anyone was watching me."

"Once I'm settled in the room, I'll know more. For starters, I'll have to make sure there really is a presence there."

With a trace of impatience Toots asked, "And how will you do that?"

"It's just something I'll know. I'll set up my voice recorder and video for backup, but if there's truly a ghost hanging around this dump, I'll know. Once I determine if it's—shit, this sounds dumb even to me—once I determine if it's a *friendly* ghost, then I can do a number of things. For starters, there's the shoes remedy, and it's pretty safe."

"Shoes? You're going to rid this place of its ghosts or whatever the hell it is with a pair of shoes? Puh-leeze, Sophie. Even I'm not that gullible."

Sophie stubbed out her cigarette. "I know it sounds like a crock, but just hear me out."

Toots gazed out at the beach, where the white foamy waves were gently reaching the shoreline. In and out, constant, always predictable. She liked knowing what was happening around her, liked knowing, or at least being able to make a pretty good guess, what each day would bring. After last night's scare, Toots was sure of one thing—she really did not like the unknown or the unpredictable. No, she liked and needed good, hard facts. But something told her that there would be very few of those available in what she was about to hear.

Resigning herself to listening to Sophie's shoe theory, she motioned with her hand. "Go on, tell me about the shoe stuff."

Sophie lit another cigarette; Toots was sure she'd smoked at least half a pack already. Then she, too, reached for one and lit up alongside her.

With the surf as background noise, the occasional seagull cawing with bursts of laughter from an unseen group on the stretch of beach below them, Sophie sat on the edge of her deck chair and explained herself. "I'm not sure of its origins, but somewhere I recall reading about the shoe theory. It's said when you go to bed at night, the person seeing or feeling the presence of a ghost—and in this case that would be you—is supposed to place the shoes you'll be wearing the next day at the foot of your bed. You then point one shoe in one direction and its mate in the opposite direction. This is said to confuse the ghosts. After a few nights of discombobulation, the ghosts leave."

Toots glared at her in disbelief. "That's it? Please tell me you're joking."

Sophie instantly appeared deflated at Toots's reaction, collapsing in on herself like a balloon that had lost its air. "What do you mean, joking? You asked me to tell you about the shoe theory, and that's what I did. It's not rocket science, Toots. It's not something you major in physics at Harvard, Yale, or Caltech to learn. Don't look so damned disappointed."

"Guess I was expecting something more . . . I don't know, concrete. I haven't dealt with this type of . . . bullshit before."

"Most people haven't and never will, Toots. This isn't the everyday normal stuff that we're used to. Why do you think it's so difficult for the average person to believe?"

Toots agreed that she had a point. Still, in broad daylight, with the ocean stretched out before her and a warm breeze blowing tendrils of hair loose from her topknot, it was hard to adjust to the fact that they were discussing ghosts and ways to get rid of them.

"Sophie, if word of this gets out, I could be in real trouble. What if someone at *The Informer* learns my identity, then discovers I'm seeing ghosts? This would not help Abby or the paper. In fact, it's this kind of story that could sink us."

"What in the hell would make you think the paper could

even find anything out about this? It's not like I'm going to start running off at the mouth. Ida does enough of that for all of us."

"Sophie, you should be ashamed of yourself. She doesn't wag her tongue that much, but don't you see, that's just it? We can't afford to let anyone, and I mean absolutely anyone, find this out. Whatever you do, we have to keep this between us."

Sophie held up her hand to stop further conversation. "Remember, Toots, I can keep a secret."

Toots nodded. How could she ever doubt Sophie? She'd kept Walter's abuse hidden from her for years. Toots trusted Sophie as much as she trusted herself. This craziness would stay between the two of them.

"I know you can, Soph. Now that that's settled, you want to share another ghostbusting theory with me? I am not spending another night in that god-awful purple room. I'll go back to the Beverly Hills Hotel first."

Sophie laughed, her brown eyes sparkling with mischief. "Of course you will. Now, tell me. What do you know about electronic voice phenomena?"

Chapter 3

Abby Simpson gazed around her newly remodeled office, which had once belonged to Rodwell Archibald Godfrey III, her former boss and editor in chief of *The Informer*. Known as Rag to most of his employees, he'd made headlines himself when he'd disappeared several months ago. Days after he'd gone missing, she'd searched his house, called a few old girlfriends, and come up empty-handed. Rag was famous for pulling weekenders in Vegas and not showing up on Mondays, but Abby knew this was more than just your average recovery from a weekend binge. Concerned because it was unlike her boss just to up and vanish—he usually had the decency to at least call or send an e-mail—Abby reported him missing to the authorities, after which all hell had broken loose. *The Informer*, a third-rate tabloid with its offices housed in the former building of *The Examiner*, the building in which William Randolph Hearst had printed his first paper, had been set afire by Michael Constantine, a local lowlife with mob connections who'd been searching for Rag since he'd skipped town. Apparently her former boss had ripped Constantine off for fifty grand. Constantine was spotted leaving the scene of the fire and was caught and arrested within hours.

The paper had to close for a few weeks in order to undergo cleanup and remodeling. Abby, along with a skeleton staff, had used her garage as a temporary office. Rag was still on the loose, with the authorities on his trail. It was thought he'd embezzled $10 million from the new owners of *The Informer,* who wished to remain anonymous. Abby had used every source she had, and still she hadn't been able to learn the new owners' identity. She told herself it didn't matter. Whoever they were, they had not only doubled her salary but also appointed her temporary editor in chief. Though not out pounding the pavement for celebrity news, she still made a point to remain in touch with all of her sources. She wasn't giving up tabloid reporting completely. If a story jumped out at her, something exclusive, she would write it, no matter what her position at the paper. Maybe when the new owners decided to come out of hiding, she would jump back into the swing of things full-time, but for now she had a third-rate tabloid to run, and she was a person who took her responsibilities very seriously.

Rag's old office had consisted of a metal desk with an equally tacky lump-filled chair and an outdated computer. Several portable black-and-white television sets had been shelved on the wall opposite his desk. Most were always tuned to E!, Fox News, or CNN. With the fire damage, everything in his office had been destroyed. Apparently the new owners had deep pockets. Abby learned that during the remodeling she was to update all of the offices with nothing but the best. Abby had done her best, and with the help of a professional office decorator, Rag's office—*her* office now—was sleek and efficient, equipped with every high-tech gizmo on the market.

The seventies-style brown paneling had been replaced with modern white walls. The wall that formerly held the old plywood bookshelves now featured custom-made shelves from which six LCD flat-screen televisions glared at her. A giant flat-screen monitor provided constant updates from the Associated Press, even though it was rare that she actually used the information coming through. But one never knew.

A custom-made desk sat in the middle of the room. On top were three iMac computers, all top-of-the-line. One came equipped with high-speed Internet, the second gave her instant access to stories in progress at *The Informer*, and the third was hers to use as needed.

Though it was old and shabby, Abby had insisted on bringing the old blue Barcalounger from her former office across the hall. She was thankful it hadn't burned during the fire, grateful a good cleaning was all it had needed since Chester, her ninety-seven-pound German shepherd, had practically grown up in that chair. Come hell or high water, she wasn't about to part with it. Abby felt sure that Chester wouldn't appreciate a replacement either.

With Chester sleeping in his chair, Abby checked her e-mail to see if she'd been one-upped on any breaking news. She skimmed through a dozen messages and, seeing nothing earth-shattering, checked the Associated Press wire. Again, she came up empty as far as tabloid news went. Then she used the master remote control to flick through all of the local TV stations. Apparently it was going to be a slow news day. Abby hated days like that, wished she could zap up some headline-making news herself. If only. Deciding there was nothing that required her immediate attention, she read through tomorrow's copy one last time before it went to press. Half an hour later, she figured it was as good as it was going to get and decided that she and Chester were due for a quick break.

"You ready for a trip outside, Chester?"

At the sound of his name, the big dog sprang into action. "Woof, woof!"

Abby laughed. What would she do without Chester? He was her best friend in the world, at least he was her best *male* friend in the world. She didn't want to think about men right now because doing so brought Chris Clay to mind, and she absolutely, positively did not want to have thoughts about him. Her brow furrowed in disgust as she followed Chester to the exit.

"Woof!" Chester held the leash in his mouth as though he were walking himself. Abby always got a kick out of this. He was such a smart animal. When she was working a story, she'd always taken him with her. He was her very own second-stringer/doggy guard.

Abby led Chester to the fenced-in parking lot, still amazed every time she walked outside. With its lighting at night, plus security cameras, Abby felt very safe there now. Before the fire, anyone could walk in and out of the back door leading to the offices. No more. The new owners had hired a well-trained security crew that worked around the clock. Abby guessed they weren't taking any chances on their investment. She and her staff were very well protected. No crazy-ass wannabe arsonist or anyone else who wasn't authorized could get past the tight security. The building was very old, and Abby truly respected its history, but she was smart enough to realize some things simply had to be brought into the twenty-first century.

The new owners had insisted on keeping the original printing presses downstairs and asked that they remain untouched. Abby didn't know what their future plans were, but that was fine by her, since she rarely went downstairs anyway. The last time she'd been downstairs, she'd given her mother and godmothers a tour. That was right before the fire.

After Chester personally anointed each and every newly planted shrub, he ran back to the entrance. "Okay, boy, let's get back to work." Abby bent down to allow Chester a doggy kiss, then headed inside to her office.

As soon as Abby returned to her desk, Chester jumped on his chair, and she sat in her own plush leather chair behind her sleek onyx desk. With news so slow, Abby logged on to her e-mail account and what she read about blew her away. She read it a second time, then a third time. No frigging way! Tabloids and legitimate magazines across the country were offering millions for this story. She instantly became suspicious. Was it possible that Rag, wherever the hell he was, was screwing with her? This seemed like something he would do, but Abby wasn't sure he'd go this far just to mess with her.

She was being offered an exclusive interview, *with pictures*, of Brad Pitt and Angelina Jolie's new kids!

Why *The Informer*? Why not *People* magazine, or *Time*. They'd offered millions for a story and pictures in the past and the couple had turned them down. Abby read the e-mail again. It was from their publicist. She recognized the name, so at least that part was true.

An interview like this could put *The Informer* back on the map. What *back* on the map? Shit, it hadn't even *been* on the map, but with this, it would be all the push Abby would need to put it on top and keep it there.

"Chester, we just hit pay dirt!"

"Woof," Chester responded to his name.

Abby swore he was part human. "We'll stop at Ralph's on the way home for a big juicy steak."

"Woof, woof!"

Abby laughed because she was 100 percent sure that Chester knew Ralph's was a popular grocery store in California. He must associate the name with beef.

For the fourth time, Abby read the e-mail from the Pitt/Jolie publicist. They were offering an interview *with pictures*—that was the part Abby found difficult to believe, because most of Hollywood's biggest stars usually wouldn't allow photos of their offspring unless millions were being offered. Something didn't seem quite right, but then again, Pitt and Jolie were well-known for their charitable acts, so it was highly possible this was just another act of charity. She hoped so, because there was no way *The Informer* could pay for such an exclusive. *If* the e-mail proved to be for real, Abby had her work cut out for her. She'd need an absolutely first-rate photographer. For some crazy reason, she thought of Ida, her godmother. In her day, Ida had worked as a photographer in New York City. Abby had seen some of her work, and it was fantastic. Maybe . . . no, she couldn't. Her mother would kill her if she asked for Ida's help and not hers. Certainly something to think about. She made a note to ask anyway. It couldn't hurt. The photographers currently employed at *The Informer* were just so-so. Too bad she didn't know the new owners. She could have asked them for a top-notch photographer. Abby felt sure they would have fit such a request into their budget, but for the moment there were other details to attend to.

Annoyed by the distraction, Abby clicked off the television set. Something was nagging at her, something she couldn't quite put a finger on. Was it possible the new owners had arranged for this interview? Were their connections that great? She thought it odd that she'd been contacted by e-mail. Wouldn't a publicist for such an A-list couple at least call her up and ask? No, something wasn't right, but until something changed, she planned to act as though a major scoop were an everyday occurrence at the paper.

A simple interview with your average B-list celebrity would be as easy as scheduling a luncheon at one of LA's

top eateries, or, if they wanted to show off a newly purchased McMansion, Abby would simply hop into her bright
yellow MINI Cooper. Of course, she assumed that Chester
would be welcome as well—she routinely brought him along
unless the celebrity specifically said not to. Chester was
not just any ordinary dog. If something were to go awry—
and with some of the celebrities she'd interviewed it had
been iffy, almost scary—Chester would act as her protec-
tor as well. Something told her that Chester wouldn't be
allowed to attend this interview.

Abby knew an exclusive interview with the Pitt/Jolie
clan would be anything but simple. First, there would be
security. Not just some off-duty cop looking to earn an
extra few bucks to send his kid to college. No, the security
for the Pitt/Jolie interview would be equal to that of the
president of the United States. She scribbled a note to herself to make sure and ask about security arrangements
when she responded to the publicist's e-mail.

Abby knew the interview would not come without strings,
but she couldn't seem to stop wondering what they were
and why Pitt and Jolie had chosen *The Informer*. She was
smart enough to know not to look a gift horse in the
mouth, so her first order to herself was to stop questioning
why and begin her preparations.

Abby clicked on the e-mail from the publicist and read
through it one last time before she answered.

Dear Ms. Simpson:

Your publication, *The Informer,* has been chosen for
an interview with Mr. Brad Pitt and Ms. Angelina Jolie.
Photos of the children will be allowed.

The e-mail named the date, though no location was in-
dicated. All she needed to do was reply.

Dear Ms. . . .

The Informer accepts your offer to interview Mr. Pitt and Ms. Jolie. I will await further instructions concerning the location and security.

Ms. Abby Simpson

There. She hit the SEND button, and the rest was up to fate and the publicist. She wanted to tell someone but was afraid if she did, she would jinx the interview. No, she decided she would go about her day just as she ordinarily did. As it was a slow news day, she decided to place a call to Ida, feel her out, see how she was doing. Just in case.

Abby dialed Ida's new cell number. She was about to hang up when the phone was picked up, and she heard a breathless "hello."

"Ida, are you okay? You sound terribly out of breath." Abby heard a male voice and what sounded like the rustle of covers. "Are you alone?"

"Oh . . . Good morning, Abby. It's wonderful to hear from you. Of course I'm alone. I was . . . running around the room, making the bed. I have the television turned on to this new soap I've become addicted to. I wouldn't dare leave the bed unmade, you know how your mother likes a neat and orderly home."

"And you don't, huh?" Abby laughed, recalling her godmother's former affliction with obsessive-compulsive disorder.

"Not anymore. If it were left up to me, I'd never change the sheets." Ida laughed.

"And we both know that's not true." It was good to hear the happiness back in Ida's voice. A few months ago she would barely come out of her room without spending hours scrubbing her hands and every object she touched.

Now, with the help of Dr. Sameer, a specialist in treating obsessive-compulsive disorder, Ida sounded and acted like the godmother Abby had always known and loved.

"Then let's just say I only change them once a week and leave it at that," Ida teased. "Abby, would you hang on for a minute?"

"Sure."

Ida must have forgotten to place her hand over the phone's mouthpiece, because Abby could've sworn she heard muffled giggling and lips smacking in the background. Must be standing next to the television set, where the soap stars were going at it hot and heavy. Abby thought nothing was left to the imagination anymore.

A minute later, a winded Ida was back on the phone. "Sorry. I just wanted to get that bed in tiptop shape. Now what is my favorite godchild up to these days?"

"In search of the next big story as usual. There isn't much happening in Hollywood today."

"Why don't you just make something up? Isn't that what all those tabloid papers do anyway?"

Abby laughed. "Yeah, some of them do, but that's not my way. I'd like to think there is some truth to the stories I write."

Abby paused, deciding whether or not she should tell Ida about the Pitt/Jolie interview and her need for a photographer. She realized it couldn't hurt anything. Also, she would call her mother as soon as she finished telling Ida; it wasn't like she was betraying anyone's confidence. She knew she could trust Ida; she'd never failed her yet.

With a trace of the mischievous in her voice, Abby said, "You'll never guess who I'm going to interview."

"You're right, I won't, so don't keep me in suspense. Just tell me," Ida singsonged.

Abby wasn't going to let her off that easy. "I've changed my mind. I don't think you would care anyway. Mom loves the tabloid news much more than you do." A grin as wide as the Cheshire cat's spread across her face. She could just imagine the look of utter shock on Ida's face. Abby had been a terrible tease throughout her life with sweet, gullible Ida.

"If that's the way you feel, fine. I do have things to do, Abby. I don't have time for this chitchat game today."

Dear old Ida was getting a bit snippy in her old age. Abby laughed. "Oh shit, I can't do that to you anymore, can I? I'm too old for the game anyway. So"—Abby paused— "do you really want to know who I'm going to interview, or would you just rather I tell Mom instead? As a matter of fact, call her to the phone now, and I'll tell her myself."

"No, you can't do that!"

"Oh, yes, I can," Abby teased.

"No, you cannot, Abby. Please whatever you do, *do not* call your mother," Ida stated adamantly.

"Why not? Is there something that you're not telling me?" Suddenly concerned about her mother, Abby realized she'd spoken more harshly than she'd intended. "Sorry, Ida, but if there is something going on, I have a right to know. I talked to my mother yesterday, and everything was just hunky-dory. Spit it out."

"Oh, you sound just like Sophie."

Abby couldn't help but smile. Sophie and Ida were complete opposites. Prim and proper Ida always the lady while Sophie was her polar opposite. She said what she thought and usually she wasn't one to mince words. No, if something were seriously wrong with Abby's mother, Ida would've told her. Hell, all of her godmothers would've called her by now. This was Ida being Ida, the noted drama queen.

"I guess I deserved that, but seriously, if there is something going on that I need to know, I want you to tell me now, or I'll get in my car right this minute and drive over there to see for myself." Abby saw Chester's ears spike at the word *car*. Alert, he sat up in his chair and waited patiently to see if they would be going anywhere.

"If you must know, I am not at your mother's house," Ida offered reluctantly. Abby had to strain to hear her words.

Instantly alarmed, Abby asked, "*What?* Then where are you? Are you okay? You're not in any trouble, are you?" She couldn't imagine what kind of trouble Ida could possibly get into, but there was always the slim chance that trouble had found her.

"I am fine. I'm visiting a friend, that's all," Ida stated firmly. "And I would appreciate it if this conversation remained between the two of us."

Abby burst out laughing. "Why, Ida, I do believe you've taken a lover!" She couldn't help herself. The mental picture of Ida sneaking around with a man was hilarious. And that rustling of covers she'd heard, the giggles and lip smacking, that was for damn sure no soap opera. If so, Ida and her lover were the featured stars. Good for her, Abby thought, grinning, at least someone she knew was getting laid. She thought of Chris, and instantly felt her blood pressure rise. She took a deep breath. Now wasn't the time to obsess over something, someone, she couldn't have. She'd seen the recent copy of *People* magazine with that sleazy starlet practically glued to him. Abby had rules about dating, and they didn't include seeing her date's picture with other women, rather *sluts*, splashed all across the country.

"Stop! You make it sound so . . . tawdry! I am simply visiting a friend. That's all you need to know. Can I trust that this conversation will remain private?"

Abby pushed thoughts of Chris out of her head and focused on the present. "Of course, Ida. Now that we have that out of the way, I have something I've been thinking about and wanted to discuss with you."

"You do?"

"You remember when you worked for that photographer in New York all those years ago? Remember showing me those pictures you'd taken that were published in *Life*?" Abby asked, giving Ida a minute to get her mind off her lover, if that's who he was, and something told Abby she was right on the mark. Ida didn't go too long without a man in her life. Everyone knew that.

"Of course I do, they were my crowning glory at the time. I am not senile, Abby. Why do you ask?"

"Do you still have your equipment?"

Several seconds passed before Ida replied. "I suppose I kept it somewhere at home. Did you want to put it on eBay? I can have Sully, he's the super at the penthouse, look in the basement if you'd like. If you're short on funds, I can give you whatever you need, dear. You don't have to resort to selling things on the Internet. I know it's costing you a small fortune to remodel your little house."

Had Abby not been sitting in her chair, she would've fallen flat on the floor. If Abby had needed money, she'd have asked her mother. Her mother was a millionaire many times over. Besides, that wasn't her way. She'd made it this far on her own and intended to continue doing so. At twenty-eight, she was a big girl. She could take care of herself. Her mother, bless her heart, had offered to foot the bill for the little ranch Abby had purchased in Brentwood, plus the remodeling. Abby had politely refused her offer, telling her she was quite capable of making it on her own, thank you very much. Her mother had called her stubborn and bull-headed, insisting that she was just like her father. Abby had taken that as the compliment it was meant to be.

"Thanks, Ida, but that wasn't why I asked. I . . . well, I

just wondered if the opportunity ever came up and I needed a photographer, if you could help me out. I have plenty of equipment. The new owners at the paper recently purchased some top-notch cameras. Think you could learn how to use them if you had to?" Abby waited. She knew Ida was very familiar with cameras, but she wasn't sure if she'd ever used a digital camera. Hell, she didn't even know if Ida knew they existed.

"Does this have something to do with the interview you're talking about? Is it some aging star, someone I might want to meet? Clint Eastwood? God, that man is sexy," Ida said. Abby swore she heard lust in her voice. "Gregory Peck was a hunk in his day and age, too. I often wished I could've met him. Those eyes about did me in every time I saw him in a movie. Hollywood's greatest loss. When he died, I spent a week in bed."

Abby wondered who Ida had shared her bed with that week, couldn't remember if Thomas, Ida's last husband, had been alive at the time. Ida and her men. She'd probably die in the throes of passion. Abby smiled at the image, thinking it wouldn't be a bad way to go.

"Sorry, it's not Clint, and I don't think I can arrange an interview with Mr. Peck, since he's no longer among us. I just thought this might be something you would be interested in. I know you weren't that hip when Mom told you she'd be spending the next six months here in Los Angeles. She told me you didn't want to stay, said something about Dr. Sameer's suddenly changing your mind. Now that you and I know you're going to be here for a few more months, I wanted to give you something to do to occupy your time. Besides making beds and all." Abby added the last as a joke, unsure if Ida would get it or not, but it didn't matter. Ida was back to normal, and that's all that counted.

"Are you asking me to come to work for *The Informer?*"

"No, I'm asking you if you'd like to photograph Brad Pitt and Angelina Jolie and their kids when I interview Brangelina."

Abby waited for what seemed like forever before Ida replied.

"Oh my God, I believe I have died and gone to heaven for sure!"

Laughing loudly, Abby replied, "I'll take that as a yes."

Chapter 4

Ida's heartbeat was so rapid, she was sure she was about to faint. Adjusting the belt on her robe, she smoothed her hand across her hair. Dr. Benjamin Sameer, Sammy—her new pet name for him—went to take a shower when he'd heard her cell phone ring. Ida assumed he was allowing her a few moments of privacy. Though first he'd had to kiss her and make all that slobbery noise, and now Abby knew she was romantically involved with someone. Abby would keep this to herself, Ida was sure. Still, Ida had wanted to keep her relationship with Sammy private, as the girls were always telling her she couldn't live without a man. She supposed there was some truth to that, but right now she wasn't about to delve into her psyche to discover why.

Never in a million years had Ida thought she'd ever get to use her photography skills again. Abby hadn't said not to mention this to anyone, but Ida decided to keep the delicious news to herself and savor it for as long as she could.

After her first marriage, she'd tossed her photography career aside, because she no longer needed a job to pay her bills. She'd missed the thrill of creating a permanent image of a moment in time, but with her duties as one of Manhattan's newest socialites, she'd had to forgo her former passion and profession as a photographer. Four husbands and numerous affairs later, she'd assumed she would never need to use those skills again. What surprised her more than anything was that she wanted to get back into the real world again. For so long she'd lived inside a glass bubble, fearful of everything, afraid to step out of her self-imposed solitude and simply live. Thankful that Toots had forced her back into the real world, Ida found her sudden vigor for life so refreshing, so new, that she wanted to shout it to the world. However, propriety and maturity forced her to remain calm and passive and preserve the image of herself she had created for the world at large.

Sammy returned to the bedroom. "Ah, my dear Ida, you look lovely. I take it your phone call brought good news."

Ida gave him a bright smile. "That was my goddaughter, Abby. She just wanted to chitchat, you know, girl talk." Ida was reluctant to share with Sammy any part of her relationship to Abby. It was too special. This was her business, and right now Sammy didn't need to know what they'd discussed. Besides, something told her he would not approve of her working any more than the rest of the men she'd involved herself with in the past had. Ida knew she had some serious soul-searching to do, but now wasn't the time.

Sammy came up behind her and wrapped his arms around her still-slender waist. He dotted light kisses down the side of her neck, then cupped her breast in his hand. "I am the luckiest man in the world. I think I fell in love with you the first time I laid eyes on you."

Ida leaned against him, relishing his words, loving the feel of his hands on her, his lips softly tracing the contours of her neck. "I will be forever in your debt, Sammy. If not for you and your work at the center, I would still be stuck in Manhattan living inside that awful penthouse."

"I can't see living in a Manhattan penthouse as a terrible life, but if you say so, then it must be. While I hate what you've been through, I am very fortunate that you chose me as the one to help you. I love my work at the center, but sadly, I may have to close the clinic down soon. Patients are not as plentiful as they once were, and, of course, the economy is not what it used to be either."

Ida gently removed his arms from her waist, turning around so she could look him directly in the eye. He looked as sad as a lost puppy. For the first time in her life she actually held the power in her hands to make a change in a man's life instead of its being the other way around. She cleared her throat, adjusted her shoulders, and held her head high before she spoke. "You have given me back my life, Sammy. I can't ever repay you for that, but there is something I can do for you if you will let me."

"Ah, my dearest Ida, I couldn't imagine you could ever do any more for me than you have already. You have filled an old man's life with love and brightness." He reached for her hand. "And I would be remiss if I neglected to mention our lovemaking. Never have I experienced such ecstasy, not even as a young man. Like a temple, your body is made to be loved."

Ida blushed at his compliment. "You're too kind, Sammy. You make me feel young again, alive, full of passion. I know how much your work at the center means to you. How could you ever give it up? As you must know, I am a very wealthy woman. I've made, or rather my late husband made, some very wise investments, allowing me to do as I please. There is nothing that would please me more than to offer my financial help if it will save your clinic." Ida paused, waiting for his reaction. He smiled at her, slowly shaking his head from side to side.

"You are a very generous woman, my sweetness, but I am a gentleman. I could never accept such an offer, but it pleases me immensely that you would consider doing this for an old man such as I." He kissed her on the cheek. "Now, while I still have a few patients left, I must get to the clinic before Amala thinks I've abandoned her and them. You may stay here for as long as you like." Sammy adjusted his necktie while he spoke.

"Thank you, but I'd better get back to that horrid beach house Toots now calls home. I'm sure if I don't make an appearance soon, she will come searching for me. I can only use the sleeping late excuse so many times." Ida smiled, then seductively dropped her robe to the floor, allowing Sammy one last look at her nude body before leaving.

With a seductive smile, he raked his gaze across her naked body. "You will kill me, my love. Now get dressed, and I will have my driver drop you off at that 'horrid beach house' before your friends discover you're not where you're supposed to be."

Ida did not like Sammy's driver, Mohammed. She guessed him to be in his early thirties. With olive skin, dark hair, and even darker eyes, he reminded her of one of those mob characters on television. He always gave her the creeps when he looked at her. It was as though he knew exactly what she and Sammy did behind closed doors and knew all of the details. He'd winked at her once before, and she'd wished that Sammy had been there to witness it, but this was his driver, had been for many years, he'd told her, so she wasn't about to stir up trouble. Still, she would have rather taken a taxi back to the beach house, but taxis weren't quite as plentiful in Malibu as they were in Manhattan. Come to think of it, she really didn't like Sammy's house either. She hadn't the heart to tell him it lacked anything that stamped it as his. The house could have been a furnished rental for all the individuality it had. It was as empty of personal items as a burgled vault. Apparently the Center for Mind and Body had most of his personal photos. She had seen a few pictures of him and Amala displayed on his desk, but nothing more. No treasured souvenirs from his many travels, no collections of any kind. She supposed it really didn't matter, but she still did not like the empty house that sat high above the Pacific.

Ten minutes later, Ida was cruising along the Pacific Coast Highway toward Toots's new house. Ida agreed the location was gorgeous, but the house itself was another matter. Poor Toots had her work cut out for her, but Ida knew how much Toots liked a challenge, especially when it came to decorating. Ida was positive that it was only a matter of time before the beach house was as glorious as Toots's Southern plantation home in Charleston.

"Drop me off at the end of the drive," Ida said to Mohammed. She'd walk the rest of the way to the beach house. If any of the girls were to see her, she'd already planned her excuse for being out so early. She would simply explain she'd gone out for an early-morning walk. Nothing wrong with that. She'd been lucky so far. No one had caught her leaving the beach house late at night or sneaking back inside in the wee hours. Ida had mentioned to the girls how she just wanted to sleep late and relax now that she no longer feared germs and no longer had to spend hours cleaning and preparing herself for bed. They'd all promised they wouldn't try to wake her. Ida felt guilty for lying, but for the moment she decided it was for the best.

At sixty-five, she felt like a teenager sneaking behind her parents' back again; but with all the talk of her reputation with men, Ida decided to keep her affair a secret. Sammy had agreed with her, saying he feared how it would appear since she was his patient. When the time was right, Ida would reveal her romance with Dr. Sameer. They hadn't even told Amala, his daughter, yet. Both decided they would know when the time was right to reveal all.

Ida managed to enter the house undetected. Inside her room she quickly changed into a summer nightgown. She lay down on her bed, then jumped up when she saw her reflection in the mirror above her bed. That had to go. Today. She'd remove it herself if she had to. Inside the equally hideous bathroom were black velvet walls, with Elvis in various poses wearing the outrageous sequined suits for which he was so well-known. Fake sapphires created a border around the top and bottom of the walls. The bathroom fixtures were all royal blue. Ida assumed they symbolized his song about those blue suede shoes. The mirror above the sink was in the shape of a giant guitar, with more of the fake sapphires surrounding the quirky pattern. She hoped this was just someone's idea of humor and not a serious attempt at design. She mussed her hair and brushed her teeth before heading downstairs to the kitchen, where Mavis was slicing fruit.

"It's about time you got up. I was about to come and wake you. It's almost nine o'clock. Want some coffee? I just made a fresh pot. Toots and Sophie are out on the deck enjoying the view. I thought we could all have breakfast together before Coco and I take our morning jog on the beach." Coco reclined on a bright pink pillow in the corner of the kitchen.

"Grrr." Coco growled at her all the time. Ida knew the small dog hated her. She didn't like her either. All she did was yap, and poop and pee in places she wasn't allowed. Personally, Ida would rather have a fish if she were to have a pet at all.

"And good morning to you too, Coco." Ida said in a smart-ass tone. All Ida wanted to do was sleep. She'd spent most of the night having wild sex. At least it had been wild for her. Ida thought Sammy must have a lifetime supply of Viagra to keep up these all-night performances or, for a man in his late sixties, he was extremely virile. She doubted it was the latter. Three times a night at her age did have its repercussions. She was sore in places she had forgotten existed. Ida hadn't been bold enough to ask Sammy if his pecker felt as though it had been skinned like the fur off a rabbit. No, breakfast was the last thing on her mind, but she had to keep up appearances. A long soak in a hot tub would have been luxurious just then, but it would have to wait.

"That would be great. It seems like it's been days since we were in the same room together."

Mavis stopped and looked over her shoulder. "You look tired. Are you getting any rest?" she asked, while arranging sliced fruit on a plate.

"Not really. That mirror on the ceiling above my bed gives me the willies. As a matter of fact, I plan to remove it today no matter what Toots says. See if she can sleep with her own reflection staring down at her," Ida said as she located a large mug for her morning coffee.

"I'm sure Toots won't mind. She told me herself the place reminded her of a fun house, I believe her exact words were 'an ugly fucked-up fun house.'" Mavis giggled.

Ida laughed, too. "I've never heard you use the F word before. Losing all that weight and gaining a dirty mouth to boot. I love it," Ida said, as she poured her coffee.

"We've all changed since our move to Los Angeles. I've been thinking about renting my house out and living here in LA part-time, maybe even spending a few months a year with Toots when she returns to Charleston. Summers in Maine are always so busy, I'm sure I wouldn't have any trouble finding vacationers willing to rent my house. Though I'd have to remove all my personal items, Toots assured me she'd help out if I decide to do it. I do love living with you girls. It's almost like high school again, minus the nuns and curfews."

If Mavis only knew. Ida was still sneaking in and out to meet "boys" just like she had in high school. "Yes, I like being together, but I still wish Sophie would learn to curb her tongue. If she isn't careful, one of these days, someone might knock her socks right off her feet because of that smart mouth of hers."

"If that was going to happen, it would've happened years ago. Sophie knows when enough is enough," Mavis said, her tone instantly serious.

Ida shot Mavis a killer look. "I find that hard to believe. She's been nothing but mean and hateful to me since we arrived in LA."

Mavis brought a plate of sliced strawberries, oranges, grapefruit, and bananas to the table. "I'll admit she was a bit rough on you, but look at where you are now. If it were me, and please don't take this the wrong way, I would thank Sophie. You're you again, not some germ-killing fearful old woman who was afraid of her own shadow. You're better now than you've been in years." Mavis added the extra compliment, knowing Ida needed to hear one.

Ida considered Mavis's assessment of Sophie's treatment. Mavis was right. Even though Sophie could be the bitch from hell, she *had* done Ida a favor when she'd dragged her to Dr. Sameer's clinic. Never in a zillion years had Ida imagined finding a cure for her obsessive-compulsive disorder, let alone falling in love again with a foreign and somewhat mysterious, handsome doctor, who just so happened to have the sex drive of a horny teenager or an endless supply of those new hard-on drugs.

"I suppose you're right. I just hate to admit to Sophie when she's right about anything, she's such a know-it-all to begin with. Or at least thinks she is. She'd never let me hear the end of it if I did. Her and that big New York mouth of hers."

"She means no harm, Ida. She's been boisterous and outspoken since seventh grade. I wouldn't take it too personally. Sophie just wants you to be happy like the rest of us."

In order to change the subject and get Mavis to shut up,

Ida lied. "I know, and I'll try to remember that. Now, how about that breakfast? I'm suddenly famished."

"I'll meet you on the deck," Mavis replied, gathering plates and flatware.

Ida hurried back to her room and took one of the fastest showers she'd ever taken in her life. God forbid if any of the girls caught the slightest scent of sex emanating from her body. When it came to sex, their olfactory senses were equal to that of a record-holding bloodhound, and she was sure that only the aroma of fresh coffee had kept Mavis from catching the lingering scent.

Chapter 5

Cigarette smoke spewed forth from Toots's and Sophie's mouths like steam from a matched pair of locomotives as they reclined on the deck. Whirls of the exhaust fumes from inhaled nicotine rose above their heads like evanescent halos.

"God, if I didn't know better, I'd think this place was on fire. You two need to give up that nasty habit," Ida said as she pulled up a weathered deck chair beside Sophie.

"I tell you what. When you give up men, I'll give up smoking. Deal?" Sophie said as she took another drag from her cigarette.

"Kiss my ass," Ida offered.

In her usual stinging tone, Sophie replied, "I doubt there's a spot that hasn't been kissed already. No thanks, I don't want the germs."

Mavis stepped onto the deck and placed the platter of fruit on the ledge of the deck with the plates and flatware by its side. "Now, girls, let's not start this gorgeous day by bickering with one another. Let's all have a healthy breakfast and catch up on what's been going on in our lives."

Coco chose that moment to appear on the deck. "Ruff, ruff."

"I see the Queen minus her royal court has arrived," Ida noted sarcastically.

Coco, four pounds of dynamite, growled at her, revealing tiny sharp white teeth.

"Don't tease her, Ida. It scares her," Mavis said.

"Bullshit; that dog isn't afraid of anything except missing her next meal," Toots said, laughing between puffs on her cigarette. "She is a cutie, though I have to agree with Ida. She really is a bit on the spoiled side."

Ida and Sophie looked at one another and grinned.

"That's much better," Mavis remarked as she dished up plates of fruit, passing them to the three women gathered around the small glass table. "So what's on the agenda for today, ladies?" Mavis asked between bites of luscious fruit. She'd lost so much weight and so quickly that she barely recognized herself these days. She'd gone from a size twenty-two to a size fourteen in a matter of months.

Toots caught Sophie's eye. "Sophie is going to help me with a few projects around here. Right, Soph?"

"Yes, I most certainly am. Projects I've never attempted before."

Ida offered, "Please tell me one of them is removing that dreadful mirror from the ceiling in my room. It scares me every morning when I wake up and see myself."

Sophie cackled like a chicken. "It would me, too, if I looked like you did first thing in the morning!"

"You old bitch! You ought to be ashamed. I've seen what you look like in the morning, and it's not pretty. In fact, if I didn't know you, I'd be frightened to death confronting such . . . ugliness," Ida replied, a big grin spreading over her face.

They all burst out laughing. Yes, Ida was definitely back to her I-am-queen-of-the-world self once again.

And that was a good thing.

"I'm sick of your whining, but I have to agree with you on the mirror. It needs to go. The construction crew won't begin demolishing the inside of this place until next week, but I think that between the four of us, we should be able to manage to remove that god-awful thing without too much effort. We'll do it right after we finish this lovely breakfast Mavis has served us. What in the hell happened to my Froot Loops?" Toots asked. "You know I am not particularly fond of eating this healthy stuff. I think it makes me sick."

Sophie chimed in, "I was just getting used to the bad stuff when you started feeding us this crap."

Clapping her hands to gain their attention, Mavis said, "Ladies, stop it right this very minute! I love all three of you and want you to be around for a very long time. Eating healthy gives us some assurance that we'll all be around a little while longer."

"Yeah? What if some of the healthy food we eat kills us? Didn't I just hear on the news where a bunch of people died from eating peanut butter?" Sophie asked.

"That was just a one-shot incident. Peanut butter isn't all that good for you anyway," Mavis claimed matter-of-factly.

"I never thought in a million years you would be advising us on what to eat. I'm happy you're taking charge of your health, Mavis, just don't run it into the ground. I've managed to survive this long eating junk food, and I suspect I'll be just fine even if I don't eat whatever it is the FDA is recommending these days," Toots said.

Sophie jumped in. "I don't trust them either. I think they're just another branch of the government that accepts bribes from the highest bidder. Let's not forget Thomas." Thomas was Ida's last husband, who'd passed away from eating poisoned meat, or at least that is where Ida believed that the E. coli infection originated. "They don't care about

tainted meat or rotting peanuts any more than Coco does."
The small dog growled upon hearing her name. Sophie
flicked the dog a bird.

"Sophie, that's not a very nice thing to do."

"Do you really think she knows what flipping the bird
means?" Sophie raised her perfectly sculpted brows, waiting for Mavis's answer.

Mavis hesitated a minute as though seriously contemplating Sophie's question. "She may associate it with something negative, I can't know for sure. She's a very smart
animal. She knows more than you think."

Toots chimed in, "I agree with Mavis. Not about flipping
off the dog, but I think animals are much smarter than we
give them credit for. Look at Chester, Abby's dog. I think
he understands much more than we'll ever know. He certainly looks after her."

After much chatting about animals and what constituted
a healthy diet, the foursome gathered their plates and uten-
sils and took them inside to the kitchen before heading upstairs, intent on removing the mirror from Ida's ceiling.

The buzzing of Toots's cell phone stopped them all dead
in their tracks. She looked at the caller ID before answering. "Abby! What is my favorite child up to?"

"As far as I know, I'm your only child, unless you've
been keeping secrets from me," Abby said playfully.

Toots's heart raced. If she only knew. "It's nice to hear
your voice, that's all. Why aren't you out pounding the
pavement?"

"Remember the new owners appointed me editor in
chief? I have to send all my little worker bees in search of
the next cover story. Though I must admit, I do miss the
excitement of the hunt and the deadlines."

Toots should have known better, but with Abby at the
helm, she felt sure *The Informer* could turn into a much better tabloid, maybe even better than *The Enquirer* or *The*

Globe. "You can still write stories, can't you?" Toots questioned, hoping she hadn't jumped the gun. She knew how much Abby loved her job. Had she taken Abby's passion for her career away by purchasing the paper just so Abby could hang on to her job? Time would tell.

"Yes, that's why I'm calling. You'll never believe in a million years who I'm going to interview."

Toots thought for a moment and came up blank. "I haven't a clue, so you'll just have to spill the beans."

"Are you sitting down?" Abby asked.

"No, the girls and I are headed upstairs to remove that hideous mirror from Ida's ceiling."

"Why don't you let that construction company you hired take care of that? You don't need to be climbing on ladders or whatever it is you're about to do."

"Abby Simpson, I will have you know that I—along with your godmothers—am quite capable of taking that trashy mirror down. We're not too old to try something new."

"Sorry, I didn't mean to imply that you were. Just be careful."

"I'm always careful," Toots retorted, mildly insulted that Abby would think of her as old.

"Now don't go getting your undies in a twist, Mom. I'm just thinking of your well-being, that's all."

"You're right. I am getting too sensitive about my age and what I can and can't do. Now tell me who you're going to interview. I hope it's not that Britney Spears. She's old news as far as the tabloids go."

"I wouldn't want to interview her at this point. Maybe when she grows up a bit, but this is even better. If all goes as planned, this interview will put *The Informer* head and shoulders above every other tabloid publication in the country."

"Okay, you've piqued my interest. Now spit it out."

"The Pitt/Jolie clan."

Toots's heart paused for a moment. An interview like that would put *The Informer* in the number-one spot as far as tabloids go.

Toots inhaled and exhaled, visualized a mountain brook, its water trickling over moss-covered rocks . . .

"Mom, are you there? Did you hear what I just said?"

Toots took another deep, cleansing breath. "Yes, I heard you. This is fantastic. I want to know every last detail."

"You sound just like Sophie," Abby said. "There isn't much to tell at this point. I received an e-mail from their publicist saying they were offering an interview with pictures. I have no clue about anything else other than what I just told you. I sent them an e-mail letting them know the paper is waiting for further instructions."

Toots took a few seconds to absorb Abby's news. Something didn't feel right about this, but Toots wasn't going to voice her opinion for fear of dampening Abby's excitement over the interview. That bastard Rag, who'd tried to rip off her $10 million, better not be behind this, because if Toots found out he was screwing with Abby and the paper, well, to put it in words he would understand, he would get the royal fucking of his life. She crossed her fingers that the authorities would find his ass before she did.

"Tell me what I can do to help out? Anything, and it's yours."

"Oh, Mom, I know you will. Right now I don't even have a date scheduled, much less anything else. I do know security will be tight. The protection they and their kids get is almost equal to what the president gets. Just don't mention this. I don't want to take any chances on this getting out before the actual interview takes place. I don't trust any of the rival papers. They'd try to snatch the interview from *The Informer* in a heartbeat. So keep this on the QT until you hear otherwise."

Abby paused, knowing she needed to tell her mother she'd told Ida the exciting news first. Her mother was tough as shoe leather, but sometimes her feelings were as fragile as a butterfly's wings.

Here goes, she thought. "Mom, I told Ida about this interview before I told you."

Silence. Abby waited for what seemed like minutes, then she spoke into the phone again. "Mom, are you there?"

"Yes, Abby, where else would I be? I suppose I should ask why you chose to tell her first, but I'm sure you have your reasons. So, tell me, why did you tell her first?"

"This is going to sound crazy. When I read the e-mail from the Pitt/Jolie publicist, I remembered those photographs Ida took that were featured on the cover of *Life* magazine. I sort of asked her if she would be interested in taking the pictures for the piece." There, it was out. Now all she had to do was wait for her mother's response.

Seconds turned into minutes. Abby felt hot, so she fanned herself with last week's edition of *The Informer* while she waited for her mother to digest the news. This was quite common between the two of them. Abby had shared many silent phone conversations throughout the years with her mother. She waited patiently, knowing her mother would reply when she had a practical answer, and not a minute sooner.

"I think that's a fantastic idea, Abby. Ida needs something in her life other than men. I can't wait to tell the others. Do you mind? Or should I wait and let you deliver the news?"

"Let's wait a couple of days just to make sure this isn't some hoax drummed up by our rivals. Don't even tell Ida I told you about this. Let her bask in a bit of well-earned glory. She needs it after what she's been through."

"You're right. I won't mention this to a soul. Now the

girls are upstairs waiting for me. Ida is having fits about that damned mirror, so we're taking it down."

"Promise me you all will be careful? I don't want to hear about anyone breaking an arm or a leg."

Toots smiled. "I'm always careful, dear. Call me as soon as you have more news."

"I will, and, Mom, I know I've said this once or twice, but I have to say it again. You're the best."

Toots's eyes filled with tears. "No, Abby, *you're* the best."

Chapter 6

Balanced on a rickety ladder with Sophie and Mavis acting as spotters, Toots motioned to Ida. "Hand me that damned thingamabob, will you?"

"What?" Ida replied.

"That." Toots pointed to the tire iron on the floor beside the ladder. "Oh never mind," she said as she inched her way down the ladder.

"Careful, Toots, you'll fall on your ass, then we'll all be crushed," Sophie cautioned.

"Kiss my burgeoning behind, Sophie," Toots shot back.

"It'd take all day," she replied. "And I really don't want to stare at your ass that long, so what is it you want?"

Frustrated, Toots grabbed the tire iron she'd found in the garage. "This." She swung the heavy tire iron at the trio like a sword.

She climbed back onto the ladder. When she reached the top rung, she looked down. "Make sure you all have your goggles on. This glass could fly everywhere." While rummaging through the garage searching for tools to remove the mirror, Toots had found several sets of snorkeling equipment. They were now using the goggles as protective eye gear. If anyone saw them decked out in their PJs, Sophie's pink-and-purple sweats, and the swimming goggles strapped around their faces, they would surely think they were misfits from a long-lost Jacques Cousteau expedition or four lunatics who'd escaped from the loony bin. Most likely the latter.

Toots wedged the flat end of the tire iron beneath the edge of the mirror, thankful that whoever had installed the darn mirror in the first place had used those cheap stick-on mirrored squares. Maneuvering the tire iron up and down, then side to side, she was able to remove the first square without shattering it. "Someone take these as I break them loose."

"Give them to me. I want to stomp on them," Ida said, standing as close to the ladder as possible.

Exasperated, Sophie said, "You can't do that, silly ass, you'll hurt yourself. That's what we're trying to avoid."

"I didn't mean it literally, *silly ass*," Ida shot back.

"Both of you shut up and take these before I drop them on your heads." Toots handed two more squares of the tacky mirror to Ida. After thirty minutes of wedging, tugging, and pulling, Toots had removed all the mirrored squares from the ceiling. Mavis, ever the helping hand, stacked them into a neat pile in the corner. Toots climbed off the ladder and gazed up at her handiwork. The ceiling was stripped of the ugly mirrors, but the tattered drywall was just as ugly. The contractors couldn't arrive soon enough as far as she was concerned. For a moment, she experienced more doubts about having purchased the place, but the view was so damned gorgeous, she wasn't that far from Abby, and she had *The Informer*. She remembered she wasn't going to live there year-round, as she still had her beautiful home in Charleston. That was where her heart remained, but for a while she would happily adjust to a new and different lifestyle in the land of glitter and glamour. She had to admit to herself, however, that she did not for one second like living in such disorder. Hell, it was a miracle that Ida could stomach such disarray, given her former affliction.

Patience, Toots, patience.

"Looks good, Toots. I think we should draw something for Ida to gaze at until the remodeling is complete, don't you?" Sophie suggested.

Folding the ladder, then leaning it against the wall, Toots asked, "And what would you suggest?"

Enthusiastically, Mavis replied before Sophie had a chance, "A bright moon with lots of sparkling stars."

Sophie rolled her eyes. "I was thinking of something more phallic, like a giant—"

"—Don't even go there!" Toots said, grinning. Leave it to Sophie to turn an ordinary repair into something sexual. She needed a man in her life, one who would appreciate her warped sense of humor and love her for it. Someday, but Toots knew the timing was off. Even though Walter had kicked the bucket several months ago, Sophie had yet to realize she was completely free of his hold on her. Toots had observed her when she didn't know she was being watched. If glass shattered, Sophie would react more strongly than the average person. At a door's unexpectedly slamming, her eyes would widen in fear, then relax when Walter didn't materialize. No, Sophie needed time to be herself. Toots didn't see a man in her dear friend's future just yet.

"I think we can leave it as is until the repairs are made. It's not like I lie in bed at night and stare at the ceiling," Ida said.

"True. With a man blocking your view, it would be hard," Sophie added. "Especially if your eyes are closed while in the throes of passion."

Ida almost choked. "What are you talking about?"

Sophie shook her head. "I don't need to draw you a picture, Ida. You know—man on top, woman on bottom gazing into the eyes of her lover—the ceiling would be the last thing she would notice."

"Apparently the former pop tart thought otherwise," Toots said. "Or maybe she simply enjoyed the view. Either way, it's gone, and now all we can do is wait for the repairs to be made."

Ida let out a breath she didn't realize she was holding. "You're right, Toots. Have you decided what colors you're going to use in this room?" Ida wanted to change the subject. Something told her that Sophie's little comment held more meaning than was immediately obvious, as though she knew about Ida's midnight trysts, and offhand remarks were Sophie's way of dropping a hint. No, Ida told herself. It wasn't possible. She'd been extremely careful, making sure the girls were down for the night. Sophie had a dirty mind, that was all. Besides, if Sophie knew, she would come right out and say so. She wasn't one to mince words. Ida relaxed. Her secret affair was safe. But for how long, she didn't know. Soon they would have to make their romance public, because while Ida enjoyed the sex and Sammy's company, she wasn't as young as she used to be. Lack of sleep was beginning to take its toll on her.

"I thought I would let you make that decision, since this is officially your room," Toots replied.

"Thanks, but this is your home, Toots . . . I'll have to think about it. Maybe I should call Chloe; she did all my decorating in Manhattan. I'm sure she could come up with something acceptable, something you would feel comfortable calling your own."

"You don't get it, do you?" Sophie challenged.

Stung, Ida asked, "What do you mean? What am I not getting? I suppose you're going to tell me how stupid I am."

"You're not stupid, Ida, just . . ." Sophie shrugged. "Toots wants this to be your room. You decide what you want. Not some fancy-ass decorator. Right, Toots?"

"Yes, that's right. So as long as it's not purple or pink, I think you might actually enjoy designing a room of your own. With your eye for detail, I think you will surprise yourself. After all, you're a photographer. You know about light and color, that sort of thing."

Ida surveyed the room. "Well, you're right about that. I do know a thing or two about photography." She smiled. Ida so wanted to tell them about her possible new assignment, but she would wait. "I suppose I would paint the walls a soft buttery yellow. Since the sun doesn't rise or set on this side of the house, that would add some warmth to the room." Perusing the room, Ida shook her head. "Yes, I would like to do this, Toots. Thank you for trusting me. This is *your* home. I do believe I might actually enjoy this little project."

Smiling, Mavis said, "This is wonderful! Toots, you certainly know how to make people happy. Would it be too brazen of me to ask if you will allow me to do the same in my room?"

"No, it would not, and for Pete's sake, stop acting so frigging formal, both of you! I bought this house for all of us. Now, when any of us wants to spend time with Abby, we'll all have a place to stay. I'll probably be here more than the rest of you since I've purchased *The Informer.* Just for the record, let's say this house belongs to a mother and a few godmothers. It'll be our own chick hangout."

They all laughed.

"Chicks," Mavis clucked. "I like the sound of that. I don't think I've ever thought of myself as a chick, but with all the new beginnings in my life, I might as well add one more. I'm a hot, sexy chick!" Mavis laughed, blushing at her own silliness.

"You are, and you always have been. You just didn't see it through all that . . . those layers," Sophie said with a smile, knowing Mavis knew she was referring to the overweight version of her former self. "I don't see how you've stuck to that vegan diet. I would've gagged, but for the record we're all very pleased with you. Right, chicks?" Sophie looked to Toots and Ida for confirmation.

Both women agreed.

Toots spoke first. "Ida and Mavis have both come a long way in these past few months. I am very proud of you both."

"And me?" Sophie questioned.

"You're still full of shit, but you already know that. I think we've all grown, or rather made some positive changes in our lives. Losing Walter was your positive change, Sophie. Now let's get this mess cleaned up." Toots nodded toward the pile of glass squares in the corner. "If no one has anything on their agenda this afternoon, I say we all go out for a late lunch. Plus I'm dying for a cigarette."

"I do wish you and Sophie would stop that nasty habit, Toots. Sorry, but I promised Coco a run on the beach, then a bath. I plan to spend the rest of the afternoon redesigning some of those outfits you bought me at Catherine's, but I'll take a rain check," Mavis said sweetly.

"I'm going to be on the phone with my financial advisor. The time factor makes it hard to stay in touch. I promised him I would free up my afternoon for him," Ida lied with a straight face. What she planned was a long soak in the tub, even if she did have to stare at all of those Elvis figures. And then a nice long nap. She might just sleep the afternoon away.

"Then I guess that leaves just you and me," Toots said to Sophie. "Unless you have something planned."

"No, but remember you wanted to switch bedrooms? The mattress? Your back?"

"Yes, of course, but that won't take all afternoon. We'll

do that first, then reward ourselves with a long, leisurely lunch at the Polo Lounge. We haven't been there lately."

"Then what are we waiting for?" Sophie scooped up several squares of the mirror. "Let's get this cleaned up. Come on, ladies, we can have this done in a heartbeat if we all pitch in."

With each of them taking a stack of the still-intact mirror squares out to the garage and placing them in an empty box Toots found, the job was done after several trips. They all agreed that they'd done just about enough work for one day.

"Let's switch our rooms and call it a day," Toots said. "I have visions of a tall, frothy cold drink laced with all sorts of bad stuff just waiting for me. I have to say our tasteless pop tart did leave plenty of booze behind."

"Yeah, she had to. Remember, she went to that rehab clinic in Mexico? *The Informer* was the first paper to break the news."

"Yes, of course I do. That's how I was able to get this house before it was put on the market. Of course I had to agree to purchase it 'as is,' and that is why we're both huffing and puffing like two old women."

Sophie grinned. "We *are* old women."

"Bullshit. You might be, but I plan to live it up, regardless of my age."

"Old women but young at heart. How's that sound?"

"It sounds like the crock of brown crap that it is. Now, let's get something to drink before we rust."

Both women laughed like teenagers as they raided the liquor cabinet.

Chapter 7

Toots and Sophie spent the next hour switching rooms. When all was said and done, Toots didn't feel one bit better about moving into Sophie's room. "Can a ghost follow you around?" she asked when they were out of Mavis's and Ida's earshot.

"Sure, I don't see why not. Why do you ask?"

"Because I'm not sure if trading rooms is a good idea or not. What if this ghost or whatever the hell it is follows me to your room? Then what? We can play musical rooms all we want. Eventually, Ida and Mavis are bound to get a bit suspicious. Ida might even suggest I make an appointment with Dr. Sameer. I think I'd rather be haunted by a ghost than treated by him."

Sophie shot her a dirty look. "I feel the same way, but remember, he helped Ida. We have to be thankful for that. Can you imagine her living here in these conditions? We'd have to bury her."

"I'm not so sure her condition was as bad as she wanted everyone to believe. Oh, I know her hands looked terrible, but that's just like Ida. She will go to extremes to get her way. I think Dr. Sameer was good for her, but I don't believe it was his medical skills that cured her." Toots laughed.

"She's been acting very strange the past few mornings.

Have you noticed? I don't think she's sleeping well. Maybe she's being haunted, too, and doesn't want us to know," Sophie suggested.

"Now that you mention it, she has been acting rather odd. Maybe there is a . . . spirit or something in this house. It is the former home of Lucille Ball and Desi Arnaz. Maybe they're pissed at that little pop tart for what she did to their home," Toots said, though she didn't believe a single word of it.

"Could be. Maybe I can sneak into her room later tonight. I'll try the shoe trick. It can't hurt."

"I thought you had to know what shoes the person would be wearing the next day," Toots said.

"Yes, but Ida always wears those silly kitten slippers in the morning. I'll give it a try, see if her behavior changes."

Toots heard Ida and Mavis bustling about in their rooms, so she whispered, "What about the camera and those voice things you mentioned? I haven't seen them. Do you really have this stuff, or were you just feeding me a line of bull?"

Sophie gazed around the room, which looked like a low-class brothel. "Now why would I lie about something so serious? Of course I have the equipment. It was the first purchase I made the minute I collected Walter's life insurance. In case he ever tries to come back, I'll know about it, but this time I will kick his ass before he gets a chance to kick mine."

Though Toots wasn't so sure Sophie was joking, she laughed anyway. "Yeah, that's one way to get back at the old bastard if he tries to come back and haunt you."

Sophie shifted around, her eyes downcast. Toots knew what she was going to say before the words came out of her mouth. "None of the faces I saw were Walter. If so, I would've socked the son of a bitch right in the kisser."

"You don't think I'm crazy for thinking this . . . ?"

"No more than I am. Look at what I saw. It wasn't my

imagination. The cold, the puffy-looking clouds, faces whose mouths moved with no sound coming from them. That sounds crazy. However, I am smart enough, sane enough, to know it was not a figment of my imagination. I suppose Walter could materialize just as easily as those . . . things, but something tells me he's burning in hell with all the other bastards who beat up on women just so they could feel superior. Want to know what I really believe?"

"What?" Sophie asked.

"I think there is a special place in hell for men like him. Women, too. Mean people."

Sophie seemed to consider her words, "Yeah, I suppose that would be nice. Maybe Lucifer himself deals with jerks like Walter. I for one don't plan on finding out anytime soon."

"Then you'd better lay off Ida, because the killer looks she gives you could be fatal."

Again the pair laughed until their eyes were damp with tears, and both had stitches in their sides.

"Don't ever tell her this, but I do love the old bitch. I just delight in tormenting her. Those looks she gives me are priceless, so I doubt I'll stop annoying her any time in the near future."

"I wouldn't dream of raining on your parade with Ida, but don't go too far. Cut her some slack now and then. She's still a bit on the sensitive side. I can't believe she hasn't mentioned Jerry lately. She never misses an opportunity to tell me how it ruined her life when I supposedly took him away from her." Jerry had been dating Ida when he fell madly in love with Toots. Like a fool, Toots married him. He'd been nothing more than a cheapskate and an inadequate lover to boot. She didn't like to think ill of the dead, but facts were facts. Toots figured her assessment of his qualities was more than generous. "I did her a favor when I married the old schmuck."

"True, but we all know she would never admit that. What number was he anyway?" Sophie asked.

Toots paused. "Five or six. I can't remember."

"Between you and Ida, I've never been able to keep up. Good thing Mavis and I stuck with just one marriage each. Though we could have been husband-hoppers like you two. We'd have a hell of a lot more men to bash, that's for sure." Sophie grinned as she placed a stack of panties in the top drawer.

"Yes, not that it matters now. We can't remember mine and Ida's as it is," Toots said. "Husband-hoppers, huh?"

"Yeah, I gave you two that nickname way back in the day. I think I even told Mavis about it. She said that you and Ida were just having a tough time finding the perfect match. It sure sounds better than 'sluts' or 'tramps.' "

Toots raised her hand high in the air. "I ought to smack you for that. I was never a tramp. Or a slut. That was Ida, who screwed anything and everything outside her marriage. My feelings are hurt that you would think of me that way."

"Oh can it! I didn't come out and say you were a slut. Some did, back in the day, but I think they were just jealous because they didn't have dates or couldn't get laid."

Toots sat down on the bed. "Please, let's not talk about sex. It's too early in the day. I want to get this ghost business taken care of and soon. Let's get cleaned up and go to the Polo Lounge." Toots pounced off the bed like a cat with one remaining life. Suddenly, the room felt eerie, almost alive. Shivers ran down her back, causing the hair on her arms to rise. "I don't want to discuss anything else about anyone or anything until we're seated at our favorite table with an alcoholic beverage."

Sophie finished putting her clothes in the drawer. "Sounds good. Give me twenty minutes to shower and change."

Toots stood in the doorway. "Not one minute more. I

want to get out of this place. I feel creepy just being in this room. You have nineteen minutes to make yourself pretty, or I'm going solo."

"Then get out of here so I can shower," Sophie tossed over her shoulder as she made her way to the small bathroom.

Toots flipped her middle finger high in the air as she crossed the hall to her new room. If these strange ghostly, haunting feelings continued, she would return to the Beverly Hills Hotel. At least there she could be scared in a safe and familiar environment.

Toots climbed behind the wheel of the bright-red Thunderbird that she'd purchased after she bought the paper. With a two-seater, she figured she would never have to haul more than herself and one person around, and that suited her. One person at a time in a vehicle on California's freeways was as much as she wanted to handle at this stage in her life. Now when and if grandchildren came into the picture, well that was an entirely different matter.

She looked at her watch. Five more seconds and Sophie would be dining alone. One, two, three . . .

Toots put the T-Bird in reverse, then slammed on the brakes when she heard Sophie yell. "Don't you dare leave here without me! I have two seconds to go." Sophie opened the door just as Toots shifted into reverse again.

"I told you I was not going to wait longer than twenty minutes, and I meant it. I feel strange in that house, or I felt that way in your new room."

Sophie tied a bright yellow scarf around her dark brown hair. "I haven't felt anything yet, but it's early. I'm going to set my surveillance equipment up as soon as we return. I did manage to sneak inside Ida's room. I found those kitten slippers and placed one facing east and the other west, just in case." Sophie secured the knot under her chin and slid on a pair of large-framed sunglasses. "We look like two movie stars, Toots."

Knowing they'd be flying down the highway with the top down, Toots had tied her auburn hair back in a low ponytail. She'd added a thick white headband to keep her hair from going wild. She wore a pair of Christian Dior sunglasses, a gift from Chris, her stepson. She peered into the rearview mirror.

"I believe we do, Sophie. Let's not talk about ghosts or Ida or anything negative. I want to enjoy the rest of the afternoon. I so love this California weather. In all the years I've spent in Charleston, I've never gotten used to that horrible humidity in the summer. I plan to spend summers in California from now on. What about you, Soph? Have you any plans for the future?"

Sophie leaned back against the headrest and stared up at the powder-blue sky, her yellow scarf billowing in the wind. "I try not to think that far ahead. Right now I'm having too much fun with one day at a time. These past few months have been like a breath of fresh air. For the first time in forever, I'm not walking on eggshells, I can say exactly what comes to mind without fearing Walter's wrath. Did I ever tell you he wore lifts in his shoes?"

Laughing softly into the wind whipping over her head, Toots replied, "No, I believe that's a piece of intelligence you kept to yourself. Maybe he suffered from small-man syndrome."

"Who knows? I don't care anymore. That part of my life is behind me. Now I can actually look to the future. You asked me if I had any plans, I guess not having any right now is what I would like to call my plan. Does that sound ungrateful or what?"

Toots realized Sophie was being serious and considered her answer before she replied. "No. It sounds like a woman who is finally happy and has every right to feel that way.

Don't ever feel guilty, Soph. You suffered way too long, if you ask me. I think not having plans is the perfect plan."

Sophie simply nodded, a slight smile lifting one corner of her mouth.

Toots steered the small sports car down the narrow winding road over sloping hills covered in gnarled trees. Bright pink, red, and orange flowers dotted the edge of the road leading to the Pacific Coast Highway. Once she reached the highway, she pushed down on the accelerator. Toots raised her voice as the sounds of traffic surrounded them. "I love the colors here. Everywhere you look there is color," she said, coming alive, instantly revived by the fresh ocean air.

"From what I hear, this is what's known as the 'ritzy area,' where the rich and famous live. We both know that there are bad areas just like anywhere else," Sophie shouted.

Toots leaned in close so she didn't have to yell. "I know that. Everything is just so perfectly manicured. I know it's not real, Sophie. This is Hollywood, the land of make-believe. I can only imagine how much water is used, how much hard work goes into keeping these areas 'ritzy.' It must cost zillions to keep the streets in such pristine condition. Abby has told me all about the darker side of Los Angeles. I don't have any immediate plans to venture into unfamiliar territory. If and when I do, I'll make sure to drag your ass along for the ride."

Sophie grinned. "You're a true Southern bitch, Toots."

Toots removed her right hand from the steering wheel, stretching her hand out so that it was directly in front of Sophie's eyes. Then she gave her the one-finger salute.

Chapter 8

Amala was a whore and the greediest bitch he'd ever laid eyes on. A true slut if ever there was one. A guy could go far with her. Very, very far. For a price. How did he know that? Because on more than one occasion he had done so himself. But he had never paid the going rate; nor would he ever. Those luscious lips and dark seductive eyes of hers held no power over him. Unlike most men, he saw her for what she truly was. A conniving, double-dealing, manipulating scam artist. He should know. He'd lived with her for five years.

Mohammed Dasgupta laughed to himself as he parked the sleek white limousine beneath the portico in front of Ben's Place. He'd been warned to use the proper name, the Center for Mind and Body, but it was too long. He liked Ben's Place much better. Sounded much more American than the Center for Mind and Body.

This New Age crap they were trying to pass off as medical treatment was their biggest con to date. Luckily for that old woman who'd been afraid of germs, old Patel, a.k.a. Ben, did have a bit of medical knowledge, he just didn't have the degree to back it up. It was only a piece of paper anyway. Patel was as good as any licensed medical doctor.

This Mohammed knew, as Patel had personally saved his life many years ago.

He had to admit when Amala first approached him with her plans, he'd been intrigued. He was unsure if they could actually pull off such a stunt, but the payoff was worth the risk. Six months, she'd said. If they didn't have their money by then, and she had assured him it would be in the millions, they would move on to bigger and better game.

Mohammed could have killed Amala when she took that phone call from the doctor in South Carolina, a friend of the good Dr. Sameer. After a lengthy discussion, they had all agreed Patel would pose as Dr. Sameer for the visits. Ripping the old women off was a bonus, one he now thought of as the real payoff as Amala had not been able to access Dr. Sameer's accounts as quickly or as easily as she had originally planned.

Amala had worked as a receptionist at the Center for Mind and Body for the past year. She'd told him the only reason she'd taken the job in the first place was her hope to trap the *real* Dr. Benjamin Sameer into marriage by getting pregnant. Then she would be set for life. She would never have to turn another trick again, nor would she have to resort to any more con games. After a year of unsuccessful attempts at seduction, Amala's plans to marry the doctor had been quashed when he told her he was gay.

Angry and embarrassed beyond her wildest dreams, she had been ready to quit when she fortuitously learned of Dr. Sameer's plan to take a year off to travel to his native India for a sabbatical. She'd offered to stay on at the clinic part-time to make sure that everything was taken care of in his absence. She reminded him of his celebrity clientele, telling him this way she would be there to explain his absence, plus she could continue to monitor the weekly yoga sessions with Kyra, the yoga instructor. The stupid idiot had thought her offer beyond generous, or so he'd said. So generous, in fact, that he'd invited her to house-sit for him while he was away. Amala had accepted his offer, telling him she would treat the clinic and his home as if they were her very own. He'd barely been out of the country when she'd canceled Kyra's classes for the remainder of his sabbatical. Mohammed had to give her credit, she hadn't wasted any time.

If the good doctor only knew.

They were now going into the fourth month, and Mohammed had yet to see any money of any kind. Yes, he'd been living in Dr. Sameer's home along with Amala and Patel while he played the role of limousine driver, but the waiting game was getting old fast.

He was tired of playing by her rules, so he'd come up with a plan of his own. Granted, there were a few wrinkles that needed to be smoothed out, but he had faith in his abilities. Unbeknownst to Amala or Patel, he'd been watching those four old women closer than they knew. The little lady with the germ disorder wasn't the only one who had money. The tall redhead was loaded and good-looking to boot. He'd followed her, watched her pay for that beach house with a check. So what if she was old enough to be his mother? Older women were attracted to younger men, especially here in California, where a guy could get a month's free rent if he met a rich woman willing to pay for a decent roll in the hay. He knew that because it was how he made his living when he wasn't dealing drugs for Patel or participating in other criminal activities.

Mohammed had found his golden goose. Now all he had to do was train her to lay a golden egg right in his lap.

"Why did you want to come here?" Amala demanded, as they were led to a discreet table in the corner of the patio at the Polo Lounge. "This is so Hollywood. Were you hoping to catch a glimpse of a famous movie star? I didn't think you had it in you, Sammy. I thought you were above all this glitz and glamour. You surprise me."

"I have my reasons. Now relax and pretend you enjoy my company," Patel said scathingly. "This isn't always about you. There are other issues I must take into consideration if we're to see this plan through to its end. Wining and dining Ida was not my idea, remember?"

Amala swung her dark hair over her shoulder. "It was Mohammed who first suggested this. I did not want to get outsiders involved. We could have it all if you two would just be patient."

"So you say. It's been much too long for us. We have seen nothing monetary. I don't know how much longer I can pretend to, as you call it, 'wine and dine' the old woman. She's stupid and full of herself. If I were a certified medical doctor, I would commit her to an asylum."

Their waiter came to the table, interrupting further discussion. After they placed their orders, Amala said in a hushed tone, "You could have refused. No one forces you to have sex with her all night every night. I am tired of listening to her moan and groan. It is sickening."

He laughed, "Ah . . . so you listen, not that this surprises me."

Amala gave him a hostile glare. "How could I not? The rooms are not soundproof."

"Dr. Benjamin Sameer," real name Patel Yadav, smiled and replied in a cool yet sharp tone, "Then you should have thought of this, too, Miss Amala. I can walk away now. I have invested nothing; therefore, I have lost nothing. You, on the other hand, have invested more than a year of your life trying seduce a man who prefers men. Now you not only want to take away his fortune but also his identity. If these are not your intentions, then I suggest you go back to that one-room apartment you share with Mohammed, where you can listen to the rats clawing in the attic at night." Patel took a sip of water and raised his thick brows in question. "The choice is yours."

"I have said nothing about giving up. You and Mohammed are impatient."

"Then you must stop complaining about my nighttime adventures with the old woman," Patel said.

"Possibly you could tone things down a bit. Besides, I cannot keep forging prescriptions for that disgusting performance drug you need for those all-night sessions."

He was tired, but never would he allow Amala to know that.

Patel Yadav had come to the United States more than thirty years ago after leaving the All India Institute of Medical Sciences in Delhi. He'd been serving his internship there and was in his last year when he was forced to give up his internship after he and a fellow intern were charged with drug theft. The chief of staff had been easy on them. They could remain and fight the charges, or they could quietly slip away with no charges brought against them, minus their medical degrees. Both had taken the offer. Punishments for such crimes in his native country were brutal. After a year of roaming his country working in makeshift hospitals that were willing to overlook the fact that he hadn't completed his medical training, after months of seeing the poor, the hungry, and the desperate people in his country, he'd fled for the United States in search of a more promising future. Sadly, he'd fallen into the same path upon entering the States. He didn't qualify for government loans because he'd entered the country illegally, and not even the lowliest of medical schools would accept him. He was right back where he'd left off in India.

For thirty years he had pulled off hundreds of scams and made and sold illegal drugs to anyone who could pay for them. He made a decent living, but nothing like he'd dreamed of when he came to America. At sixty-seven he was still searching for his pot of gold.

He'd met Mohammed fifteen years ago when he'd stumbled upon him sleeping in the streets of West LA. Only sixteen years old at the time, Mohammed had been addicted to crack and near death. Patel had taken him back to his apartment and eased him off the street drug that had almost cost him his life. In return, Patel had asked for nothing except his loyalty. He often felt that Mohammed was the son he'd never had. There had been several times when both wanted nothing more to do with the other, as a father and son could be expected to, but they always managed to overcome their differences and remain friends.

Patel knew it was wrong to deal drugs to kids on the street. Mohammed's life was proof of that. He himself never indulged; he rarely even took a drink. Sadly, there were users who needed a supplier. With his medical knowledge and laboratory skills, he had the power to ensure that his drugs were as pure as any addicted user on the street could expect to buy. Mohammed swore to him he did not use drugs, not since Patel had rescued him. For the most part Patel had believed him. Lately, however he was not so sure.

Though he would never admit to it, Mohammed would do anything Amala told him. If she asked him to share a line of coke or a hit of meth, Patel knew that he would. Hence the reason for that day's luncheon. He also had other reasons, but they were of no concern to either Amala or Mohammed.

"Again, I will remind you that this was not my idea. I am only doing this for you and Mohammed," Patel added, though if he were to be honest with himself, he was enjoying his time with the old woman. She was as spry as an eighteen-year-old. At least in bed. He had watched her when she thought he wasn't looking. She rubbed her lower back and stretched her neck from side to side as though she were stiff and sore. It pleased him to know their late nights weren't easy on her either.

"I did not want to bilk those old bitches out of their money. Dr. Sameer has millions and millions of dollars. I am sure the old women aren't near as wealthy. That's your and Mohammed's gig. I want nothing to do with it," Amala said.

"I suppose you will want nothing to do with us if there is a large sum of money involved?" Patel suggested.

Amala swung her head from side to side. "You are a stupid old man, Patel."

Before he could respond, their waiter returned to the table with their entrées: a Caesar salad for her and his grilled Kobe burger. After assuring the waiter that they were fine, Patel glanced from left to right, making sure the conversation couldn't be overheard. "No, Amala, it is you that is stupid. You think you are smarter than I." Patel leaned forward, lowering his voice. "You are stupid to insist Mohammed partake in your little coke habit. He cannot handle himself when he is half out of his mind. You might want to take this into consideration the next time you offer him drugs. He talks. You would not know this because you are too involved with yourself. Your plans to steal Dr. Sameer's fortune will be ruined if Mohammed starts running his mouth. He does that when he is out of his mind. I suggest you stop offering him the drugs. If you have to indulge, do it when you are alone." Patel glanced at the diners seated outside on the patio. When his eyes rested on the pair entering the patio, his heart stopped.

"Whatever you do, do not turn around. Ida's friends are here."

"So?"

"I don't want them to see us together."

Amala took a bite of her salad. "Why? Is there something wrong with a girl's father taking her to lunch?"

Patel took a deep breath. "I suppose not. Do not do anything to draw attention. If they see us, act surprised, then insist we are running late. I do not want to linger with them here any longer than necessary. Just eat and keep your eyes focused on me," Patel ordered. "I mean it, Amala."

"Of course, old man. I wouldn't want to shame the good doctor."

"Your barbs are childish. I suggest you focus your anger on something or someone else. I have very few enemies, but those I have know what it is like to be subjected to my wrath," Patel said before taking a large bite of his juicy burger. Blood from the rare meat ran down the sides of his mouth. He mopped up the juices with his napkin, never once taking his eyes off Amala.

Apparently Amala decided to take his implied threat seriously. She attacked her salad as though it were her last meal. Never once did she look away from her plate to meet his unwavering gaze.

Patel took his glance away from Amala just in time to see the duo heading to their table.

Chapter 9

"Dr. Sameer, how are you? Amala?" Toots said as she held her hand out. "Not curing the world of its weird ailments on this fine day?" she added, thinking it odd to see Ida's doctor at her favorite LA hangout.

"Ah, Miss Loudenberry, Miss . . . Sophie. How wonderful to see you both." Dr. Sameer, ever the gentleman, stood and gave a slight bow to her and Sophie. "We are celebrating Amala's thirtieth birthday today. This is the only free time we have as work at the clinic never ends."

"Well, I for one think it's fantastic that you took the time to celebrate this day together. Most daughters your age would be out partying with friends," Toots said, then wished she hadn't. The look on Amala's face went from peaceful to hostile in seconds. Was she only humoring her father? Toots wasn't sure but took the young woman's look as a sign to move on. "Our table is ready. It was good seeing you both. Amala, have a wonderful birthday."

"Enjoy your luncheon," Dr. Sameer said before sitting back down.

"Thank you," Amala said.

Toots nodded to the young woman. Sophie raced ahead to their favorite table. She was already sitting down when Toots reached the table. "Something isn't right with Amala today. I think she's pissed at her father. I can't imagine why. A nice lunch at the Polo Lounge doesn't seem like a bad way to spend your birthday. Maybe it's just me," Toots rambled on as she sat down in the chair across from Sophie.

The patio of the Polo Lounge was the best place to see and be seen in Hollywood. Toots had learned that the first week she was in LA. Smack-dab in the center of Beverly Hills, the Polo Lounge was surrounded by twelve private acres, where lush tropical greenery and flowers washed the ground in every color of the rainbow. In the center of the patio was a Brazilian pepper tree, the long branches of which cast a shade over their favorite table. The brick flooring, the white wrought-iron chairs with dark green cushions, and green-and-white-plaid tablecloths were becoming quite familiar to Toots and Sophie. Their favorite waiter, Miguel, brought two tall sweetened ice teas to their table as soon as he saw that they were seated.

"Miss Toots, Miss Sophie," Miguel said. "You both look like you could use a cool drink today."

Sophie took a huge gulp of tea. "If you only knew. I'd like something a bit stronger. How about a Tom Collins? It's not too early, is it, Toots?"

"Considering we hit the liquor cabinet earlier, I don't think so. That one drink I had was enough for me. Remember, one of us has to drive. And you're not touching my damn car, so it looks like it's gonna be me. Drink all you want, but don't you dare get drunk. I will kick your butt all the way to New York if you do. Remember, we have plans tonight?" Toots kicked Sophie beneath the table.

"Ouch, that hurt!" Sophie said.

Miguel continued to wait for them to decide if they were going to have a drink or not.

"Good. I hope it left a mark," Toots added with a wink before turning her attention back to Miguel. "Just keep the sweet tea coming for me. Sophie, no more than two drinks. I don't want to drag your rump out of here, then have to keep you awake the rest of the evening."

"Piss on you, Toots. I was only going to have one. Three is my limit, remember? Or it is today." Sophie turned to Miguel. "One Tom Collins, please."

"Right away," he said.

Miguel quickly disappeared, allowing them to continue their conversation in private.

"I know that, but I also know how you fall asleep when you've had a few too many. You have to stay awake in order to set up all your equipment to capture the sounds and images of the ghosts, and I for one am going to make damned sure that you do it. My ass—hell, my sanity—is on the line here. What would Abby think if she knew I was seeing ghosts?"

Sophie finished off her ice tea. "Nothing. Abby isn't a judgmental person. You should know that by now. Unlike her mother, I might add."

"And what is that supposed to mean?" Toots flared.

Sophie picked up the white linen napkin, wiped her mouth, and reached for a cigarette.

"We can't smoke here, remember?" Toots reminded her. "Now go on, tell me what you meant. You think I'm judgmental. Give me an example."

Sophie deliberated a minute, then spoke up. "I can't think of anything offhand. But I'm sure that you are. I am, and we're two peas in a pod. So there."

Laughter from the table across from theirs forced Toots to glance at the occupants. A young girl was laughing at something her mother, or maybe an older sister, was saying. Toots wanted to make sure she hadn't overheard the talk of ghosts. Toots knew that if she heard someone discussing such an insane topic, she would laugh, thinking the speaker was one slice short of a loaf. Apparently the pair were simply laughing about something else, enjoying their lunch, because they never once looked in her direction.

Not only was she seeing ghosts but also she was becoming paranoid. She cast a glance at Dr. Sameer's table. Gone. He and Amala had managed to slip out without being noticed. Strange, Toots thought, that they didn't stop by their table to say good-bye. Then she remembered that Amala hadn't seemed to be her usual charming self. Maybe it was the thought of turning thirty.

"Earth to Toots?" Sophie fanned her hand back and forth in front of her face.

"What?"

"You're not listening to anything I'm saying, are you?"

Miguel appeared with Sophie's drink, saving Toots from having to reply.

"How can I not hear you? You haven't stopped flapping your jaws since we arrived. And we are not two peas in a pod, absolutely not, no way. I'm not judgmental either. I simply call things as I see them."

"Oh, and that's not being judgmental? I see. I guess the rules don't apply to you." Sophie grinned.

"Shut up, and let's order. I for one am damned sick and tired of eating all those fruits and vegetables Mavis has been shoving down my throat." Toots scanned the menu, then tossed it aside as their waiter approached the table to take their order.

"Two Kobe-beef burgers, medium rare, loaded with extra cheese and triple the mayo. And I'll have a double order of fries. Add some ranch dip, too. I haven't had a decent meal since forever."

"Mavis would kill you if she were here," Sophie said, then added, "I'll have the same."

The waiter wrote down their order and scurried away.

"Yeah, well, thank goodness she isn't. I don't think I can

survive much longer on that junk she's been feeding us. My body isn't used to all that fiber."

Sophie laughed. "We're a friggin' pair, aren't we? Bitching about poor Mavis, who'd give anything to be eating the artery-clogging meal we're about to have. Whatever you do, don't tell her we had beef. She's all but stopped eating red meat."

Toots took a sip of her tea. "Good, she doesn't need it anyway. I want to take her shopping, but she keeps insisting on remaking her old clothes. I wish I were more like Mavis."

"Yeah, she is one for the books. She likes to sew, so let her. Some of her new designs, or remakes as she's calling them, are much better than the originals. Maybe she could have a second career in fashion. Who knows? I need a cigarette. I'm going out front to smoke while you wait for our food."

Toots rolled her eyes. "Be my guest. That's considered rude, just so you know."

Sophie looked left to right, and when she saw no one was paying her the slightest bit of attention, she stuck out her tongue. "Like I give a good rat's ass. I'll smoke one for you."

Sophie raced off before Toots could respond. Toots needed a few minutes alone with her thoughts anyway. Last night's event—no, she couldn't call it an event; that word was reserved for funerals only—last night's *haunting* had scared her much more than she'd let on. Part of her questioned what she'd seen. Had she actually seen a ghost? Ghosts? Or, and this was what really frightened her, were the mysterious figures just figments of her imagination? Was she losing touch with reality? Maybe the haunting was an early sign of Alzheimer's disease, or a brain tumor. When she'd mentioned those possibilities to Sophie, she had been serious. Toots wasn't sure which was worse—the possibility that she had a mental illness or that the $3.8 million house she'd purchased had come with its original owners: ghosts. Either way, she was not a happy camper.

Before she continued down that depressing path, Miguel appeared with a heavy tray laden with four giant-sized plates. "You ladies have the appetite of bears."

"Yes, we do. I was never one to order lettuce and act like I wasn't hungry. Give me a good burger, and I'm a happy woman."

"Yes, Miss Toots," Miguel said as he set a huge plate in front of her.

"I'm guessing we'll want dessert, too," Toots added. Her sweet tooth needed a major fix.

Sophie slid into her empty chair. "I love to smoke. I don't care how bad it is. I was considering quitting, but why bother?" She raked her gaze over the plates of food. "You know we'll never eat all of this."

"Speak for yourself," Toots said before taking a large bite of her hamburger.

Sophie leaned across the table. "You're never going to guess what I just saw." She plucked a fry from her plate, dragging it through a mound of ketchup.

With her mouth full she couldn't speak, so she motioned with her hand.

"Don't talk with your mouth full," Sophie said.

Toots swallowed and was about to reach across the table and slap Sophie in her smart-ass mouth, but thought better of it. "What? I'm only asking once."

"Dr. Sameer and Amala were waiting outside. Apparently they have a limousine, not sure if it was his or maybe he rented it for Amala's thirtieth birthday. Whatever, I thought it rather odd when I saw Amala practically shove her tongue down the limo driver's throat. She kissed him like she couldn't wait to drag him into the sack. Hell, for all I know, they could be knocking one off in the backseat as we speak, though I doubt it. With her father present, it's unlikely. I'm sure she's learned a bit of control. I'm just saying . . ."

Toots considered this bit of news, unsure what to make of it. Then she decided she agreed with Sophie. "Not if she's tonguing the driver in the parking lot; that's anything but control. This is rather strange. She doesn't look like the type to go for the hired help. Maybe the limo belongs to her father, or maybe the limo driver owns the damned thing and he's her boyfriend. I'll mention this to Ida. If Dr. Sameer owns a limousine, she would know."

"True. I think Ida is having a fling with Dr. Sameer." Sophie took a small bite of her hamburger. "This is what food is supposed to taste like. Poor Mavis."

Engrossed in her meal, Toots waited until her hunger was satisfied before continuing their conversation. "Ida loves all men, Sophie. She acts like a slut no matter who they are. What makes you think she and the good doctor are an item? She hasn't been to see him in . . . I can't remember when her last visit was. Maybe I *am* getting Alzheimer's. Have you noticed anything odd about me lately? Have I been acting strange, forgetting things?" Toots feared her grip on reality was slipping and she had no control.

"Oh, frig! To quote you, 'You're as full of shit as a Sunday outhouse.' No, I don't think you have Alzheimer's; nor do I think you've been acting odd. You always act weird, Toots, that's just the way you are. You've let this ghost story frighten you too much. Ghosts aren't necessarily a bad thing. I tell you what, when we get back to the house, not only will I set up the camcorder and the electronic voice-phenomena recorder, but we'll have a séance, too. We can have Ida and Mavis join us. We need more than two people. We'll tell them it's just for fun."

Skeptical, Toots asked, "And you think they'll believe you?"

"They have no reason not to unless you tell them otherwise."

Toots pondered Sophie's idea of a séance. "Exactly what happens if a ghost does appear?"

"Hell if I know. I've been to a few séances when I lived in the city, but I never saw any ghosts or anything even close. A séance is simply a means of trying to make contact with the ghost, spirit, or a dead person. You can use a Ouija board, but I've heard that's dangerous. Some believe it opens portals into the unknown, allowing evil spirits to enter. We won't be doing that."

Toots took a bite out of her second hamburger. "I still can't believe we're talking about this . . . craziness. You sure you don't think I'm losing my mind?"

"Not at all. If I thought that, I would drag your old ass to Dr. Sameer's clinic in a heartbeat." Sophie laughed.

Toots almost choked on her food. "Don't you dare! I would kill you first. I'm going to tell Abby about him. Maybe she can do a bit of investigating on the side, see if he's registered with the American Medical Association and all the places any good doctor would register."

"Don't you think it's a little too late for that? You said he came highly recommended by your doctor. Are you having second thoughts about him? He sure as hell fixed Ida's problem in a hurry, I'll give him credit for that." Sophie tossed her napkin on top of her plate. "I'm ordering dessert before I get too full."

Toots smiled and took one last bite of her burger before giving up. As usual, her eyes had been bigger than her stomach. She should've ordered dessert first. She swigged the last drop of her ice tea. "Yeah, I'm ready for a sugar rush, and if Joe Pauley recommends someone, you can bet they're the best. I've trusted the man with my health for more than twenty years. Sameer did cure Ida of her weirdness, so he can't be all that bad, but there's something about him that gives me the creeps." Toots removed her lipstick from her clutch purse, reapplying her favorite warm peach color. "Again, it's probably nothing more than an old woman's paranoia."

Miguel appeared at their table with the dessert menu. "Ladies, will you be having another beverage with your dessert?"

Toots rolled her eyes, "Yes, we'll both have coffee, heavy on the cream and sugar. I'll have the red velvet cake."

"Ditto for me," Sophie said.

Toots waited for Miguel to leave before she resumed their conversation. "The next time I talk to Abby, I'll ask her if she can run a check on Sameer. Though she might not have time, since she's going to have her hands full with her new assignment, which, by the way, will put *The Informer* on the top of the tabloid totem pole." Toots hadn't told Sophie about the upcoming interview with pictures of the Pitt/Jolie clan. She'd kept quiet long enough.

"Oh, I didn't know she was out pounding the pavement again. I thought editor in chief was her new job."

"She's not, and it is. For now anyway." Toots took a deep breath, knowing Sophie would be as excited as she was. "Abby received an e-mail from Brad Pitt and Angelina Jolie's publicist inviting *The Informer* to interview them, and, get this, they're letting Abby take pictures of the kids!"

"What the hell! When did this happen?"

"This morning. And it gets even better."

"How so?"

"She's asked Ida to be her photographer," Toots said.

Sophie shook her head. "Ah-ha! So this is why you're suddenly so concerned about Sameer's credentials. I knew there was something you weren't telling me."

"I'm probably being paranoid again, but this interview is big-time news. I have to protect the paper and Ida, plus

I have to make sure my identity isn't revealed. I would hate for Ida to make a slip of the tongue. Call it a sudden case of I need to cover my ass. And if you're right about Ida and Sameer, who knows what might slip out of her mouth while she's wallowing in ecstasy."

Miguel delivered their coffees and dessert.

"Why don't we just ask Ida if she's sleeping with the doctor? There isn't any reason for her to deny it," Sophie said.

"If it were anyone else, that would be true. With Ida, not so. She likes to stir up controversy any way she can. We will start watching her closely. Starting tonight. After the séance."

"You're sure you want to go ahead and do this?" Sophie asked.

"What choice do I have? It's either get rid of that . . . presence in the house, or I go nuts and lose $3.8 million."

"Then let's get out of here. I have a lot to do."

Toots took four twenties and tucked them beneath her dessert plate for Miguel. "Come on, let's go. I don't want to put this off any longer. Who knows, this time next week I might be locked up in a loony bin."

Chapter 10

"**O**uch!" Mavis said when she stuck herself in the thumb with the needle for the third time. "You would think I'm a novice at this."

"Why won't you let me or Toots buy you a sewing machine? It would make your work much easier," Ida said.

"I have one at home. There's no need to spend money on something I already have. Besides, I enjoy hand sewing. Keeps my fingers nimble," Mavis said.

Ida was heading to her room to soak in the tub when Mavis had asked for her assistance with a piece of fabric. Not wanting to appear rude, Ida had said yes, having no clue what she was in for. Now that she stood in the center of the horrid pink-and-purple kitchen like a designer's dummy with a teal piece of material draped around her, she wished she'd said no. Her ankles hurt and her neck and back muscles screamed for a long hot soak in the tub. However, dear Mavis never asked for a thing, and when she did, it was almost impossible to tell her no. So there was Ida, stuck in the center of the kitchen while Mavis pinned her new design together. Though she was hesitant to speak up, Ida wanted to tell Mavis that she was a size six. Whatever she was making for herself, Ida wasn't her size, and she would just have to let out all the seams anyway, unless she lost another thirty pounds. Deciding that was what Mavis must be thinking, Ida didn't say anything, didn't want to hurt her friend's feelings, so she continued to hold her arms out like the Tin Man in *The Wizard of Oz*. Just waiting for a heart. In her case she was waiting for a bath.

Mavis turned her around for the tenth time. "Just a little tuck here, and I'm finished." She had several straight pins with colored heads sticking out of her mouth, making it difficult to understand what she'd said.

Ida wondered how Mavis was going to lift the fabric off her without jabbing her with all the pins, but she kept the thought to herself, knowing that Mavis was an expert seamstress and wouldn't put her in a position where she could get hurt. Mavis was like that, Ida thought. Kind, loving, caring, not a mean or spiteful bone in her ever-thinning body. She'd often wished she was more like her friend but accepted the fact that she wasn't.

Ida knew she was mean-spirited, spiteful, and wicked to her three best friends, but that was just the way she was. They seemed to accept her that way. After fifty years, not one of them had declined her friendship. They'd loved her just the way she was. She loved them all in return, but wasn't the kind to gush on and on about it. They knew she cared about them. Why else would she be there allowing Mavis to poke and turn her around as though she were a mannequin? Friends do such things for one another. That was what she kept telling herself. She looked at the clock on the stove. She'd been in the center of the kitchen for almost an hour. If Mavis didn't finish up soon, she would have to tell her it was time to quit.

She simply had to pee.

Mavis spun her around, eyeing her up and down. "There, it's perfect! Hold your arms up." Mavis gently lifted the fabric up and over the top of Ida's head. Not once did she feel the slightest pinprick.

"I don't see how you do that, but I'm about ready to bust. I'll be back." Ida raced to the downstairs bathroom, took care of business, then returned to the kitchen. In her absence Mavis had set up the ironing board and was stretching the teal fabric on top of it.

"You mean you actually iron that before you've finished," Ida said in complete and utter amazement. "I can't imagine why you would do that. Isn't it a waste of time when you know you'll have to iron it all over again after you've finished?"

"I'm ironing the seams down. It makes it easier to sew. I don't mind ironing. I used to spend Sunday evenings ironing Herbert's dress shirts when he was alive. It's a mindless task, Ida, not laborious." Mavis ran the iron along the fabric, weaving in and out, avoiding all the pins she'd inserted.

"Oh. Well then if you don't need me anymore, I need to go . . . uh, I have to call my broker." Ida was about to head upstairs when Mavis called out to her.

"Ida, I saw you this morning."

Ida stopped dead in her tracks, then turned around to face Mavis. "What are you talking about?" She knew. She just wanted to hear Mavis say the words. Kind of.

"I saw you get out of that limousine."

Damn! Now what to do?

Temporarily stunned, Ida wasn't sure what to say. She remained rooted to the floor for several seconds before she gathered her thoughts enough so that she could speak. "Oh, well then . . ."

Mavis interrupted her. "You don't owe me an explanation. As long as you're happy and safe."

Ida contemplated what to say and what not to say. She was an adult and didn't like all this sneaking around. In fact, she was going to tell Sammy it was time to go public with their relationship. They were both free, there was simply no reason to keep their feelings for one another hidden. With a lightened conscience, Ida found her voice. "I have been seeing someone."

Mavis continued with her ironing, though Ida saw the slight smile on her face. "I guessed it was something like that."

"You don't think I'm a tramp, do you?" Ida asked.

Mavis placed the iron on the edge of the ironing board, then unplugged it from the outlet. "Oh Ida, of course not! I would never think such a thing. I think it's wonderful that you've met someone."

"Really? I wasn't sure how you would react. Toots and Sophie are always teasing me. They think I can't live without a man, but that's not true. It's just . . . I just seem to attract them." Ida smiled. Well, it was true. She didn't go searching for them. They came to her.

Mavis dipped her head like a bashful teen. "Actually I've met someone, too. His name is George. He has a dachshund named Albert."

For once Ida smiled a genuine honest-to-goodness straight-from-the-heart smile. "Let's go outside and sit on the deck." Any thoughts of spending the afternoon bathing and sleeping were gone. Ida perked up when the topic turned to men. "And you can tell me all about him."

With a lightness in her step, Mavis beamed when she spoke, "I'll bring a pitcher of lemonade. I can't wait for you girls to meet him."

"Let me help you," Ida said.

"No, no, you go on out and wipe the sand off those old deck chairs. I'll only be a minute." Mavis grabbed a damp sponge from the sink. "Are you sure you don't mind?"

Ida took the sponge from her. "I'm okay now. Truly. I can sit on sandy deck chairs, Mavis. As a matter of fact, I want to sit on dirty chairs. It reminds me just how grateful

I am for Dr. Sameer's help. I don't know what I would do without him."

Mavis took the pitcher of lemonade from the refrigerator and grabbed a tray of ice and two glasses. "Come. I want to hear all about your new love," she said.

Out on the deck, Mavis poured them each a tall glass of fresh-squeezed lemonade before settling into the weather-beaten chair next to Ida's. "So tell me about George," Ida said cheerily. She simply loved to talk about men.

"We met on the beach. Coco saw his dachshund, Albert, and fell madly in love. I've never seen her so taken with another dog. Albert refused to walk when he saw Coco. I think it was love at first sight for the two. George and I just started talking, and one thing led to another. We've been meeting on the beach for the past two weeks. We're going out to dinner as soon as we can find a sitter for both dogs. He's very hesitant to leave Albert with just anybody. Of course I understand, and I told him so. I said Toots and Sophie would watch the dogs, but he said he wasn't sure and would have to meet them first. So, when they meet, and if Albert takes to Sophie and Toots, then we're going out on a real date."

Ida couldn't recall Mavis ever being quite as animated as she was at that moment. Her eyes sparkled, and her skin glowed like she'd just had one of those facials that Ida paid hundreds for in Manhattan. Love. Mavis looked like a woman in love!

"I can watch the dogs, Mavis. You don't have to ask Toots or Sophie." Ida said this knowing Mavis wouldn't accept her offer. Coco hated her, and she figured Albert would, too. Dogs didn't seem to like her for some reason.

"Oh no, but thank you. Coco really likes Toots." Mavis shifted her eyes downward. "Not that she doesn't like you, it's just that Toots is more of a dog person."

Somewhat chagrined and not exactly sure why, Ida just nodded. "Well, the offer still stands. You know, in case of an emergency. So tell me more about your George. Is he tall, dark, and handsome?"

"Yes, he is. He's also kind and loves animals. He is a widower, too."

"He sounds nice," Ida thought. Just like dear Mavis.

"Oh, there's much more to him than that. He owns a string of dry cleaners, and says he'll never fully retire. He travels a lot, too. He's never been to Maine. I asked him if he would like to come and visit me sometime in the future, but he didn't answer. I wonder why? Do you suppose he doesn't like easterners?"

Ida almost fell out of her chair. Mavis was so naive. Poor thing. Ida would have to teach her a thing or two about men. Maybe she should start a dating service or an advice column; she certainly had enough experience. Something to do with her free time. Or maybe she would just enjoy herself by taking pictures of whatever she wanted whenever she wanted. She'd thought about that many times but never dreamed it was possible. Once she took the photographs of the Pitt/Jolie kids, who knew where that would lead? Ida promised herself she would be open to all the possibilities regardless of where she was in her romantic life. She really did not have to have a man in her life. Someday she would prove this to Toots and Sophie. She smiled at the thought.

"Ida? Are you all right, dear?" Mavis asked.

Ida shook her head, "Yes, I was just woolgathering. No, I don't think being an easterner has anything to do with George's not answering you. It's quite possible he didn't hear you." Ida smiled. Poor Mavis spoke in such soft tones it was all Ida could do to hear her.

"Really? Now that you mention it, I suppose it is possible. He does seem to lean toward me when we're talking. I'll just have to speak loud and clear the next time the subject comes up. What do you think?"

"I think you should invite George and Albert over for dinner. I'm sure Toots wouldn't mind. You could make that fish dish of yours that I like so much. Of course we could call out for something if you don't want to cook. This way we would all get a chance to meet George, and he could decide if Toots and Sophie are worthy enough to dog-sit."

Mavis clapped her hands together. "That's a wonderful idea. Why didn't I think of that? We meet every morning at sunrise. I'll make sure to ask him. Of course, I want to clear it with Toots first. She's been so good to me. I would hate it if she thought I were taking advantage of her generosity. And I'm not sure if she would even want a stranger in the house now. Maybe I should wait until all the remodeling is finished. I wouldn't want to embarrass Toots."

Ida took a sip of her lemonade. "I'm sure Toots wouldn't want you to wait, but it's probably a good idea to ask her first. She can be moody when she wants to be." Ida shouldn't have said that, but it was true. Toots could be as big a bitch as Ida. That's why they fought like cats and dogs. They were very much alike, though Ida was sure Toots would never agree with her. As the old saying goes, "It takes one to know one."

"Well she did just lose her husband, Ida. Of course she's moody. It took years for me to recover from Herbert's death. Sometimes I'm still not sure that I'm over it. I still miss him, and it's been almost fifteen years." Mavis gazed longingly out at the Pacific.

"She's had eight husbands. I think grieving has become routine for her. It's an event for her, she told me so herself. I don't believe Toots's moodiness can be attributed to grief."

"Well, I for one don't care what kind of mood Toots is in. She's my dearest friend." Mavis paused as though she'd made a massive blunder. "And of course so are you and Sophie. I love each one of you."

"Oh Mavis, you're too sweet to be hanging with three old women who do nothing but complain about one another. You should be with people who are more like you."

"And what kind of people would that be?" Mavis asked.

Ida brushed sand from her lap. "Nice people, people who don't bitch all the time."

Mavis laughed. "I wouldn't change one thing about any of you, so you can stop right now. Now, you haven't said one word about this mysterious man that you've been sneaking out to see every night for the past few weeks. I want to know all about him."

Shit, it was confession time.

Chapter 11

Abby had checked her e-mail at least ten times since she'd replied to the publicist's message. Nothing. She thought that she should have heard something by then. E-mail was practically instantaneous. If the Pitt/Jolie publicist wanted to arrange for an interview, one would assume they would check their e-mails often enough to get the process going. Abby glanced at her watch again. Damn, only four minutes had passed since she looked at it the last time. Chester lay curled up in a ball on the Barcalounger, fast asleep. Dogs, they could sleep anywhere. Almost like men. Men. No, she would not think of men because thinking of men would remind her of Chris Clay. And Chris Clay was not someone she wanted to think about. Not after she'd seen his face plastered on the cover of *People* with that sleazy-ass star of the month. No, men were jerks. Men made promises they couldn't or wouldn't keep, unlike women, who always kept their promises. At least she did.

She remembered her so-called date with Chris right before the fire. They'd gone to Pink's, a hot-dog stand made famous for its "cuisine" and the stars who often dined there. They'd gone together. She'd eaten three hot dogs. He'd kissed her fingers. Each and every one of them. One at a time. Abby had promised herself she wouldn't wash her hands for at least a week, but she had eaten those words almost as fast as she'd gobbled down the hot dogs.

She'd spoken to Chris on the phone in the wee hours of the morning, had asked him for a favor. And he'd flat out told her no. He hadn't minced words either. She'd been avoiding him ever since. He'd told her he liked her. As in really liked her. Her mistake, she'd believed him. Her dear stepbrother, whom she'd had a crush on since she'd first laid eyes on him. She had been fourteen and he was eighteen, and now at twenty-eight she still couldn't stop thinking about him. Damn!

She heard the bell on her computer ding, letting her know she'd received a new e-mail. Maybe the publicist. She clicked on the yellow mailbox. An e-mail from Victoria's Secret. Yes, just what she needed. A sexy pair of panties with a matching bra. No one to appreciate them except herself, so she definitely wasn't in the mood for designer lingerie. No need. Her love life had been stuck in slow motion for so long, it would take more than sexy lingerie to lure her out of . . . what? There wasn't anyone she wanted to date, except Chris. He'd ruined any chance they had when he'd refused to offer his legal advice, telling her he was working for her mother. Abby believed him; she'd even asked her mother just to double-check. Still, he could've helped her out. Conflict of interest, he'd said. Conflict of interest my ass, Abby thought.

Chester stood up in the Barcalounger and stretched languidly before jumping off his favorite chair. "You want out, I bet." Abby found his leash on the back of her chair. She clipped it to his collar, grabbed her keys, and headed outside for Chester's afternoon stroll so he could water the bushes.

Once out in the parking area, Abby removed Chester's leash. Now that the parking lot was completely fenced in, there was a nice safe area where Chester could run loose and do his business while she didn't have to worry about keeping him collared. Rag would've had her ass if he'd known she allowed Chester to roam freely. He'd been real big on insisting she keep him on a leash, always reminding her of the liability if he were to bite an employee or, God forbid, an advertiser. She wished that Chester had taken a bite out of the old bastard. Would have served him right after all the trouble his leaving caused. Abby had high hopes that he would be found someday. Until then, she had more important things to worry about.

The Jolie/Pitt interview would put *The Informer* up against *The Enquirer* and *The Globe*. They would pay millions for this interview, she knew that. Hell, *The Informer* would pay big bucks if they could. But luckily for them—and for her—they didn't have to.

A germ of an idea began to form in the back of her mind. What if she were to build up this interview before it actually took place? What if she hinted to the readers that *The Informer* was about to land the mother of all exclusive interviews? She could do it, build up reader momentum, not to mention sales, then boom. She'd have every tabloid reader in America lining up to buy *The Informer* when her interview, with pictures, was front and center at every grocery store, airport, newspaper stand, and every discount department store in the nation. Yes, she could do it. She was sure it would be at least two to three weeks before the interview actually took place. That would allow her enough time to write the teasers. She'd do them herself. Of course, she would have to have the approval of the new owners, but Abby figured if they were smart businessmen, or women, they would give her the go-ahead. The only way she could contact them, though, was via e-mail.

"Come on, Chester. We've got work to do."

Upon hearing his name, the German shepherd raced to Abby's side. She stooped down so he could cover her face with dog kisses. She ruffled his ears, then patted his muzzle. "You're such a smart boy, you know that? I do believe you're smarter than Mr. Clay, the jerk."

Chester barked.

Abby grinned. "I see you agree with me. A smart move, old boy."

Back inside her office, Abby refreshed Chester's water and grabbed a Coke from the minifridge before sitting down to draft an e-mail to her unknown employer, LAT Enterprise. How was she to address them? she wondered as she clicked on her e-mail account. She went with the obvious.

Dear LAT Enterprise:

Yesterday I received an e-mail from the publicist for the Pitt/Jolie team. They have granted *The Informer* an interview. They also requested photographs of their twins. As of this writing, we have not scheduled an exact date. I would assume two to three weeks before all involved are ready. I believe *The Informer*'s sales would skyrocket if we were to build up our readers' anticipation with teasers on the upcoming exclusive interview. As editor in chief I will take full responsibility for writing them and doing the upcoming interview.
I ask your permission to begin this project immediately.

Respectfully,

Abby Simpson,
Editor in Chief

She read through the e-mail twice before hitting the SEND button. That was direct and right to the point. She had no clue if the actual owners would read it, but assumed the information would somehow reach the decision maker. If they were smart, they'd jump on this like white on rice. Done properly, the interview could launch a whole new readership and keep their regular subscribers satisfied as well.

Abby scanned her new e-mails, hoping for a response from the publicist, but so far, nothing, nada, zilch. "Damn, come on, answer your e-mail," she thought as she typed short, succinct answers to her three stringers covering Revlon's Woman of the Year luncheon, which amounted to nothing more than older out-of-work actors vying for a chance to rub shoulders with producers and directors. Still, one never knew. She'd instructed Elizabeth to hide in the ladies' room on the off chance she'd hear something newsworthy, tabloid newsworthy. She hated to sink so low, but it was commonplace in the business nowadays, almost so much so that it was next to impossible to overhear the tiniest bit of gossip. Today's stars were savvy where the press were concerned, yet they knew how to play right into their hands when they needed a headline. Trouble was, *The Informer*'s "hands" always seemed to be last in line.

When she finished answering her e-mails, Abby turned off the computer, covered her keyboard with a protective plastic cover, and grabbed her purse and Chester's leash. "Come on, boy, it's time to go home. Maybe we'll both get lucky tonight."

Chester leaped off his chair and followed her to the door and down the long hallway to the back exit. Once inside her MINI Cooper, Abby strapped Chester's seat belt in place before adjusting her own. She had promised Chester a steak that night. She'd make a pit stop at Ralph's. She needed food, *real* food. She'd been existing on takeout for weeks. Between running *The Informer* out of her garage, then settling into her new office, not to mention trying to stay on top of her remodeling projects at home, Abby hadn't bothered with grocery shopping, let alone cooking. As her mother would say, that's what restaurants are for. While she agreed wholeheartedly, she was sick of fast food.

She weaved the little car in and out of traffic, stopping every so often for one of LA's world-famous traffic jams. Forty-five minutes later, she hit Brentwood, where she lived just minutes from a Ralph's grocery store.

"You'll have to stay in the car, Chester, but I promised you a big steak, and that's exactly what you're gonna get."

Before she got out of her car, she lowered the windows just enough to allow fresh air to flow through the car, but not enough that Chester could jump out after her.

Abby entered the store, grateful for the wash of icy air. She was about to reach for a shopping basket when her hand collided with another hand, another large male hand. "Wait a minute buddy . . ."

"Well, if it isn't my favorite reporter. Abby Simpson. What are you doing in a grocery store? Please tell me you're not making dinner tonight."

Her first instinct was to run out of the store, her second was to sock him right in the kisser, but her third, the one she acted on, was to remain calm. She was an adult. She could handle this.

"I suppose I should ask you the same. I hope you're not making dinner for one of your Hollywood starlets. I might have to report that some of them actually eat real food." Abby yanked the shopping basket out of Chris Clay's hand.

He jumped back. "Testy today, aren't we? News must be slow. I remember that about you. You're always pissy when you don't have something to write for that sleazy paper."

Abby had turned her back on him. She was going to purchase her groceries, go home, and cook dinner for herself and a steak for Chester. But no, Chris just had to remind her what he thought of her chosen profession. Something he knew would tick her off.

Abby turned around to face him. She gripped the shopping basket so hard her knuckles were white. "What do you want? Are you following me?" Damn, why did she say that? Of course he wasn't following her. Why would he follow her? He knew where she lived. Damn, damn, and double damn.

He laughed, shaking his head. "No, Abs, I'm not following you. It just so happens this is where I buy my mint-chocolate-chip ice cream. I can't cook, or don't you remember?"

She felt like jerk of the month just standing there staring at him. But he was so hot to look at. Faded jeans with a few holes in all the right places, a tight black T-shirt that only emphasized his broad chest and narrow waist. She focused on his feet. When she saw the bright orange Crocs on his feet, it was all she could do to keep from laughing. She couldn't help but smile. What a jerk.

"It was good seeing you, Chris. Have a nice day." Abby turned and walked away, giving herself a mental high-five. Let him stare at my ass, she thought. Maybe he'd see what he was missing. Shit, now where did that come from? She wasn't one to play on her looks. She'd been told by more than one person that she should've been in movies. Her token reply was always, "Too bad I can't act." That usually shut them up. Abby knew looks were important in the movie industry, but they didn't count for anything in her line of work.

Not wanting to leave Chester alone in the car any longer than she had already, she raced up and down the aisles, grabbing a few items before turning back to the meat counter for Chester's steak. Of course her luck was tough that day because as soon as she emptied her basket for the cashier to ring up her items, who stepped in line behind her but Chris Clay? She'd been in such a hurry to get out of the store she really hadn't paid that much attention to what she'd tossed in her basket. She observed Chris as he watched the cashier drag her items across the scanner. One New York strip steak. A pack of hot dogs. Buns. Mustard. Sour cream and onion potato chips. Cherry Pop-Tarts. What the hell was she thinking? Abby thought it obvious her subconscious had chosen those particular items with Chris in the store. She only prayed he didn't make the connection.

"You should've told me you were craving hot dogs, Abs. We could go back to Pink's."

She wanted to kick him, but refrained. "Thanks, but they're for Chester. He likes hot dogs with mustard and relish. I have relish at home," she added. TMI, she thought. Too much information. More than he needs to know.

The cashier totaled up her purchases. Abby scanned her debit card through the machine. She sneaked a side glance at Chris, praying he wouldn't discover her PIN number. He was watching. Shit. Before the cashier could ask again, Abby quickly punched her PIN number in the machine— 24747—C-H-R-I-S. She was sure she moved her hands over the keypad fast enough. Unless he stood right beside her or directly behind her, she was fairly certain he couldn't decipher her password. And if he did, tough shit.

"Of course you do," Chris said as he dropped two gallons of mint-chocolate-chip ice cream on the checkout counter.

Abby felt her face flame, and it pissed her off. Why she should feel so . . . *antsy* she didn't know. This was Chris. Her stepbrother. Sort of. And he'd kissed her fingertips. One at a time after they'd had hot dogs at Pink's. She hated the feelings brought on by that memory. She did not want to get involved with Chris Clay. No way. He was a heartbreaker, a player, and her mother's current attorney. She didn't even want to think about all the stars he dated. They were like revolving doors. In and out, constantly. Everything about him screamed no.

When the cashier finally finished bagging her groceries, Abby grabbed the two plastic bags and hurried over to the automatic doors. She couldn't get out of the damn store fast enough. She juggled the two bags in one hand while she used the other to dig inside her purse for her car keys. When she located the jangling bunch of keys, she hit the unlock button. Chester was dragging his tongue up and down the passenger window. *Lovely,* she thought as she slid into the driver's seat. "You are going to help clean those windows when we get home."

"Woof!"

"And you're getting a bath, too," Abby added. The weather was perfect for grilling that night. While the steaks cooked, she would hose down her car and Chester. After dinner, she would check her e-mail one last time before calling it a day.

If she hadn't heard from the Pitt/Jolie publicist, she would . . . wait. What other choice did she have?

Chapter 12

"A séance? Are you out of your mind?" Ida exclaimed. "Next thing I know, you'll be asking us to set up a hotline like that Miss Cleo from the Psychic Friends Network!"

"Oh, get a frigging grip, Ida," Sophie said. "We're trying to have fun. If you don't want to join us, then you can sit out here all night and pout. None of us gives a good rat's ass. Right, girls?"

Mavis clapped her hands to get their attention. "Sophie, let's not argue. I think it would be fun. I have to say I've never tried this before, but it sounds exciting. I'm all about trying new things now. You'll enjoy yourself, Ida. Look at this as another new experience. Please join us."

Toots took one last puff of her cigarette before crushing it out in the seashell. "Make up your mind, Ida, this isn't all about you and what you think. If you're scared, just say so," Toots challenged. If they only knew. She was shaking in her shoes. Her act of bravado was just that. An act. No way would she let Ida know she was the least bit frightened.

Sophie sat on the edge of the deck, finishing her cigarette. "If you're in, you're in. I have to get things ready. Toots, you want to help me?"

"Of course. I, for one, can't wait. Who knows? Maybe we'll contact one of my deceased husbands. Ida, you might get in touch with Thomas. He might reveal where that tainted meat came from."

"Okay, I'm in. If you are all trying to pull something on me, tell me now. I don't like surprises," Ida said.

"She's just pure chickenshit," Sophie teased.

"Count me in. And Sophie, why don't you just . . . fuck off?"

Toots, Sophie, and Mavis burst out laughing.

"Now that's the spirit, Ida!" Sophie cheered. "See? You'll be cussing and smoking real soon, and before you know it, you'll be stopping all that prissy-ass behavior. Ida, you and Mavis gather up as many candles as you can find. I'm sure that pop tart has some stashed somewhere in this seaside whorehouse. Toots, come upstairs with me." She looked at her watch. Mimicking a ghostly voice, Sophie said, "We'll meet in the dining room in one hour. Don't be late."

Together they raced upstairs. Once they were inside Toots's new bedroom, Sophie sat down on the bed.

"What can I do to help?" Toots asked, then added, "I will not go in that room, so don't even ask."

"You don't have to. All we need are those candles and a tablecloth. I was going to use one of the silky sheets from the ghost room. Maybe our resident spook will be more amenable if they see something they recognize. I'm going to set up the camcorder and the electronic voice recorder, too. Just in case we actually hit pay dirt."

"Don't you think this . . . ghost or spirit—I still can't believe we're having this conversation—don't you think they'll know where they're at?" Toots asked. "Because I sure as hell know what I saw, and it was not something normal. Whatever you do, don't say anything about last night. If—

and this is a big if—something appears, don't say I told you so. Pretend you're surprised."

"Trust me, Tootsie, I won't be acting if something manifests itself. I will be just as scared as the rest of you."

Suddenly unsure, Toots asked, "Are you sure about this? Shouldn't we have the house blessed or something before we do this?"

"I have some holy water left over from Walter's funeral. We'll sprinkle some around and say a prayer. Now let me get my things. You go on and help the girls. Make sure that god-awful dining room doesn't have any flowers or fruits lying around. Spirits, or so I've heard, don't like sweet or fruity scents. If there are any metal or glass objects, take them out of the room, too. Minerals supposedly interfere with the spirits' ability to show themselves. Don't ask. That Madam Butterfly lady told me that once."

"I'll make sure to check. See you downstairs." Toots hurried out of the room.

Sophie made her way across the hall to her bedroom, hoping that whatever Toots had seen would show itself while she was in the room. She rummaged through her luggage until she found the small bottle of holy water that had been blessed at Walter's funeral. She took her camcorder and a small tape recorder just in case the spirits decided to make themselves known through sounds. Sophie was excited, but she was scared, too. She trusted Toots, knew she wasn't off her rocker, wasn't seeing things. If Toots said she saw a ghost, a spirit, puffy clouds with faces inside, Sophie believed her 100 percent.

She pulled the purple silk top sheet off the bed, rolled it into a ball, then tucked it beneath her arm. She glanced around the nightmarish room once more. When she saw there were no floating clouds, cool gusts of air, or faces struggling to speak, she went downstairs.

Sophie closed the door to her room, then opened it. If there were something inside the room, she wanted to do everything in her power to help it make its exit. Who knew? It could just as easily walk through the door, but she left it open anyway. She wasn't taking any chances.

Racing downstairs, she found Toots, Ida, and Mavis in the dining room, lighting candles. "Not too many, just enough to add a touch of light to the room. We don't want a bonfire."

Sophie shook the sheet out and draped it over the round wooden table, thinking it odd that the pop tart who'd rented the place actually had a decent piece of furniture that wasn't pink, purple, or white Formica. The table was solid wood. Sophie wasn't sure what kind, but she remembered reading somewhere that when wood was charged with an unnatural entity, it acted as a conductor. Therefore, it wasn't necessary to hold hands or touch one another.

"Mavis, put one of the candles over here," Sophie said, pointing to the center of the table.

"Oh yes, of course. You need to see."

Once Sophie had all her props in place, she scanned the setting. It looked like something from a B movie. The round wooden table with a candle glowing in the center, the sheet's edges billowing from the movement around the table, and three women who already looked as though they'd seen a ghost. All that was lacking was the proverbial crystal ball. She looked down at her cream-colored blouse, thinking maybe she should have dressed for the part as well. After all, this was Hollywood. Sophie could have wrapped herself up in one of the purple sheets on her bed.

In her most serious voice, Sophie said, "If you ladies are ready, I say we get down to business."

Toots, Ida, and Mavis each stood behind a chair, their faces already pale with anticipation.

"First, I want to say a prayer. Bow your heads," Sophie instructed.

They did as she asked.

"Oh great one, bless this dump and those who inhabit it, living or dead." It was all Sophie could do to keep from laughing even though she was trying her hardest to act serious. The utter stupidity of what she was doing suddenly hit her, but it was too late to back out now.

"I'm not saying 'amen' to that one," Toots whispered.

Sophie ignored her and began walking around the room. She sprinkled the holy water, saying, "We come in peace. Please don't be frightened." She remembered an old sci-fi movie where they'd said words similar to hers. After she'd circled the room three times, Sophie took her seat.

"Let's sit down and join hands."

Again the women followed her directions.

Mavis was on her left, Toots to her right and—thank God—Ida was seated between Toots and Mavis. Sophie really didn't want to hold her hand.

Sophie chuckled to herself, thinking that under other circumstances it would have been almost too bad that Ida was cured of her obsessive-compulsive disorder. She would've loved nothing more than to have arranged for Ida to sit next to her and to have Ida reach for her hand, only to find it dirty and smelly. Sophie could've found a dead fish or something and rubbed it across her palm. Ida would have had a heart attack.

Next, Sophie pushed the candle away from the center of the table and put a drinking glass in its place.

"I want everyone to relax, think of something pleasant. Ida, think of a man. Take a deep breath," Sophie said, getting into her role. "Now imagine someone from the past, someone you would like to connect with. Deep breaths in. Now out." Sophie's hypnotic words were having an effect on the three. They looked as though they were in a trance. Wasn't she the one supposed to be in a trancelike state? She cleared her head. Didn't matter, they were into this now, and she wasn't going to do anything that would ruin it. They would all have a good laugh about it later.

"If there is someone in the room with us, make yourself known." Sophie paused, waiting for something to crash. When nothing did, she continued. "We're not here to cause harm. We are friendly." God, had she actually said that? Yep, Sophie Manchester, you certainly did. "Is there someone out there who would like to communicate a message to someone? We want to help you."

The room was silent except for the sound of their breathing. "Girls, think of someone who has passed, a friend or family member you would like to give a message to." Sophie saw the three around the table, their eyes squeezed tight in concentration.

Several minutes passed before Sophie spoke again. She remembered reading in one of her psychic books that if an hour passed, and there were no signs of paranormal activity, then it was time to stop.

Suddenly, the room became icy, bone-chilling cold. Sophie's eyes grew to the size of saucers. Mavis looked like she was ready to faint. Toots didn't appear to be frightened, but Ida seemed to be in a state of shock. Sophie was in control. She could do this. Take a deep breath. In and out, she told herself.

"We're not here to cause any harm, please know that." In a whisper, Sophie said to the girls, "Place your fingertips on the glass, very lightly." They did. "Good, now, whoever is here, we want to talk to you. There is a drinking glass in the center of this table. If you see the glass, try to move it." Sophie waited. "Use your fingertips to move the glass." Again she waited several seconds. Nothing happened.

"If you're a male, could you try to move the glass to my right? If you're a female, move the glass to my left. We want to help you." Sophie paused, focusing her attention on the glass. Without warning, the glass slowly moved to the right, then stopped.

The women drew in their respective breaths in one giant gasp. "Nothing to be frightened of, ladies. Take a deep, calming breath." They followed her instruction.

Sophie's gaze went back to the glass. "You are a man. Move the glass to my right for yes or to the left for no."

Except for the fizzing sounds of the candles' burning wicks, the room was silent. All stared intently at the drinking glass. Ever so slowly the glass moved to the right. "Son of a—" Sophie stopped herself. Deciding to go with it, she asked, "Are you a movie star? If your answer is yes, please move the glass to my right."

All four women observed the glass as it moved to Sophie's right for the third time. The chill in the room soaked in clear to her bones. "If this house we are in belonged to you, please move the glass to the right for yes, to the left for no," Sophie repeated.

Again all were mesmerized by the movements of the glass as it slid ever so slightly to the left. Sophie gasped. "Were you ever married to any of the women is this room?" Sophie asked in a small voice. What if Walter showed himself? Sophie looked up to find Toots staring at her. Toots offered up a weak, but reassuring smile. She knew what Sophie was thinking.

They all focused their gaze on the glass as it slowly moved to the left. Sophie let out such a deep breath that the flame on the candle wavered. Relief was etched across all of their faces. Suddenly the candle went out, a breeze swept through the room, and the glass, wavering on the edge of the table, slid off and crashed to the floor.

"Oh my God!" Mavis shouted.

Sophie glared at her. "Shhh!"

Mavis nodded.

Sophie regained control of the séance. "If you are angry, it's okay. Are you angry?" Sophie realized there wasn't a solid object for the spirit to use as a means of communication. Not wanting to get up and go to the kitchen for another glass, Sophie eyed the burned-out candle. "Let's place our fingertips around the candle."

Again, they followed her instructions.

They'd barely touched the candle when it fell to the right. Sophie's eyes never once left the candle.

"You are angry." The candle rolled to the edge of the table, stopping abruptly. The women jerked their hands back as though they had been burned. "It's okay. Nothing to be afraid of. Just relax. Let's join hands."

Again their hands formed a circle around the table. Their hands were bitterly cold now, almost stiff. Sophie was beginning to fear she'd bitten off more than she could chew. She squeezed Toots's hand; Toots returned the squeeze.

"Are you angry at someone in this room?" Sophie asked, afraid of the answer as she gazed at the candle teetering on the edge of the table.

The candle rolled back to the center of the table, then to the left. Sophie looked at Ida, who was deathly pale. Mavis's eyes were closed, and Toots had a death grip on her hand.

Sophie continued to guide the spirit. "You are *not* angry with someone in this room?" The candle rolled slowly to the right.

All at once the room returned to its normal temperature. Sophie knew that whoever had been there was gone. She eyed the candle. It remained on its side. Their hands no longer felt quite as cold. "Bless all who reside in this house, past, present, and future," Sophie said, then let go of Toots's and Mavis's hands. They in turn released their hold on Ida.

They looked at one another, unsure of what to say.

Sophie took charge. "Let's go out to the deck. I need a cigarette."

"Me, too," Toots added in a shaky voice.

They were all silent as they followed Sophie out to the deck. She grabbed her pack of Marlboros, lit one, handed it to Toots, then lit another for herself. Nothing was said, as each of them tried to come to terms with what had just taken place in the dining room. Sophie had more or less thought the entire séance thing was a joke until the biting cold had swept through the room. Their having contacted someone/something wasn't funny. Not in the least.

"So"—she took a deep drag from her cigarette—"what just happened back there . . . we shouldn't tell anyone."

"Absolutely not!" Toots said. "If Abby finds out we're talking to . . . whatever that was, she'll have each and every one of us committed."

Mavis and Ida nodded their agreement.

Toots crushed her cigarette out in the shell, then lit another. "Let's have a drink."

Before they could answer, Toots went back inside, returning minutes later with a bottle of scotch and four shot glasses. Words were unnecessary as she poured the amber liquid into the glasses. Toots passed the drinks to her friends. They tossed back the liquid as though it were water. Toots poured a second round. After the third, they relaxed a bit, and their tongues loosened as well.

"What the fuck just happened in there?" Toots asked.

"This frigging dump is haunted, that's what happened. I don't know if I even want to spend the night here," Sophie said. "Ida, Mavis? What do you two think happened in that room?"

Mavis was drunk from the three shots of whiskey. "Like you said"—her words slurred together in one sentence—"thereisaghostinthishouse."

Sophie smiled. "Ida?"

"I never thought I would be saying this, but I think this place is haunted. I for one am not going to spend another night under this roof."

"I agree. I think we all should go to Abby's for the night. We can tell her we lost power," Sophie stated firmly.

"No! I don't want to do that. Abby will know right away something other than losing the power is wrong. She knows each and every one of us like the back of her hand. We can't go there. I don't want to leave. This is my damned house, and I will not let a . . . ghost chase me out of it. Besides, I think our resident spirit is harmless." Toots poured herself another shot of whiskey.

In a shaky voice, Ida asked, "How do you know that?"

"If he meant us any harm, he would have harmed us tonight. Right, Sophie?" Toots questioned.

"You're probably right. I think whoever this is . . . is frustrated. I think we should call those people on TV, tell them this place is haunted. We might even get to go on the show. We could be reality stars. Sort of . . ." Sophie's words fizzled when she saw the look on Toots's face. "Okay, that's not a good idea."

"We are going to do nothing. At least for now. We cannot let what happened here tonight leave this house. I want you all to swear to me that you will not repeat what happened here tonight." Toots placed both of her hands down on the small glass table, one on top of the other. Sophie followed, then Mavis. Ida was last as usual, but this was their secret handshake. They only used it when they were serious. And this ghost stuff was serious business.

"Okay. It's agreed. We won't tell anyone about this. Not now. Sophie, when can we have another séance? Is there a rule about how often you can hold one of them?"

"Not that I'm aware of. Let's try it again tomorrow night. Same time. We'll try to make sure the scenario is as close to tonight's as possible, see what happens. Meanwhile, I think I will go online and do a bit of research. Maybe something terrible happened in this house. Maybe that's why you were able to purchase a Malibu beach house for three-point-eight million dollars." Sophie raised her brow. "Wasn't Sharon Tate killed around here somewhere?"

"Oh shit, Sophie, stop it! No one was murdered in this house. The real estate agent would have told me. Besides, I don't think that little pop tart that lived here would've stayed as long as she did if she thought the place was haunted, or if someone had been killed in the house."

"We don't know that for sure. It can't hurt to look into it," Sophie said.

"Yes, it can. What if someone at *The Informer* found out the editor in chief's mother thought she was living in a haunted house? I can just imagine the headlines *The Enquirer* and *The Globe* would have splashed across their front pages!"

"Okay, you're right. I didn't think of that."

"You can't think of everything, Soph. So . . ." Toots looked at her three closest friends in the world, Abby's godmothers. "Do I have your word that what happened here tonight won't leave this house?"

"Of course," Sophie said. "I don't run my mouth." She looked at Ida.

"Are you insinuating I do?" Ida asked.

"No. It's not a matter of 'insinuating' anything. You have been known to run your mouth, and you damn well know it!" Sophie said a bit too loud. The booze was getting to her.

"We all swore we wouldn't tell. I trust all of you," Toots said.

They all nodded, agreeing that what they'd witnessed wouldn't leave the confines of the house.

In order to change the subject, Toots said, "Then let's

get back to our routines. I am so behind on my e-mail, it will take days for me just to catch up."

"Yes, and I have been longing for a soak in the tub," Ida said.

Mavis and Sophie just nodded. They were too drunk to do anything else.

Chapter 13

Three weeks after *that night*, which is the way Toots and the godmothers referred to the night of the first séance, Ida checked her image in the mirror one last time before heading downstairs. She wanted to look her best for her first official public date with Sammy. She'd chosen to wear a pale yellow skirt that clung in all the right places and an opalescent blouse that shimmered in the light. She'd used two gold combs to pull the sides of her hair away from her face. She wore a simple gold chain around her neck and her smallest diamond earrings, along with a slender gold bangle bracelet. That was all the jewelry she wore. Sammy had hinted that he had something special to give her tonight. Ida was sure he was going to propose and that the "something special" he had mentioned was an engagement ring.

She looked at the clock on her night table. He would be there any minute if he wasn't already. He was very punctual, something she was not. Toots, Sophie, and Mavis were downstairs waiting for her. She felt like a schoolgirl facing her boyfriend's parents for the first time. Mavis was thrilled for her. Toots and Sophie hadn't let up when she had finally told them she was dating Dr. Sameer. Ida had to admit that they hadn't been too hard on her. Sophie said she'd suspected as much, and Toots had warned her to be careful. Of what, Ida had asked, but Toots hadn't elaborated.

Just in case Sammy was waiting at the bottom of the staircase, Ida practically floated down the stairs. When she reached the bottom, she was greeted by none other than Coco, Mavis's spoiled Chihuahua.

"Grrr," the small dog growled at her, then ran up the stairs. Ida hated the dog and wished Mavis would train her to behave.

She heard voices and followed them outside to the deck. Toots, Sophie, and Mavis were gathered around the new patio table with Sammy. She took a deep breath. "Hello, it looks like you've started without me." Ida observed that their glasses were almost empty.

"You take too long to get ready. Your date was thirsty," Sophie informed her.

"Oh Sammy, I'm sorry. I didn't mean to keep you waiting."

Dr. Sameer, Sammy, stood up, then walked over to where she was standing. He placed a light kiss on her cheek, then stepped back to admire her. "You are as beautiful as ever, my dear. Take as long as you need. Your friends are very entertaining," he said, smiling.

Ida feared what her "friends" would tell Dr. Sameer now that they were out of his office in a relaxed atmosphere. Ida prayed Sophie hadn't said anything that would embarrass her. "Yes, they are very, very entertaining, to say the least. Now, if you don't mind, I am famished. You did say we were going to dinner?" Ida asked, knowing that he had but wanting to get away from the house as soon as possible. Ever since that first ghostly séance three weeks ago, Ida felt strange just being in the house. Other than the regular séances they held, there hadn't been any remotely ghostlike encounters, or at least she hadn't had any. And if any of the others had, no one had told her about them. But maybe that was because they knew that she was uncomfortable in the house, that she felt like someone or some-*thing* was watching her. Sometimes she wished that they had not acted on Toots's suggestion that they have a second séance the night after the first one, which since then had grown into twice-a-week meetings with the spirits.

"Ah, yes, I did. Now, if you ladies will excuse us. Ida . . ." He linked her arm through his, leading her inside. The trio followed them like lost puppies. Ida smiled. She liked the idea of her friends trailing behind her.

"Don't be late," Toots said.

Sophie chimed in, "And don't do anything I wouldn't do."

"Just enjoy yourself," Mavis said. "Take good care of her, Dr. Sameer."

"Of course. Now if you ladies will excuse us." Ida let Sammy lead her outside. When she saw the limousine, her heart fell flat to her feet and back. She had hoped Sammy would drive tonight. If they were going to get married, she would have to tell him how she felt about his driver once and for all. Of course, she wasn't totally sure Sammy was going to propose, but she wasn't stupid. She'd been this route more than once and knew when a man was about to ask her to marry him.

Mohammed jumped out of the driver's seat and opened her door, "Ma'am."

Ida simply nodded. She eased into the backseat, inching over to make room for Sammy.

Once they were situated, Sammy spoke to his driver. "Take us back to the house."

Ida was crestfallen. Sammy just wanted to have sex tonight. She'd been sure he was going to propose! Damn. She'd gotten all dressed up for nothing. Not that an evening in bed was a bad idea, just that she'd thought this evening was going to be special.

"Ida, my love, do you mind if we have dinner at my house? I wanted us to have some privacy tonight. You look disappointed."

She did, but she wasn't going to tell him that. "No, not at all. I just assumed since this is our first date . . . I just thought we would be going somewhere besides your place to celebrate our decision to take our relationship public."

Sammy took her hand in his. "Ida, love, I am afraid I have disappointed you. I can change our plans. Where would you like to go? I feel like such a fool, you must forgive me. I am an old man, remember? It has been many years since I've taken a beautiful woman to dinner. Please forgive my thoughtlessness."

Ida took a deep breath. Poor Sammy. He wasn't as worldly as he wanted her to think. "There is nothing to forgive. I don't mind not going out, truly. Now put it out of your mind. At least we don't have to sneak around like teenagers anymore."

"That is true, but if you would rather we have dinner out—"

Ida placed a finger over his lips. "Not another word about it. Now tell me, what have you prepared for our dinner?"

"Ah, I see you are intrigued. I must admit I am a terrible cook. Amala has prepared something for us. She said it was a surprise."

Ida looked at Sammy. Really *looked*. Olive skin, deep brown eyes. Sammy was extremely handsome for a man his age. Ida was sure his raven-black hair was dyed, but she hadn't the heart to ask him about it. For a man who was sixty-seven years old, he was in excellent shape. His body was still lean and muscular, with only the beginnings of an old man's paunch visible when he was naked. He was a superb lover, and he was rich—two qualities Ida required in a man.

"I do love surprises, Sammy."

"Good, my dear, very good," Sammy said, then patted her hand. "I am pleased this makes you happy. You are very dear to me, Ida. You do know that?"

"Yes, yes. Of course I do. You sound . . ." Ida thought he sounded weak, old. "You sound as though you're having doubts about us. Are you?"

Sammy smiled, revealing chalk white teeth. "If I keep up this behavior, I will scare you away. No, my dear I am not having doubts about us. Never! It's the—" Sammy waved his hand in the air. "Please forgive me for telling you this on such a special night. I just received some very disturbing news today concerning the clinic. Forget I said that." He leaned over and kissed her on the neck. "Tonight is for us to celebrate. You don't need to be burdened with an old man's troubles."

Ida wished he would stop referring to himself as an old man. He was only two years older than she. If he thought of himself as an old man, then surely he must think of her as an old woman. She wanted to tell him that, but if that wasn't the case, she didn't want to bring attention to her age any more than necessary.

"Sammy, if there is something you need to talk about, please do. I am not the delicate flower you believe me to be." Ida thought that was an understatement, but he didn't need to know that.

"You are *my* delicate flower," he said with a trace of possessiveness.

Ida loved that he felt that way. She needed to feel this sort of love, she thrived on it. Maybe Toots and Sophie were right, and she did need a man in her life. That wasn't the worst thing in the world. She could be a drunkard or a thief. Or even worse, she supposed, a serial killer.

Mohammed steered the limousine up the winding road leading to Sammy's house. Ida decided that if they were going to get married, she would have to redecorate. The beach house was all chrome and glass, the furniture modern and sterile. While Ida wasn't quite as talented as Toots in the decorating department, she did know a thing or two about what she liked and disliked. Soon she would have Sammy completely wrapped around her little finger. He would allow her to do as she wished with his home.

As soon as they came to a stop, Mohammed jumped out of the driver's seat to open their door. Ida hated that. Hated Mohammed. There was something about him that gave her the creeps. She would have to discuss it with Sammy. He would have to decide just how important a limo driver was if he wanted to marry her.

The door was yanked open. Sammy got out first, then assisted her before turning to his driver. "That will be all for tonight. You may park the car."

"Sure thing, Pops," Mohammed said, then smacked Sammy so hard on the back that Ida about jumped out of her skin. If that was the way he treated Sammy once they were married, she would fire him regardless of what Sammy said.

"Do not pay any attention to Mohammed, this is just his way. He means no harm," Sammy offered as an explanation for his driver's behavior.

"I don't like him, Sammy." There, she'd said it.

"Yes, I am aware of that, but there is more to the man than meets the eye. Someday I will tell you his story, then you will understand why I am so tolerant. Now, forget Mohammed for tonight. Let's not allow him to spoil our time together."

"If you insist," Ida said a bit too sharply. He'd already ruined their evening by showing up, she wanted to say, but stopped. She would give Sammy a chance to explain himself, but not just then.

He was silent as they entered the dimly lit house. Windows facing the Pacific provided a stunning view. Outside on the deck, which ran the length of the house, Ida saw that a table for two had been set up. On it was a white linen tablecloth, a single rose lying across each dinner plate, and a candle flickering in the slight evening breeze. A bucket filled with ice and a bottle of wine or champagne was placed to the side of the table. A scene for seduction. Ida smiled. Her Sammy was a die-hard romantic. Seeing this and all the preparations he'd made for their evening, Ida forgave him for not taking her out to a fancy restaurant. She couldn't wait to see what kind of ring he'd chosen.

They stepped outside together. "Please sit."

Ever the gentleman, Sammy pulled her chair out, waiting for her to sit down before seating himself.

"This is perfect," she said, meaning it.

"I am glad you approve." He removed the bottle resting in the bucket of ice. Ida saw the label, recognized the Dom Pérignon, and was disappointed that he'd picked something so common. She must remember to tell him that after they were married. He uncorked the bottle, filled two crystal flutes with the bubbly liquid, and handed one to her.

"I would like to propose a toast." Sammy held his glass out in front of him. "To the future, to *our* future."

Ida clinked her flute against his and again felt a deeply rooted seed of disappointment begin to sprout. This was so . . . trite and common. She had expected more from him. Or at least something original, more classy and polished.

"The future," she said glumly.

Maybe it was only the chase that was so tantalizing. She'd had better marriage proposals from younger, less experienced men. But he hadn't really proposed yet. She owed it to him to wait and see if he measured up.

"You sound so bleak, Ida. Have I upset you?" Sammy asked, concern all over his face.

He hadn't. Not really. It was just her. She had been anticipating this date all week, and now that it was happening, she'd been let down by her own expectations. Straightening up, she took a sip of her champagne. At least she had good sex to look forward to.

She smiled at her thoughts, thinking she sounded just like Sophie. "Not at all, Sammy. I was just woolgathering." Wasn't that what Toots would've said? She was more like her friends than they gave her credit for.

"Good, because I have something I want to ask you. I wouldn't ask if you were upset."

Here goes, she thought. "What is it you wanted to ask me, Sammy?" She knew but didn't want him to know she knew.

He took a deep breath, reached for her hand, placed a soft kiss on her palm. "Do you remember our conversation a few weeks ago when I explained the clinic wasn't doing well?"

She did, but what did that have to do with proposing? "Yes, I do."

"As much as I hate to, I must relent and accept your offer for financial assistance. It pains me to do this, my love, but I have no other choice, as my patients are dependent on me for their continued care."

Shocked, Ida didn't know what to say. She had made the offer, but he'd refused, and she'd never given it another thought. Apparently Sammy had thought about it enough to stage this scenario.

"How much?" The words were out of her mouth before she had a chance to stop them.

Apparently taken aback by her bluntness, Sammy replied, "Oh, . . . well if I were to name a figure off the top of my head, I would say three million."

Three million dollars?

To say that she was shocked would have been putting it mildly. Flabbergasted was more like it.

Three million dollars!

Sammy emptied his champagne glass in one swallow, then poured another. After he drained the second glass, he looked at her. "Please forget I asked this. I don't know what came over me. I will go to the bank. I am so distraught over the clinic's finances that I am not thinking clearly. Please accept my apology."

Right then Ida wasn't sure what to think, but she had made the offer. Sammy was a caring man, of that she was sure. Concern for the clinic and his patients always came first with a doctor. Ida knew that, too. Did she want to be number two in Sammy's life? She wasn't sure she could accept second place and knew she would have to give the question some serious thought. Soul-searching, Toots would say. But she was a very wealthy woman, so why not share her wealth?

"You have nothing to be sorry for. I did make the offer. If I'm anything, I am a woman of my word. I'll call the bank first thing tomorrow and have that amount transferred to your account. I'll need your banking information."

Sammy reached for her hand again, bringing it to his mouth. His lips barely touched her palm, but it was enough to send sparks shooting straight to her stomach, settling just below her waist.

"You are an amazing woman, Ida. I don't know what to say or how to thank you. I will think of something. Now that business is out of the way, let's eat. Suddenly I am famished."

Ida felt like a glass of ice-cold water had been tossed in her face. So much for romance. "And suddenly I am feeling sick. Please, take me home now. And I don't want your limo driver anywhere near me!" Ida jumped out of her chair and raced inside, Sammy chasing after her.

"Ida, my love, what has come over you? What can I do?" Sammy seemed genuinely concerned.

Ida took a deep breath. "Just take me home. I think the champagne went from my stomach straight to my head."

Without another word, Sammy helped her out to the limousine. He slid into the driver's seat. Not a word passed between them on the ride home, as neither knew what to say. Ida feared she'd just been screwed.

Royally.

Chapter 14

When Patel returned from taking Ida to Toots's house, Amala was waiting to give him a piece of her mind. "You are a stupid old man! I can't believe you would ask her to lend you $3 million. What's even worse, I can't believe the old broad would even consider doing it." Mohammed smirked.

"No, it is you and Amala who are the stupid ones. This is our chance to make a small fortune without even committing a crime. There is no law that prevents a wealthy woman from lending her money to whomever she pleases. Amala, your plan is not working. Part of being in this business is knowing when to walk away," Patel explained. "You are young and beautiful, there will be other opportunities, other gentlemen."

Patel watched Mohammed. He got angry when Amala's name was mentioned in connection with another man. Patel knew this but could not stop himself. He did not want to hurt Mohammed, only to remind him what kind of woman she really was.

"Both of you are stupid. Go on and rip off your wealthy old women. They will soon tire of you and see through your schemes. Mohammed has been watching the redhead. I think he wants her," Amala said.

The three were seated around the empty table Ida had run away from earlier that evening. Amala had just returned from smoking a joint on the beach. The breeze from the Pacific carried a tinge of the sweet-smelling weed with it as a gentle wind blew across the deck. Mohammed had refused when she'd invited him to join her, but Patel was not a fool. Had he not been there, Mohammed would have enjoyed smoking weed with her.

"Shut up! You don't know what I want, bitch." Mohammed stood up, preparing to go inside. "I am staying at the apartment tonight. You two can stay here in the good doctor's house. I am sick of this scam." He yanked the glass door aside as he entered the house, not bothering to close it behind him.

"He is angry. Serves him right," Amala said. "You like it when he is this way. I see it. You think you know Mohammed better than I do, old man? I sleep with him. I know his secrets, private things he will never tell you."

Patel stood, brushed the sand from his slacks. "Your plan is falling apart. You need to cut your losses while you still can."

"And then what will you do? What about your clinic? The old woman really thinks you're a doctor. Without *my* clinic, you have nothing to bargain with."

"You are wrong. With $3 million in my bank account, I will not need your clinic, Amala. By the time dear, lovely Ida discovers she has been taken for a fool, I will be long gone, and you, my dear, will be left to explain my absence."

Patel watched as Amala realized what he had just said. "Then I will turn you in myself!"

"You will not. Why would you want to involve the law when you are trying to pilfer millions from a well-respected doctor?" Patel raised a thick brow.

"Go on, get out of my sight. You and Mohammed make me ill."

"I would not be so quick to make such demands if I were you."

Amala's laugh was wicked. "You do not frighten me, old man. It is you who should be frightened of me. All it takes is one anonymous phone call to Immigration, and you will be sent back to your nasty country without your dear Ida's money, and poor Mohammed will be left to live his life in peace."

Patel stood and put his hands in his pockets. It would be pointless for Amala to see how his fists were clenched in rage, how badly he wanted to wrap them around her slender neck and squeeze until all signs of life drained from her. Lucky for her, that was not his way. She would orchestrate her own demise if she continued to use the street drugs she believed to be of the highest quality.

Patel was much more concerned with Ida's reaction earlier that night. He had been confident she would lend him money for his clinic without a second thought. After he took her back to her friend's home in Malibu, he replayed the evening's events in his head over and over again.

He was almost ashamed of himself when he realized why Ida had suddenly left, why she had been so hurt and upset. The champagne, the roses, a romantic dinner for two. How could he have been so blind? Amala was right. He *was* stupid. Tonight had been a very stupid move on his part.

Ida had been expecting a marriage proposal. Asking her to lend him money was not a wise decision on his part. Had he not been blinded by greed, he would have known Ida's desires. He would have proposed first, then once she accepted, he would have asked her to help save *their* clinic. Stupid. *Yes, Patel, tonight you were a stupid old man.* He considered calling Ida on her cell phone and apologizing but decided against it. If he wanted Ida's $3 million, he was going to have to ask her to marry him. She would want a large wedding. Large in a monetary sense. Patel knew Ida had few friends. He understood why, since she was a whiny old bitch who wanted nothing more than to be catered to. He would cater to her all she wanted if it meant she would *lend* him that $3 million.

He looked up to find Amala staring out at the ocean as the waves crashed against the shore. It would be so easy to get rid of her. Once she was out of the picture, he and Mohammed could relocate to another country. With $3 million, Patel was confident he could buy his way out of the United States as easily as he had bought his way in many years ago. However, he was not a complete fool. Mohammed was entranced by Amala's beauty and sexuality. Though Patel knew he would never admit to it, if something tragic were to happen to her, Mohammed would be devastated. He was like a son to him, and because of that, Patel put aside any further thought of how much easier their lives would be if Amala were to disappear, never to be seen again. An old man's wish, he thought.

"I am going to bed, you can stay out here all night if you want to. I am locking the doors. I don't want Mohammed tonight. Maybe you would like to take his place, see what a younger woman is like," Amala said, though she continued to lean over the balcony overlooking the ocean.

Patel was almost tempted to give her a shove, but again that was not his style. He turned to go inside. "You are nothing but a small-time whore, Amala. I am going inside. Good night." Patel quickly covered the distance from the table to the door before the temptation to rid himself of her overwhelmed him.

"Night, old man," she tossed over her shoulder.

Inside his room, Dr. Sameer's room, Patel paced back and forth. Amala was a walking time bomb. Trouble followed her wherever she went. He had observed it firsthand. He knew nothing of her background other than that she had lived in several foster homes until she ran away at the tender age of fifteen. She had been living on the streets much like Mohammed when she tried to sell her body to Patel for a hit of meth. Knowing she was much too young for him, Patel had ignored her. For two weeks she followed him, begging him for drugs. Since she was neither a paying customer nor likely to become one, Patel wanted nothing to do with her. Children were nothing but trouble.

But one of the occasions when she had tried to score drugs from him, Mohammed had been with him. He laid eyes on Amala and never looked back. That had been almost sixteen years ago. Patel regretted not giving her the drugs. Had he known then what he knew now, he would have supplied her with enough drugs to send her to eternity.

Hindsight, people called it.

Mohammed raced through the empty streets, not caring that the limousine stood out like a sore thumb. He was going to ditch it anyway once he and the redhead were finished. He'd planned and plotted for weeks. Now it was time to put his plan in motion.

Though the concept was simple, he knew things weren't always as easy as they seemed. Amala had thought ripping off the gay doctor would be easy. But other than the normal allowances for the clinic's expenses, she had been unable to get her hands on any of the doctor's money. She kept telling him and Patel to be patient, but Mohammed knew nothing would come of her half-baked attempt to steal millions from the doctor, and that was why she wanted, no, *needed,* his and Patel's help. She wasn't smart enough to pull off a con this size without some assistance. And now it was too late. He wanted no part of her little scheme; it was not working.

When she came up with the bright idea to steal Dr. Sameer's identity, he'd thought about it but knew she couldn't pull that off either. That was when he started looking elsewhere for a means of income. And the redhead had big bucks. More than once he'd stolen mail from her mailbox and taken it back to his shabby apartment, where he carefully steamed the envelopes open, hoping to find a check, anything that he could gain from financially. The day he discovered he had her bank statements, he decided he'd hit the big time. She had millions and millions of dollars just waiting to be spent. He'd planned and plotted how to get his hands on the money. While it wasn't the most original idea, it would work because he would make it work.

Patel and the old woman he was screwing had given him an idea. Every morning when Mohammed brought the old bitch back to her beach house, he would hide the car and watch the four old ladies. No one came to their house except the girl in the bright yellow car, and she had only been there a handful of times. He'd followed her home once, then he broke into her little house. A reporter for one of those trashy papers that Amala liked to read when she wasn't stoned out of her head. He'd rummaged through her personal belongings only to learn that she was the daughter of the tall redhead. The other three women were her godmothers. Who had three godmothers? How stupid, he thought.

It was time to put his plan into action. The only chink in the armor was Patel's Ida. The old woman was pissed at Patel. He'd been spying on them earlier when they were together on the deck. She had been completely caught off guard—and he was, too—when Patel had asked to borrow $3 million to save that yoga center he called his clinic. He'd laughed when she told Patel she didn't like his chauffeur. He wanted to shout out and tell her the feeling was mutual, but he hadn't. If Ida stopped her nightly booty calls, he would have to make other arrangements to get to the redhead.

Again, he believed his plan to be quite simple. When he brought the old woman home, his plan was to scare her into getting the tall redhead to come outside to the limo. How he was going to scare her, he hadn't yet figured out, but he knew that if he had to, he could get a gun. If that didn't scare her, then she really was a wacko. Once the redhead came to her friend's rescue, he would shoot her up with one of Amala's dirty needles filled with some of Patel's most potent heroin, which would send her on a trip to hell. After she'd been there a few times, Mohammed was confident she would be more than willing to pay him a few million for a return ticket to freedom.

He laughed. His life was about to change.

Chapter 15

The day after Ida's unfortunate date with her Sammy, Abby opened her e-mail account for the zillionth time, hoping, praying, she would see the e-mail she'd been waiting on for over three very long weeks. One that gave a location and security arrangements for the exclusive interview and picture session *The Informer* needed to gain a bit of respect among the tabloids.

She scrolled through several names, scanning for the e-mail address that she'd memorized. The publicist for the Pitt/Jolie crew, as she had come to think of them. Nothing.

"Son of a bitch!" Abby got up and paced her office. Chester jumped off his chair and paced alongside her.

Abby had jumped the gun, and now she was in the deep brown stuff. Piles of it. She'd been so hyped about interviewing one of Hollywood's most famous couples that she'd thrown caution to the winds. She'd been given the go-ahead by the paper's mysterious owners to write the teasers, anything to build up the readership. Sales meant money. As long as *The Informer* was making money, she had a job. According to LAT Enterprise, sales had almost doubled since she'd penned the headlining teasers. And now she had nothing. No Pitt/Jolie interview, not even a half-assed, mediocre, down-on-his-luck actor to interview.

Abby should have listened to her gut instinct. When she received the e-mail inviting *The Informer* to interview Hollywood's first family, she should have known something was awry. She'd tried numerous times to call the publicist in question. Each time she called explaining who she was and what happened, some little smart-ass twit laughed at her, then hung up. Abby had to face the facts: The Pitt/Jolie interview wasn't going to happen. She'd been screwed, blued, and tattooed, and now she had to suffer the consequences.

All she had to do was find an actor or actress that would be considered front-page, headline-breaking news and write something so newsy that it would live up to the buildup she'd created. Abby considered calling Chris to ask him for any dirt on the many starlets who passed through his arms, but she couldn't bring herself to stoop that low. Chris wouldn't have told her anything worth printing. He might be a player, but Abby knew he kept any newsworthy gossip to himself.

Briefly, Abby wondered about that doctor her mother had asked her to check out. He ran a clinic that catered to the stars. Maybe there was something there. Hell, at this point I'll try anything, she thought. Deciding a trip to her mother's was needed, Abby clicked off her computer and turned the televisions and lights off before she left. Surely the new owners would appreciate her economizing.

"Come on, Chester, we're going to the beach."

"Woof!" He ran out the door and down the hall before she had a chance to hook his leash to his collar. Didn't matter, she told herself, as the offices were all but empty anyway. Her reporters were covering small-time events for the back pages. The way things were going, she might have to bring some of that small-time news to the front page. Worse, she might have to take that same news and spiff it up a bit, make it more interesting without telling any flatout lies. Yes, if she had to, that was exactly what she'd do.

The Globe and *The Enquirer* did it all the time, and that was the reason they were the numbers one and two tabloids in the country.

"Come on, boy, let's go see what Coco is up to." Outside, Chester ran around in circles, letting her know he was excited. She laughed. Smart dog.

Traffic on the Pacific Coast Highway was bumper-to-bumper. Abby popped Britney Spears's latest in the CD player. The girl had made a comeback, but her music wasn't anything to rave about. Abby turned the volume down as she inched her way toward Malibu. She should have called first, but her mother wouldn't mind her just popping in. She hadn't been to the house since the inside remodeling had been started.

She couldn't wait to see what magic her mother and the contractors had performed. The inside of the house had been beyond tacky. Her mother was one talented woman. Abby knew she would be turning the place into the perfect beach house.

Forty-five minutes later, she parked her MINI Cooper next to her mother's bright-red Thunderbird. Chester was pulling at the bit to get out of the car. "Hang on, boy, let's get you unbuckled." Abby released the seat-belt buckle just in time. The shepherd jumped across the seat before Abby could get out of the car.

"Coco, that's what you're all excited about."

Chester ran back and forth, digging his hind paws into the dirt. "Chester, stay!" Abby commanded. The big dog stopped in his tracks. Abby scratched his back. "Good boy. We're learning patience, aren't we?"

Abby knocked on the door, causing it to open. Must not have been closed all the way. Abby held Chester by the collar in order to keep him from flying through the house knocking down whatever was in his path. "Mom?" She called out.

She heard her mother talking to someone. Abby hoped she hadn't come at a bad time, interrupted anything important. "Mom, Sophie?"

Abby walked through the kitchen, surprised at the total makeover. White cabinets, sleek blue granite countertops. Chrome appliances. Very beachlike. "Mom, where are you?"

Her mother whizzed out of the dining room like a rocket. "Abby! I thought that was you! What in the world are you doing here? If I had known you were coming, I wouldn't have . . . I would have made dinner."

Abby laughed. "Then I would've left hungry."

Toots hugged her daughter. "You're not very nice today."

Her mother pulled her arm. "Mom! What are you doing? My arm!"

"Sorry. Follow me."

"Okayyy, what's going on here?" Abby said as she followed her mother through the house to the main deck outside.

"Nothing. Nothing at all. What makes you think there's something going on?" She practically dragged her through the sliding doors. "I just want to . . . smoke."

"Chester, no!" Abby ran down the steps leading to the beach. Chester sat at the bottom of the steps next to Coco's carrier. She lugged him back up the stairs. In her most commanding voice, she said, "Stay." She turned to her mother, who was sucking on a cigarette as though her life depended on inhaling every last bit of the tar and nicotine.

"Where's Mavis's dog? I can't say her name without Chester going bonkers. I think he's in love."

"Stay here. I'll be right back." Toots put her cigarette in a bright green ashtray.

"Mother, what is going on?" Abby called before Toots had a chance to open the glass doors.

"Nothing, Abby. I'm just going to get the dog. Stay put for two minutes. I'll be right back, okay?"

Abby nodded, then plopped down on a blue-and-green lounge chair. Her mother was acting beyond strange. Not that she didn't act strange any other time. Her mother was keeping secrets from her. She laughed, thinking there might be a man involved. No wonder her mother wanted her out of the way. Abby could've sworn she heard her mother say she was swearing off men after Leland.

"I'm back," Toots said. She held Coco in her arms like a baby. "Just be careful. Mavis would kill me if something happened to her."

"Where are Mavis and the others?" Abby asked as Toots gently placed little Coco next to Chester. The large dog nudged the Chihuahua with his nose, then Coco licked Chester's ears. "True puppy love. Now tell me what's going on."

Ida, Sophie, and Mavis stepped outside.

By the time the round of greetings was over, Abby was certain that each of her godmothers had hugged and kissed her at least ten times. After a prolonged episode of oohing and aahing over how adorable Coco and Chester were, they all gathered around the new table. "You three—four—are up to something, and I want to know what it is. Right now. No ifs, ands, and buts."

"Abby Simpson, we are grown women. We are not 'up to' anything, and if we were, it would be our business. I don't know what makes you think that we're doing anything we shouldn't be doing in the first place," her mother said, her nose tilted up just a tad too high in the air to be believed.

"Oh shit, Toots, Abby's a big girl. Let's tell her what's been going on. She might want to write a story for the paper," Sophie said.

"You have the biggest frigging mouth; has anyone ever told you that? I'd like to stuff a great big—"

"—Girls! Let's stop fussing. Abby dear, what your mother

meant to say is . . . is, well, we seem to have a new friend.
Yes, we have a new friend. He's a man. I have a new
friend. His name is George. He has a dachshund named
Albert. We meet on the beach every morning at sunrise."
Mavis looked at Toots.

"Yes, Mavis is in love again. Isn't that just peachy?
We're trying to find out if she's made it with George, but
she won't tell us."

"That's great, Mavis. But there's more, and I'm not leaving until you tell the truth." Abby glared at her godmothers
and her mother. "The whole truth and nothing but."

"If you won't tell her, I will," Sophie said.

"Tell me what?" Abby demanded. She was starting to
get concerned. Maybe her mother was hiding a fugitive.
That would be so like her and her godmothers.

"This house is haunted," Sophie stated.

Abby's jaw dropped halfway to her chest. She raked her
gaze across the four most important people in her life, the
most loved. They all looked to be sane. No wild eyes or
electrical-socket hairdos. Nope, they looked the same as always. Four attractive older women. Abby took a deep
breath. "Okay. Let's start over. Say what you just said.
Slowly."

"She said this house is haunted, and we were getting
ready to hold a séance when you interrupted us. Now,
Abby, don't look at me that way. We're not crazy." Her
mother shot Ida a glance.

"Don't look at me when you say 'crazy,'" Ida quipped.

"I wasn't," Toots said.

"Yes, you were. I saw you."

"Would you two just shut the fuck up? Sorry, Abby. Both
of you quit picking on each other. It's getting old. And, Abby,
your mother is telling you the truth. This dump is full of
spirits, ghosts, whatever you want to call them. I think some
of them are old movie stars. We've been holding séances

twice a week trying to figure out exactly who they are. We were pretty sure that one of them is Bing Crosby, but we couldn't verify it until last week. We were just preparing for another séance when you arrived. Unless you want to join us, in the future make sure you call ahead before driving all the way out here."

Abby was truly, totally, completely struck dumb. "I see." No, she didn't, not really, but what else could she say? Briefly she thought of calling Chris, then changed her mind. If word got out that her mother and godmothers were seeing ghosts, it might float back to the owners of the paper and somehow reflect badly on her. She would be out of a job. Hell, she was going to be out of a job anyway for flubbing up her so-called exclusive. This was simply the icing on the cake.

"I told you she would think we're loony," Toots said, a cigarette dangling out of the corner of her mouth like she was an old-time gangster's moll.

Abby remained as still as a statue. She needed to think. "Give me a minute."

Toots nodded, drew a long drag off her cigarette, then blew the smoke out through her nose like a dragon.

"Now let me get this straight. You're saying that this house is haunted? By Bing Crosby?" Abby paused, praying she was mistaken but knowing she wasn't.

"Yes it is," Sophie stated matter-of-factly, thinking back to the confrontation between Bing and Aaron Spelling.

Like a marionette, the quartet's movements were jerky and quick, as though each were orchestrated by an unknown puppet master. Each woman stared in awe as the two eerily cloudlike bursts of fog appeared to argue with one another.

The man, rather the spirit they knew as Bing Crosby, shook his fist at the other spirit, his pale purplish lips moving with the speed of light.

"Why have you followed me here? What have you got to complain about? The place was a treasure! You . . . you bulldozed it down as if it were nothing more than an old tree stump!"

More fist shaking.

The other cloudlike mist who they recognized as the famous movie mogul, Aaron Spelling, shook his head as though amused, his close-cropped silver hair shimmering in the dark like glistening crystals.

"Look, old pal, you were dead when I bought your . . . house. The other one, of course, not this one. You're dead now, so why should you care?"

The four women continued to stare at the two spirits, who'd made several appearances since Sophie had started conducting her twice-weekly séances. In the other séances, however, it was one or the other, never both at the same time. And it was clear that, for some obscure reason, the Aaron Spelling spirit was looking for the Bing Crosby spirit.

The Bing spirit threw up his hands, which took the form of two gauzy appendages flowing from his torso, high into the mist that surrounded him. "And you're not? You're dead as a doornail, my friend, or haven't you figured that out yet?"

The Aaron figure dropped his head to his fading chest. "I think you're hallucinating. I just finished a nap, I'm not dead."

Bing's spirit laughed a hearty lifelike laugh. "You haven't been dead long enough to realize you're dead. Takes a while. Took me almost a year to realize I wasn't among the living. Don't worry, it will hit you when you least expect it."

The Aaron apparition looked down at some unseen object, appeared to bend over to pick it up, then held out his hand to Bing. "These are the keys to my homes. Dead men don't have house keys."

The Bing spirit reached into a translucent pocket and

pulled out a key ring with at least a dozen keys. "These were placed in my coffin before I was buried. I sure don't know why, but I have keys, too." Bing appeared to be contemplating something. "Your keys have any special meaning?"

The four women remained rooted to their chairs as they watched the interchange between their two resident ghosts play out.

The Aaron ghost considered the question. "I have a key to every house I've ever owned on here. I guess you could call that special."

"I bet someone you loved placed them in your casket."

The Aaron ghost shook his semitransparent head vigorously. "No, my wife would never part with them, knowing how special they were to me."

Bing laughed again, then floated over beside Aaron. "So, that just proves my point, Mr. Spelling. You, too, are as dead as a doornail."

Suddenly the foglike mists whirled around the table, then began to spin like mini whirlwinds. The purple satin sheet on the old wood table snapped off the surface and draped itself around Sophie's shoulders like a cape. The whirling mists disappeared as fast as they'd appeared.

Toots, Ida, and Mavis gaped at Sophie, who had turned as pale as the images of their two now-departed spirits. She seemed to be in a mild state of shock.

Knowing they couldn't remain like that all day, Toots leaned across the wooden table and snapped her fingers directly in front of Sophie's face.

Sophie jerked to attention, slung the purple sheet off her shoulders, and stood. "I don't know about the rest of you, but I am about to get sloshed." She left the séance room, heading straight for the liquor cabinet with Toots, Ida, and Mavis right on her heels.

* * *

"Haunted by Bing Crosby? You actually saw him?" Abby asked.

"Yes," Sophie confirmed.

"I see."

"No, I don't think you do. I'm guessing you think we're just a bunch of old fuddy-duddies who have lost their marbles." Sophie stared at Abby. "Am I right?"

Abby reached down to pet Chester and Coco. They were real. Okay, this wasn't a dream. She was really at her mother's new beach house in Malibu. And her mother, her strong-willed, no-nonsense, cut-out-the-bullshit mother was talking about ghosts as though they were her new neighbors.

If only one of them believed she'd seen a ghost, Bing Crosby's ghost, then Abby could explain it away. Too much to drink, not enough sleep, a trick of the light. It could be a number of things. But all four of them? And her mother? No. Her mother wasn't flighty, airheaded, or someone with an overactive imagination. So, Abby had a decision to make. She could either believe them or tell them they were all losing their minds.

"Tell me about them, the ghosts. Who saw them first?" Abby asked. She could see that she had their undivided attention. The four of them gathered around the patio table, and Abby pulled her lounger as close as she could without bumping into Chester and Coco, who continued to bathe one another with kisses.

"I did," her mother explained. "It woke me out of a sound sleep."

"You were awakened by Bing Crosby's ghost?" Abby asked.

"No, I think I woke up because of the chill in the room. I don't remember exactly. I just remember feeling as though someone was watching me. Then the next time I opened my eyes, I saw these clouds. They were sort of translucent, almost like fog, but they were shaped like a cloud. There were faces in them. Just heads and the mouths were moving like they were . . . arguing with one another."

"You never told me that," Sophie said.

"No, it just occurred to me that that's what they were doing. They were male faces, or at least I think they were. One woman, too. Her hair was blond, fixed in one of those bouffant styles of the sixties."

"How is it you're able to recall these images with such vivid detail when you couldn't remember anything about them the day after they materialized?" Sophie questioned. "Don't make this up just so Abby won't think you're nuts. If this is true, then we might be onto something."

"Sophie, kiss my ass. I wouldn't lie about something this crazy. You know I never lie. I don't know why I can recall these details now. They just came to me all of a sudden."

Abby held up her hand. "Stop it. Both of you. This is too weird. Ida, Mavis, what are your thoughts on this? Neither of you has said much."

"I didn't see the ghost clouds your mother saw, but I did see Bing Crosby. This experience has opened up an entire new belief system for me. I never believed in ghosts before now. I know it's a lot to absorb, but it's true." Mavis smiled, a sad smile.

Ida piped in, "They're telling the truth, Abby. The spirit we saw was definitely Bing Crosby. It's beyond bizarre, but it's the truth, I swear."

Abby nodded. "Show me where you hold the séances. Inside, Chester."

Mavis scooped Coco up in her arms, and Chester followed right on her heels.

"In the dining room. It's the only room that we haven't finished remodeling. Sophie thinks we should leave it alone until we find out more," Toots said.

Inside the house, Abby entered the dining area and saw

the round table with the purple satin sheet draped on top. "Nice touch." She flipped the light switch but nothing happened. "What about lights?"

"Just candles," Sophie said. "Spirits don't do lights, but I was able to pick up some movement with the camcorder. I've ordered a motion detector and an infrared camera."

"Okay, I want to see the video, but later." Abby paced the length of the dining room several times, always returning to the table. It was as if there was a magnetic force pulling her toward it. "Where did this table come from? I know it's not yours," Abby said to her mother.

"It was here when we moved in. I can ask the Realtor if she knows its original owner. What are you thinking, Abby?" her mother asked.

"This table looks very old. I've always believed things, such as furniture or clothing or a house, can hold a person's spirit. Maybe this table is connected to the spirits in some way."

"You've never told me that," Toots said.

"You never asked, and the issue never came up," Abby said to her mother. "Let's just say I have always kept an open mind. Growing up in Charleston, you can't help but know something about ghosts. All those old plantations that are supposedly haunted, Fort Sumter, the ghost tours. Didn't we take one of those when we first moved to Charleston?" Abby asked.

"We did; if memory serves me right, you were scared to death. I can't remember why, only that when it came time for you to go to bed that night, you wouldn't let me turn out the light or close your door." Toots smiled at the memory.

"I do remember that. What was I, ten or twelve?"

"Something like that."

"So do you want to join us at our next séance?" Sophie asked.

"I think so, but I'm not sure. It depends on how things go at the paper. I'm probably going to get fired, so I'm sure I'll have a lot of free time on my hands."

"Let's go in the kitchen. I'll make us a drink and, Abby, you can tell us why you think you're about to be fired," Toots said.

"You don't want to know, trust me."

Toots turned to her daughter. "Trust me, I do."

Chapter 16

Toots, Abby, and her three godmothers were seated at the white country French kitchen table with their drinks and a plate of fresh fruit with cheese and crackers courtesy of Mavis.

"I was so excited about the prospect of interviewing the famous couple, I lost sight of important details, such as actually meeting with the publicist. I admit it was totally unprofessional. If I lose this job, it's my own fault. I don't know why I fight so hard to hold on to the damn job in the first place. It's not real news. Just silly stuff of no importance."

"Don't you dare say that, Abby Simpson! Those tabloids got me through many a lonely night between husbands. I cherished every word I read. Don't think I'm the only one in this room who thinks that way either." Toots looked at Ida, Sophie, and Mavis. Their heads bobbed up and down like Halloween apples in a barrel of water.

"We grew up in an era in which movies were magic, and so were the stars that played in them. Every Saturday the four of us would trek to the matinee. Then we'd spend the rest of the day wishing we were movie stars," Ida said, her face softening with the memory.

"There are a lot of us out there, Abby. Don't sell yourself short. What you do has value, you just don't hear about it." Toots reached across the table and took Abby's hand in hers. "Is there anything we can do to help you?"

"Short of kidnapping the Pitt/Jolie crew?" Abby shook her head. "I don't think so, but thanks. It's nice to know that, between ghosts and séances, you're willing to help me out. If only I had some magical way to create the news, I'd be a happy girl."

Sophie's eyes brightened. Toots grinned.

"Maybe we can help out. What if you were to write about this?" Sophie gestured toward the dining room.

"You mean write about the séances? Bing Crosby's ghost?" Abby asked.

"Why not? It's Hollywood, where anything is possible," Toots said.

"I don't know, Mom. This generation probably doesn't have a clue who Bing Crosby is. I'm not sure I would, if not for you watching all those old movies. I doubt if my boss would go for something so . . . out there."

"You could ask them. It can't hurt. *The Enquirer* writes about aliens, and it hasn't hurt their reputation," Toots advised her daughter. She wanted to tell her right there on the spot that she owned the paper and she read the tabloids. It was an excellent idea. With all the new television programs on ghosts and haunted houses, Toots was sure that a ghost story would be quite popular with the public, but she couldn't reveal her ownership to Abby. Not yet; maybe someday, but not anytime soon. Abby loved her job, and Toots would do whatever needed to be done to keep her daughter happy.

"I suppose I could ask. I'm sure that after they realize the mess I've made with all the teasers leading up to this so-called exclusive interview, I'll be on the chopping block anyway. I might as well go out with a bang."

"Nonsense! I bet they would love the idea," Mavis said, smiling encouragingly at Toots and Sophie.

"I agree. I think it's a wonderful idea for a story." Ida paused. "And I don't read the tabloids as often as your mother does. I do enjoy a good romance novel, though."

Sophie shot Ida a dirty look. "I bet you only read the sex scenes."

They all burst out laughing.

"Lucky for me, I don't need to fantasize about a sex life. I have one," Ida replied haughtily.

"You're a real rip," Toots said.

Mavis clapped her hands together to get their attention. "Stop it before it starts. I swear you three are worse than some of my former students."

"Oh stop trying to change the subject, Mavis. You know we're going to ask if you're boinking George. You might as well spill the beans," Sophie teased.

Mavis blushed. "It's none of your business. I was taught it wasn't polite to kiss and tell."

Abby stood up. "I would love to sit here and discuss your sex lives, but while I still have a job, I'd best go home and get a good night's rest. Chester, are you ready to go?" The dog dropped to the ground. He whined, then licked Coco. "Let's go, Chester. Go! Now!" Abby pointed to the door, grabbed his leash. He wouldn't budge. "I guess he doesn't want to go. I've never seen him like this. It must be true love."

"Leave him here for the night. Coco would love to have company," Mavis said.

"I can't. He's sort of like my security blanket. I don't feel safe without him," Abby explained. "Sorry."

Toots took over. "Why don't you and Chester stay here tonight? It's too late for you to drive all the way back to Brentwood alone anyway. We have plenty of room. And who knows, you may be graced by old Bing's ghost while you're here."

Abby looked at her mother and her three godmothers. It'd been forever since they all had been together for an entire night. She could get to work from Malibu just as easily as from her house in Brentwood. "You've talked me into it. But if I stay, I want to sleep in the room where Mom saw the ghosts."

"That would be my room," Sophie said. "The bed is huge. You can bunk with me."

"You've got yourself a deal. Now how about another drink? I want to hear more about these séances you've been conducting. How do you know about this stuff anyway?"

As usual, Sophie was delighted to be in the limelight, especially when Abby was involved. "Back in New York, I had a friend who had an interest in anything paranormal. She told me all these creepy stories. After a few years with Walter, ghosts started looking really good to me. I spent some time learning how to read tarot cards. I used to read cards for a few of the girls in the office. I've always been fascinated with ghosts and ghouls. Haven't you heard about all the haunted hotels here in Los Angeles?"

Abby nodded. "Sure, but I never truly gave them much thought. They're part of the Hollywood legend. All those old hotels have a ghost story connected to them. A few of them are said to be haunted: the Roosevelt, the Knickerbocker."

When Sophie got excited, anyone who was remotely acquainted with her knew to stay out of her way and let her do whatever she wanted. She became so animated, arms flapping all over the place. She'd knock over anything in her path. She was getting overly excited now.

"Yes, the Roosevelt. I've seen it, but I haven't been inside. I want to go there before I leave. I hear Marilyn Monroe's haunted mirror is still hanging on the wall in the lobby. I remember reading where some of the hotel's guests said they saw a blond woman's reflection in the glass. Some die-hard fans believe that her life was so sad that her image was permanently impressed in the glass."

"I hope you're not stupid enough to believe that," Ida said.

"After what I've seen the past three weeks? Are you kidding? I'd be afraid to say I didn't believe. You better watch what you say. You never know when they're listening. I wouldn't want to get on the bad side of a ghost."

"Tone it down, Soph," Toots said.

"Why? Am I scaring you, too?"

"No, you only do that in the morning," Toots commented dryly.

"Kiss my ass," Sophie suggested.

"I'll pass."

"Mother, you two stop it. I swear, you act like two schoolgirls."

"I know it may be hard to fathom, but dear old Sophie and I were schoolgirls. Once. A hundred years ago."

They all laughed.

"It's getting late. I'm tired, and I've had too much to drink. Come on, Abby." Sophie stood up and stretched. "Maybe we'll catch a glimpse of a spirit tonight."

"Okay. Mom, Ida, Mavis, I'll see you in the morning. Chester, I assume you're sleeping with Coco tonight?"

"Woof!"

"I'll take that as yes," Abby said.

"Night, Mom."

Mavis cleared the table and put the dishes in the dishwasher. Toots locked all the doors and turned off the lights. Ida made her way up to her room. She was going to soak in the tub and think about lending Sammy $3 million.

Chapter 17

Abby didn't bother to stop off at her house on the way to the office. She had showered at her mother's house before she left. Lucky for her, she always kept an overnight bag stuffed inside the trunk of her car. She'd been doing that for years. In her business, she never knew when the need might arise for a fast change of clothes or an unexpected overnight trip. Abby's bag contained a perfect little black dress that never wrinkled no matter how she wadded it up, a pair of black trousers made of the same material, a black turtleneck top with quarter-length sleeves, and black heels that worked with the dress or trousers. She carried the usual mishmash of female toiletries and a copy of her passport, which looked almost identical to a driver's license. She also had a small bag of stuffed dachshunds for Chester and a plastic bag filled with doggie treats. Once a week she replaced her six-pack of water with fresh bottles. She liked being prepared for anything. That morning it had saved her at least an hour.

As soon as she got Chester fed and settled in his chair, she made a pot of coffee, clicked on all the television sets, and booted up the three computers on her desk. She needed news. Not that shitty stuff that made the back pages. She needed front-page, blockbuster news. Otherwise, she was seriously going to have to consider her mother's idea. Not that it was bad; it wasn't. Abby just needed something timely. That was always the key in tabloid reporting. Entertainment news had to be timely. If the news was old, no one cared about it. She needed news that coincided with movie premieres, celebrity divorces, trips to spas where one might find a star trying to knock off ten pounds before a public appearance.

The aroma of coffee filled the room. Abby filled her cup and took several quick sips before sitting down to check her e-mail. She hoped to find an e-mail from the Pitt/Jolie publicist. Abby figured that was wishful thinking at this stage of the game. Even if the interview and photography session were to come to fruition by some stroke of luck, Abby wouldn't have a chance to make all the necessary arrangements in time for next week's edition. She simply had to move on to another story. She opened her e-mail account, scanned through the subject lines. Nothing from the publicists, just as she'd expected. Expect nothing, and you would never be disappointed. Someone had said that to her years ago, and she'd always remembered it. How true it was today.

Abby answered three e-mails from the staff and two from a local TV news show that had been trying to get an interview with her since Rag's disappearance. No way was she going to grant them an interview. She knew what it was like to be turned down repeatedly, but Abby was in no position to give interviews connected to Rag. His case was being handled by law enforcement. That kind of trouble she didn't need. She hit the DELETE button, then blocked that e-mail address. One less worry.

Abby saw an e-mail from her mother. Strange, she'd just left her house. She saw the time stamp on the e-mail. She'd already been gone half an hour when her mother sent the e-mail. She quickly read through it, then again.

Abby—

I didn't have a chance to catch you alone last night as we were all tired and a bit sappy when we went to bed. Ida has been dating Dr. Sameer. As you know, they kept this a secret until a few days ago. The day before you came over, they had their first open date, but something happened and Ida came home very early and very upset. Sophie and I are having second thoughts about him. I know Dr. Pauley recommended him, but there is something not right, though I am not exactly sure what it is. A gut feeling. Could you, on the QT of course, look into his background? I know you have all kinds of contacts at *The Informer*. If not, I will call Chris and have him check his background. Also, we are planning another séance next week. I would love to see you there.

Mom

P.S. Poor Ida. She is devastated over losing the opportunity to photograph the stars!

Abby hit the REPLY button:

Mom—

You were still sleeping when Chester and I left—sorry! Didn't see the need to wake you. Tell Ida I'm sorry, too. Maybe something else will come along. I'll see what I can find out about Dr. Sameer. His credentials are impeccable, but . . . I will get on this right away. Yes to the séance—call me with details.

Abby

She hit the SEND button.
Abby made a note to ask a staff member to check into

Dr. Sameer and the Center for Mind and Body. Maybe there was a story there. Abby was getting desperate.

Now she had to write the e-mail she'd been dreading for days. If this got her fired, then so be it. She couldn't postpone this any longer.

LAT Enterprise:

It is with regret that I write this e-mail. I have been informed that the Jolie/Pitt interview is off. I am currently working on a story that I hope to be of equal interest to our readers.

That was nothing but a big fat lie. Abby hated lying.

It involves a story concerning a dead actor. While not breaking news, I believe that *The Informer*'s readers will be open to the possibilities of our take on the supernatural.

I ask your permission to proceed with the story.

A. Simpson.

Abby didn't even bother reading through the e-mail before hitting the SEND button. It was too bizarre. She was sure this would be her last day as editor in chief. She looked around her office. She could be out of here in minutes provided she had assistance with Chester's recliner. Saddened at the thought of losing her job, Abby had an idea. If she could find out who and where those e-mails had come from, she might be able to use them in her defense when she was fired. It couldn't hurt. Before she changed her mind, Abby reached for the phone on her desk. She dialed the three-digit number that would connect her to Josh, their resident computer guru.

"Yeah?"

Abby heard computer keys clicking away in the background.

"Josh. Abby. I need you to come upstairs to my office as soon as possible. I need your expertise."

The clicking stopped. "Sure thing, Abby. Give me ten minutes."

"Thanks, Josh," Abby said before hanging up.

If anyone could find out the origins of the publicist's e-mail, it was Josh. Rag had hired him right out of high school, and he'd been here ever since. One of the few things the jerk did that had paid off.

If the e-mail really was from the Pitt/Jolie publicist, Abby considered what kind of story she might be able to get out of that. It wasn't much, but she was scraping the bottom of the barrel, anything to fit beneath the banner that read EXCLUSIVE!

A knock sent Chester bounding to the door. "Good boy." Since the fire, Abby hadn't left Chester at home. He was her own personal bodyguard. Josh jumped away from the doorway when he saw Chester. "Man, I didn't know you had an attack dog in your office." He hesitated before stepping inside.

"Don't tell anyone, but he only bites on command. Go sit, Chester." The German shepherd immediately jumped back in his recliner.

"Good, now what is it you needed me to do?"

"I've been receiving e-mails, and I'm not sure they're from the person who sent them. Can you find out where they're being sent from?"

Once she had that information, she would launch her own investigation.

"Easy to do. You want me to find out now?"

"That'd be great. Here"—Abby pulled out her chair for Josh—"I use this computer for *The Informer*'s business." She pointed to the computer in the center of her desk.

"This should only take a minute," Josh said, and began to type with bionic speed.

While Josh's fingers flew across the keyboard, Abby sat on the edge of her desk, waiting for a miracle. If the e-mails originated from the publicist, her job would be safe. No way would LAT Enterprise fire her. She might not have the headline news, but she wouldn't be without a job. Abby could ask for her old job back in San Francisco, or she could move back to Charleston, but that wasn't what made her happy. Life and work were all about being happy. Her mother swore by those words. Abby thought she'd lived by them, too, for the most part.

"What the—"

Abby leaned across the desk to look at the computer monitor. "What is *that*?" The screen was filled with computer codes no one in his right mind should be able to read, let alone understand.

"Computer buzz," Josh answered without taking his eyes off the screen. He continued to type with amazing speed.

"Of course, I don't know why I asked," Abby said. While she knew her way around a computer, she had absorbed only what she needed to know. Codes, encrypted files, logarithms, she could live without the knowledge thank you very much. She had enough stuff floating around upstairs in the gray matter.

"This is weird," Josh said.

Abby slid off the edge of her desk to stand directly behind her chair so she could view what Josh called weird. "What?" Abby hated waiting around doing nothing. "What did you find?"

Josh's hands flew across the keys, "Man, this is some serious shit."

"Josh, if you don't tell me what you've found right now, I'm going to go downstairs and start smashing all those computers." Abby was smiling, so she knew he wouldn't take her comment seriously.

"It looks like arrest records. Here"—he slid away from the desk so she had a better view of the monitor—"take a look."

Abby skimmed the pages. "I don't get it. These are booking reports. I've seen a few in my day. I don't understand how or why this could show up in an e-mail. It doesn't make sense."

"My guess, and remember this is just a guess, I would bet someone in jail with access to computers sent these e-mails. I don't know if they're computer geeks, or it's possible the system this came from has a virus and managed to attach them to your e-mail without the sender knowing."

Abby raked a hand through her hair. "In a nutshell, you're telling me it's possible someone is sending me e-mails from jail? Do inmates in the county jail have access to computers?"

"I'm not one hundred percent sure, but I'd safely go with ninety-five," Josh said, grinning from ear to ear.

"Okay. Then the next step is to find out if anyone I know is incarcerated. I don't personally, but professionally I suppose anything is possible. You can go back to your command center. I'll make a few phone calls. Thanks for your help, Josh."

"Anytime, Abby. You know where to find me," Josh said.

Alone, Abby plopped down in her chair and whirled around so that she faced her monitor. Her first thought was that Rag had been apprehended, but she ditched that idea immediately. She would've been told if that were the case. No, it had to be someone who held a grudge against her and the paper. But who? Abby racked her brain in search of an answer, but she came up empty.

Chris would know. Without thinking, she dialed his number. He picked up on the second ring.

"Chris Clay," he answered in his most professional voice, the one he reserved for clients.

"Chris, it's Abby." She waited to hear the dial tone. When she didn't, she continued. "It seems I've been receiving some bogus e-mails from an inmate in the LA County Jail."

"Hello, Abby."

She could hear the smile in his voice. Knowing he couldn't see her, she smiled back. "Hello, Chris. How are you? How was the ice cream?"

"That's better. You really need to work on your telephone etiquette."

"I will, I promise, later. Did you know inmates had Internet access?"

"Yes, and it's a shame, too. How is your mother? I haven't talked to her lately."

"She was fine when I left her house this morning. Could you just listen to me for one minute without being such an . . . ass? Sorry, but I need to find out what person I know is residing in the county jail, someone with a grudge against me, or the paper. Don't you have connections there? Someone who can look up a name without a major ruckus? I have my sources at the jail, but I don't feel comfortable using them, since I don't know what or who is behind these e-mails." Her heart was beating so fast she had to take a deep, cleansing breath. This was business, nothing personal.

"I do, Abby, but I must advise you if I go to all the trouble to call and ask around, you're going to owe me. Bigtime."

"Owe you? As in money, owe you?"

"No, as in you'll have dinner with me."

"Oh, well, if that's all. Sure I can have dinner with you. We'll go to Pink's, and I'll bring Chester along. He loves hot dogs, too."

"Yes, I remember you telling me that. With mustard and relish, I believe."

Abby couldn't help but laugh. Chris had a killer memory to go with that killer body.

"So you'll go to dinner with me if I find out who is sending you e-mails from the county jail? I want to make sure I'm hearing you correctly because the last time I saw you, you weren't all that friendly."

No, she hadn't been a bit friendly, but that didn't matter now. "Okay I was a bitch. I must've had PMS or something that day. Now, if you'll find this information for me, I'll buy you dinner, you pick the place."

"You've got yourself a deal. Let me get back to you. Keep your cell phone on," Chris said, reminding her that she'd left the charger at home last night; therefore it was highly probable her battery was dead.

"I think the battery is dead. Call the paper or my house if you can't reach my cell. I really do appreciate this, Chris."

"I'm sure you do, Abby. Glad to help. I'll get back to you as soon as I have an answer."

"Works for me." Abby placed the cordless phone back in its charger.

A dinner date with Chris was the last thing she'd expected when she called, but she had been rude to him that day in the grocery store. He didn't know how he'd hurt her when he told her he really liked her, then never called her, never mentioned it again. She could forgive him for representing her mother, the whole conflict-of-interest thing.

Even though it was highly possible she could lose her job for jumping the gun with those teasers, Abby felt like shouting to the world how fantastic her life was. Especially since she and Chris were going to dinner again.

"Whoopee!" She did a little dance, stopping when she saw Chester's head tilted in question.

"It's called happiness, old boy. Happiness."

Chapter 18

The same morning that Abby had agreed to go out to dinner with Chris, Ida heard her cell phone ring just as she stepped out of the shower. The only person who called her on the silly thing was Dr. Sameer, and she really didn't want to talk to him at the moment, so she let it ring.

Ida dressed quickly in a pair of white capri pants with a crisp navy short-sleeved blouse. She fluffed her hair and swiped pink lipstick across her mouth. Since she had no plans to go out that morning, she didn't bother with her usual thirty-minute morning routine. What she needed at the moment was some caffeine. She'd had too much to drink the previous night and would suffer for it the rest of the day if she waited too long.

She hurried downstairs, still amazed at all of the changes Toots and her contractor had made, and in such a short time. The royal-blue-and-white kitchen was now light and airy. She'd finished her room a few days ago. She loved the creamy yellow she used on the walls and had bought the bedroom furniture herself. The bleached oak went perfectly with the pale green sheets and bedding set. The bathroom now housed a Jacuzzi tub. She used the pale yellows and greens throughout the room. When she'd finished, she'd been so thrilled with the results that she couldn't wait to tackle that dreary dining room. Toots wanted to wait until she was sure their ghostly visitors had crossed to the other side before starting the work. Ida still had a hard time believing how casual the four of them had become, talking about ghosts and dead people, but they had, and Ida didn't care if anyone thought it weird. She was happier now than she'd ever been in her sixty-five years. She didn't have to pretend to be something she was not. The girls loved her, cussed at her, called her all kinds of names, but Ida took it all in stride. She knew they loved her regardless of her faults. And she was just starting to learn to love them back the way they deserved to be loved.

Ida poured herself a cup of coffee and followed the smell of smoke to the deck, where she found Toots and Sophie, still in their pajamas, puffing like two old freight trains. "You two gag me, smoking those old nasty things this early. I bet your lungs are black as coal. I wish you both would quit."

Sophie took a deep drag from her cigarette, blowing the smoke in Ida's direction. "I'll make you a deal. You give up men for one whole year, and I'll stop smoking." Sophie grinned, winked at Toots, then took another puff from her Marlboro.

"Men and smoking aren't the same. Smoking can kill you," Ida said.

In a much more serious tone, Sophie said, "Men can kill you, too, Ida. Trust me. At least with smoking, it's your own choice."

Ida shook her head. "All right, I agree, is that better? You hate to be wrong, don't you? No, don't answer that. Where is Mavis? I haven't seen her or that pesky dog this morning."

"She went with George to inspect one of his dry-cleaning stores. Can you believe that? Sweet old Mavis fatter than a plump chicken, loses all that weight in record time, then meets a rich man while walking her dog. I think that our friend has finally met Lady Luck," Toots said.

"Have you met this George?" Ida asked. She brushed the sand off her chair, then sat down.

"Not yet. Mavis says she's going to invite him for dinner as soon we finish our work in the dining room. She doesn't want to scare him away. Can't say that I blame her. Four old women living with the ghost of Bing Crosby. No—" Toots paused to light a cigarette. "She's smart to keep him away, at least for now."

The beach crowds were starting to emerge, dotting the beach with brightly colored beach towels, blankets, umbrellas, and coolers. Parents opened bottles of sunscreen, slathering it on backs, bellies, and faces. Kids young and old raced toward the water, screaming with delight as the cold water took their breath away. Laughter, shouts, and the occasional cry drifted up to the deck.

"All this time we've been here, and I haven't been to the beach yet, or not like that." Sophie looked below at the crowds. "I am going to do that soon. Just sit out there and people watch and smoke." She laughed. "You want to join me, Ida? I'll puff, and you can look for a man. Maybe Mavis's new man has a brother?"

"I am not interested in finding a new man. I wish you would lay off. You haven't stopped for six months. I am getting quite tired of listening to you. Why don't you have a man in your life, Sophie? Can't find one? Too much work? Or are you afraid I might snatch him up like Toots snatched Jerry away from me?" Ida took a deep breath, crossed her arms over her chest, and waited, the hint of a smile lifting the corner of her mouth.

"Well shit, Ida, I am proud of you! You have a set of iron nuts after all. I always knew they lurked somewhere beneath all that perfection. Not that it's your business, but since you seem to believe a woman's happiness is dependent upon her abilities to capture a man, I choose to remain single, and it's not much work when you're with the right man and I would never ever date a man that would look twice at a woman of your . . . caliber. So does that answer your questions?" Sophie smiled, knowing it irritated Ida. "One more thing to remember—Jerry was a dud?"

Ida laughed. "Yes I seem to recall hearing that a time or two. Toots, have you heard from Abby this morning? I wanted to tell her good-bye, but she was gone when I woke up. I do hope her boss isn't planning on firing her!"

"I was so close to telling her that I was the mysterious owner of the paper last night, but I held myself back. I sent her an e-mail this morning, but I haven't checked my computer to see if she's responded. Let's go inside. Sophie, you can make a fresh pot of coffee. Let's see if Abby's penned an e-mail to her 'employer.' She will kick my old ass when she finds out about me and the paper. I'm looking forward to it and dreading it at the same time."

Inside, Sophie made coffee while Toots booted up her laptop. Ida brought milk and sugar to the table.

"Okay, here it is. Damn, she says she's considering telling our ghost story. She says she'll come over when we have another séance. Sophie, make sure you have that new equipment set up just in case we actually catch a movement, an apparition, a puffy cloud with faces talking with no sound. I still cringe at the image. If Abby had a photograph of an actual paranormal event taking place or a recording she could use and transcribe, those A-list asses over at *The Enquirer* and *The Globe* would get a bit of good old healthy competition."

Toots scrolled through the rest of her e-mail. "Would

you look at this! I can't believe it. Dear old Bernice has sent
an e-mail. Wonders never cease. She says the Confederate
jasmine is blooming, Dr. Pauley has stopped by three times
this week wanting to know when I was coming home. I
once thought about going after Paul, did I ever tell either
of you that? No, I don't think I did." Toots hurried through
the rest of the e-mail, reading out loud when it pertained
to the girls or Abby. "I miss that old broad. We may have
to make a quick trip to Charleston."

"I'm game, you know that," Sophie said. "I always
wanted to travel whenever the urge hit me."

"I'm going to write Bernice and tell her to expect us; I'm
just not going to tell her when. That way she'll be on her
toes every time she hears a car pull in the drive. Poor Bernice—I wish she would retire. It's not like I haven't made it
easy for her. I am so proud of her for trying the computer.
I bought her a laptop for her birthday last year. She looked
at me as though I'd handed her an alien spacecraft fully
equipped with little green men. I think she's lonely. Oh
shit." Toots's eyes teared up just talking about Bernice.
She missed the old gal.

"Stop the caterwauling; you can go home to Charleston
anytime you want. I know you have this so-called job at
the paper, but Abby is running the paper all by herself. All
we're doing is encouraging her. She thinks a big-time cor-
poration is lurking behind the scenes. Come to think of it,
when put that way, why are we here? We aren't running
the show like you said, Toots, we're having séances and . . .
What the hell are we doing here? Abby doesn't need us."

It was a rare sight to see tough, street-smart Sophie's eyes
pool with tears. "I don't know why I just said that. I think
I'm feeling old and useless today. I need to do something
constructive, something with purpose and meaning."

"You did that months ago when you buried Walter, remember?" Toots replied. "It seems like you've forgotten about your plan to not make any plans. Did you forget, Sophie?"

"No, I didn't forget, but it just hit me that I am doing absolutely nothing! For the first time in my life, I don't really have any responsibilities. I'm not so sure this is a good thing, Toots," Sophie said. "I feel like a loser with a capital L plastered across my forehead."

"Will both of you just be quiet? I swear, you get an e-mail from Bernice, and everything begins to unravel. You are both acting like two silly old women, not the intelligent, liberated, freethinking, complaining women that I have come to admire and love more than ever." Ida stopped talking when she saw she had their undivided attention. Their jaws dropped, and they were staring at her as if she had three heads. A two-legged Cerberus.

"What?" Ida asked.

"What? I think that's what I need to be asking you. What the hell has gotten into you, Ida? In all the years I've known you, and it's approaching fifty-one years this fall, I have never once heard you tell me or Sophie or Mavis that you loved us! What the hell was in the coffee we drank this morning?" Toots looked at Ida, then back at Sophie. "Did you drug her or something?"

"No, I didn't. I think old Bernice's e-mail hit home, really. Reminded me that I don't really belong here or in Charleston. And forget New York. I'd rather live in Outer Mongolia. Toots, I am going to pack up that dreary-ass-ugly apartment and sell the son of a bitch to the highest bidder! I know the real estate markets are in a slump right now, but I've never heard of anyone who had an apartment in the city waiting years before it sold. Yes, this is what I'm going to do. Then I might buy a place out here, or in Charleston. I need a kick in the ass, something to keep me busy." Sophie opened a fresh pack of Marlboros, lighting two. She passed one to Toots.

"What the frick? Is this the woman who plans to have no plans?" Toots asked, then blew a funnel of smoke in her friend's face.

"I still don't want to make plans, Toots. I have to plan to sell the apartment, or to take trips. Yes, I plan to do all that. I want to do something other than nothing. I think it's the choice now. I've spent most of my life making choices that, while they affected me, were choices I had to make because of the poor choices I'd made in the past. Now that's gone, I'm free to choose or not." Sophie took a sip of coffee from one of the new royal-blue mugs. "That doesn't make any sense at all, does it?" Sophie looked to Toots for confirmation.

"I got what you were trying to say. You want to make your own choices because you can, not because it's something you're being forced to do. Does that about sum it all up? Because if it doesn't, then no, you're not making a lick of sense." Toots cast a glance at Ida. "What about it, Ida, is Sophie making any sense to you?"

"Yes, I understand exactly where she is coming from. I think we're in the middle of a massive epiphany. Bernice's e-mail was just the kick in the pants Sophie needed. I needed it, too. Talk about wasting your life doing nothing." Ida got up and brought the coffeepot to the table. She refilled their cups, returned the pot to the burner, then sat down. "I wasted a whole year of my life washing my hands and anything around me. I can't believe I'm over that. Toots, Sophie, if not for you two, I would still be in that lovely penthouse apartment washing my hands, trying to sanitize the world. That's what Dr. Sameer told me. He said because my life had slowly fallen apart around me, I needed to have control over the things that were in my power to control, like keeping my environment clean."

Sophie was the first to speak; at least that hadn't changed during the past fifteen minutes. "You actually believe that crock of shit?"

"In a way, because it's partially true. Thomas died, and I no longer had control of . . ." Ida stopped short. "I think I liked controlling people. Thomas let me have complete control during our marriage."

"Now that's news. Shit, Ida, I could have told you that and dunked your hand in the garbage for free. How much did you say you paid Dr. Sameer?" Sophie grinned. "Maybe I missed my calling. I should have been a shrink."

Toots stood up and stretched. "I've had enough psychobabble for one day. I'm going to get dressed and do something proactive with the rest of the day. Sophie, when you have a minute, I need to speak to you. Alone. Nothing personal, Ida. It's a surprise."

"You don't have to explain, Toots," Ida said.

"Good, I've never liked explaining myself to anyone. I'll see you two later."

Ida heard her cell phone ringing again. "I better get that." Ida carried her coffee upstairs and grabbed the phone off her night table. "Hello."

"Ah, Ida, my dear. I thought you were never going to speak to me again. I have been calling you all morning."

Ida rolled her eyes, thinking she was getting more like Toots daily. "I was outside having coffee with my friends."

"I must see you today, Ida. I have something I want to ask you. Please say that you will. I'll send a cab for you when it's convenient. I have not slept one wink since you left the night before last. I owe you an apology, too."

Ida's heart melted. Sammy loved her—she could feel it in her bones—but he also loved being a doctor. Maybe it was time for her to stop thinking about what she wanted and think about what others wanted. She'd been selfish for so long. "Yes, Sammy, do send a cab over as soon as you can. I'll be waiting at the bottom of the drive."

Ida hung up, grabbed her purse, and hurried outside before Toots or Sophie could ask her where she was going. In spite of all her talk about control, Ida knew it would take more than a morning of girl talk to end her desire to share herself with a man.

Chapter 19

Toots felt out of sorts after her conversation with Ida and Sophie. Her intention had been to operate *The Informer,* but, unless she was willing to show her cards, she had to stay behind the scenes. She'd convinced herself that she and the girls could create news stories for Abby, but it wasn't that easy. She didn't have any connections in show business, wasn't an actress, and had never aspired to become one. Purchasing the paper hadn't been the smartest investment, she was quite aware of that, but it all came back to Abby. What she should do, could do, and would do was anything in her power to keep her daughter happy. Abby's happiness made Toots happy.

Though she'd buried eight husbands, she still kept a positive attitude, but Sophie was right. Abby didn't need her to run the paper. She was doing quite well as editor in chief. Having said that, Toots knew Abby's passion was the reporting itself, chasing the stars in search of the big headline of the day. Now Toots was having doubts, and she didn't like feeling this way. She'd felt this way when she was in Charleston. And that was why she'd called her dearest friends together. She wanted to stir up trouble, kick some ass or, as Sophie would say, "open a can of whoop-ass."

"Screw this!" Toots stomped across the room, pulled a denim skirt and bright green blouse off their hangers and grabbed her sandals. She was not going to let a pity party take over her life. Life was for the living. She was going to live it up as long as there was breath in her.

For starters, she was going to call Chris, invite him for dinner, and pick his brain. He ran around with starlets almost every night. If he had the tiniest bit of gossip, she was going to force him to spill the beans. Abby needed headlines. Toots was going to step up to the plate and do whatever she could to see that she got them.

Dressed and impatient as hell, Toots raced down the hall searching for Sophie. She tapped on her door. "Sophie, you in there?" She waited outside. She couldn't bring herself to go inside that room even though she knew the spirits or whatever the hell they were calling them weren't bad spirits. They had frightened her something terrible, and she wasn't ready to go back inside and face her fears just yet. She had too many other important things to tend to. She knocked again.

Sophie came up behind her, poking her in the ribs. Toots almost jumped out of her skin. "What! Oh, you about gave me a heart attack." Toots's hands shook. "Don't ever do that again or I'll toss your ass down the stairs just like Bette Davis tossed that head down the stairs in *Hush* . . . *Hush, Sweet Charlotte.*"

"Damn, Toots! Don't be such a mean bitch. I was teasing, all right?" Sophie elbowed her way around her to the bedroom door. "Go on, get out of here, you've pissed me off." She slammed the door in Toots's face.

"Wait! I need to tell you something."

Sophie yanked her door open. "What? I'm still pissed at you."

"You'll get over it. Listen, Abby has asked one of her reporters to check out Dr. Sameer." Toots lowered her voice so Ida wouldn't overhear.

"You can speak up. She's not here. The minute her phone rang, she raced up the stairs like a horny teenager. A taxi just picked her up at the end of the driveway. You know where she's going, don't you?"

"Dr. Sameer's place?"

"Yes. Probably going to have hot and heavy sex while she's there."

"And that means what?" Toots asked.

"What it means is that we aren't. Now go on, but I am still pissed at you."

Sophie was about to close the door when Toots put her foot next to the door frame. It was now or never. Toots entered the bedroom. "I need to get over this now. I don't want it to take over my life like Ida's OCD. Now move." Toots entered her old bedroom and waited for the temperature to change. When nothing happened, she stood next to the bed, knowing nothing would happen, but she needed to do this anyway. The room wasn't the same as it was before. Sophie had chosen clean whites and different hues of peach. The room looked warm and inviting. Maple furniture. Though Toots thought it out of place in the beach house, she'd given Sophie and the girls free rein to decorate as they pleased. Sophie liked this, and that was fine with Toots.

"Okay, this room isn't so frightening anymore. I'm over it. You can go back to being pissed at me."

"I haven't stopped," Sophie said.

"So be pissed, then get over it. We've got things to do," Toots insisted.

"I will in my own time, okay? Now go do your thing. I want to take a shower and get dressed. I may go to the beach and hang out today after I contact a Realtor in New York."

"Okay, you've made your point. I'm going to call Chris,

see if I can pick his brain for anything gossipy for the paper." Toots turned around to leave, stopping only when Sophie reached for her arm.

"Just so you know, I will stop being mad in an hour."

"Good, I'll look forward to it. Now git." Toots removed Sophie's arm from hers, then walked down the hall to her own room, where she booted up the laptop, checking to see if she'd received a reply from Abby. There it was, Abby's response to the e-mail she'd received from LAT Enterprise:

TO: LATEnterprise@yahoo.com
FROM: ASIMPSON@THEINFORMER.COM

Thank you for permission to pursue the ghost theory. Also, thank you for your confidence in me, allowing me to act as editor in chief, granting me final approval of *The Informer*'s content.

The e-mail continued with a few stories Abby had planned for the back pages. While this wasn't exactly owning and operating a tabloid as Toots had first envisioned, for now Abby was content, and that made Toots happy. Hers was a one-day-at-a-time business. There could come a day when Abby might have a change of heart and tell LAT ENTERPRISE she no longer wanted the position and responsibilities of being editor in chief. Until that happened, Toots would remain in the background as LAT ENTERPRISE.

Toots answered the e-mail to the point, professionally. Too much, and she might give herself away. For now she was content knowing Abby was happy with her job. At the first sign of her unhappiness, Toots would . . . she would do whatever needed to be done.

Next on her shit-to-do-list: Call Chris. She used her cell phone to make the call.

"Chris Clay." He picked up on the first ring.

"Morning, Chris. How is my very favorite attorney today?"

Toots smiled when she heard Chris laughing.

"Okay, old girl, what is it you want? I know you."

Was she that obvious? Did she only call her stepson when she needed something? She would think, and if she did, then that, too, was about to cease. She loved Chris as much as if he were her own flesh and blood.

"I called to invite you to dinner. You name the time and place," Toots stated succinctly.

More laughter from Chris. "I must be the luckiest guy in the world, because this is the second invitation I've had in the past twenty-four hours to have dinner with a beautiful woman. What gives, Toots? Everything okay with that paper? The house, you're good with the contractor I recommended?"

"Yes, the paper is up and running, thanks to Abby, and the house is finished on the inside. The contractors were awesome. Who is the other woman that invited you to dinner? Hope it's not one of those fly-by-night starlets of the moment."

"If you must know, it's Abby. She promised me dinner if I did her a favor." Chris paused. "Like mother, like daughter. I do favors, I get dinner. Good thing I've got healthy self-esteem, or I would start to wonder if you two weren't trying to bribe me."

"No, well, I am not trying to bribe you. It's been too long since I last saw you. I want you to see all the changes at the house. I could have Mavis fix something and we could dine in. What do you say?"

"I say yes, but I need to get back with you on the time. Will that be a problem?" Chris asked.

Sort of. Kind of, Toots wanted to say, but didn't. She needed to pick his brain as soon as possible, but if not, that was okay. Poor Chris, she didn't want him to feel like he wasn't appreciated, wasn't a member of the family. Maybe in her own way she had been using Chris.

"No, it won't. You just call me when you have a free evening. Mavis has the freezer and pantry so well stocked, I'm sure there's enough food for fifty. So, you'll call me?"

"Sure thing, Toots."

"I'll be waiting," she said, then clicked the END button. Abby hadn't mentioned Chris lately. Toots assumed they weren't speaking. The two had been back and forth for years. Abby would rant and rave about what an ass he was, but Toots knew different. She'd seen the way they looked at one another when they thought she wasn't paying any attention. The attraction between them had just started a few months ago. She'd seen the sparks in their eyes. Abby hadn't said anything to her, and Toots wasn't going to ask.

She would have liked nothing more than to see Abby and Chris in a relationship, maybe even marriage. Chris was a wonderful man. If Abby and Chris had a thing going on, then it was fine with her. Maybe she should invite Abby to dinner when Chris confirmed a date. Yes, that's what she would do. After she picked his brain, she would watch them, see if what she'd observed between them was more than a mother's imagination.

Another item to be added to her shit-to-do-list.

Chris was about to head for the shower when his cell phone rang for the second time. He picked up on the second ring. "Chris Clay," he said.

"Hey, Chris, what gives?" His source at the jail.

"Nothing much. Work, work, and more work, you know how it goes."

"Yeah, I do. Listen, I have that information you asked for. Is this line secure?"

"Yes, go ahead, tell me what you have." Chris listened while his contact at the Los Angeles County Jail relayed the information to him.

"Hey, I owe you one, thanks for getting back to me so quickly," Chris said.

"Anytime, man."

Chris clicked the END button on his cell phone. He wanted to call Abby with the information, but first he was going to pay a visit to the son of a bitch who'd been sending her those e-mails.

He showered, shaved, and dressed in less than ten minutes. Chris didn't want to waste another minute. He made it to the jail in record time and found a parking place within reasonable walking distance. That in itself was a small miracle.

Inside the jail, he went through the metal detector, and tossed his keys, cell phone, and wallet into a small bowl, stepping aside when a sheriff's deputy ran a handheld scanner up and down the length of his body to search for any kind of contraband. Once he'd passed inspection, he was allowed to roam throughout the building. Chris found the reception desk and signed in as counsel in order to prevent waiting in the lengthy line. A deputy led him through a maze of doors leading to a long row of chairs that faced a wall of glass. The county jail in LA was no-contact, hence the phone and wood dividers that separated each visitor. This provided a bit of privacy, but Chris wasn't concerned about protecting this slimeball's privacy. If anything, he wanted anyone within hearing distance to find out what an ass he was. Maybe he'd get a good old-fashioned jail ass-kicking when the other inmates discovered what he did with his allowed computer time. Chris had learned that a select few inmates were allowed to use the Internet for one hour each day if they were enrolled in a county-sponsored program.

"You can have a seat." The deputy motioned to a metal chair that had seen better days. Chris wished for one of those disinfecting wipes when he saw a thick white clump of something—he was sure he didn't want to know exactly what—stuck to the chair. The deputy watched him. "Formula. Mom bringing baby to visit Daddy."

Chris nodded, then sat on the edge of the chair. He picked up the phone, saw more of the white gunk, and used his sleeve to clean the phone's mouthpiece. He was glad Abby wasn't here with him to see what a dump the jail was, but for all he knew she'd seen this before and, knowing her, thought nothing of it. She was a reporter. Chris couldn't remember if she'd reported on any celebrity jailbirds. A tap on the glass brought his attention to the man wearing the typical LA County Jail one-piece orange designer suit.

Michael Constantine. Arsonist, small-time hood.

Chris spoke into the phone. "Your ass is in a load of crap, you know that?"

Michael Constantine, "Micky" to his friends, lifted the wall phone from the cradle, laughing, which showed his nasty, yellow, nicotine-stained teeth. "Who the fuck are you? I ain't done nothin' to you. I don't even know your ass."

"No, and I for one am glad. I'll get straight to the point. You've been sending Abby Simpson bogus e-mails when you're supposed to be studying for your high-school diploma. I've advised the jail what you're doing with your computer time. If the state brings some charge against you, good. If not, I will see that your ass suffers, and I mean that quite literally, if you know what I mean? Stop sending e-mails to *The Informer* or else. Do you get it?"

"Yeah, man, I get it. You must be the boyfriend of that hot little blonde. Give her a message for me. Tell her I said her ass is mine as soon as I'm outta this place. You got it?"

Chris hung up the phone and walked away. If he stayed,

he might've been tempted to break the glass and strangle the sleazy dime-store hood. He collected his wallet, phone, and keys, then hurried outside to his car. He dialed Abby's cell-phone number. It went to voice mail. She'd told him to call her at the paper. He scrolled through his list of phone numbers, found the main number for *The Informer*, and dialed. He was put on hold, then Abby picked up. "Chris, what's up? I take it you found my mailer?"

"You're not going to believe this, Abby. The jerk that tried to torch *The Informer*. He's your man."

"Michael Constantine? How?"

"He's enrolled in a county program that allows him access to a computer. Apparently he wasn't using his time just to study."

"That ass! I . . . is there something I can do? Legally?" Abby asked.

"I'm not sure. Probably not. I don't think it's against the law to send bogus e-mails as long as they're not threatening in any way."

"What about those booking reports that I saw? Isn't there a law against that?"

"I'm sure there is, but again you'll need proof that he accessed encrypted files. This is probably nothing more than a glitch in the county's system."

"He better thank his lucky stars I didn't lose my job over this. I've printed teasers for the past three weeks building up to this *exclusive* interview. I would like to choke the bastard, but since I can't, I'll have to chalk this experience up to desperation and unprofessionalism."

"So, now that I've fulfilled my duty, when are we having that dinner you promised me?"

He heard her sigh over the wires. "Let me call you back; I need to check my calendar," Abby said.

"Don't wait too long. I promised your mother I'd have dinner with her and your godmothers. She invited me to come out to the beach house and see all the changes. Personally, I think she has something up her sleeve. I told her I would get back to her with a time and date. I was waiting to see when you wanted to go to dinner first."

"Oh. She didn't tell me that."

"Your mother doesn't tell you everything, Abby," he observed, then wished he could take the words back before she read something into them.

"How do you know that? Is there something you know and you're not telling me? Because, you know, if there is, and I find out you've been keeping secrets, I'll have to kill you."

Relieved, Chris laughed. Yes, there certainly were things he knew about her mother that she didn't know, but he wasn't about to tell her what they were.

"I don't have anything on your mom, Abby."

"That's good to hear. Seriously, though, I do have to check my calendar before I can confirm dinner plans. Truly, I am not lying to you."

"I didn't think that you were," Chris said, knowing that that was exactly what he'd thought. Abby had her information. Now she would try and squirm out of having dinner with him.

"Yes, you did. I know you, and I know me. I usually make excuses. You have my word I am not doing that this time. I really want to have dinner with you."

"Okay. I'll wait for your call."

"Count on it," Abby said, then hung up.

The acorn didn't fall far from the oak. Abby was certainly her mother's daughter, big on having the last word. Chris smiled. Suddenly he had that kid-at-Christmas feeling again.

Damn, life was good.

Chapter 20

Before she had a change of heart, Ida took her cell phone from her purse and dialed her banker in New York City. After several minutes, she was put through to her personal account manager. Though she didn't have all the banking information she needed, she instructed her manager to be prepared to wire $3 million to an account in California as soon as she called back. He, Russ was his name, had asked her if she was buying property. If so, he could send the funds directly to the seller. She'd quickly told him it was none of his business, just make sure that amount was ready for transfer when she called back. If not, she would take her business elsewhere. Banks were falling like rain these days. Ida was sure she and her fortune would be welcomed with open arms at any number of banks. She told him this before she ended the call.

Ida gave the driver a fifty-dollar bill and told him to keep the change before she got out at the end of the drive-way. She thought Sammy would be waiting for her when she arrived, but he probably didn't know she'd left so soon. It didn't matter, she told herself, as she walked the length of the drive.

She heard raised voices when she reached the front door. Undecided whether to knock or just walk inside, her manners got the better of her and she knocked, then waited. When no one came to the door, Ida knocked again. Hand on the knob, she was about to turn it when the door opened.

"My dear, Ida. I was about to walk to the end of the drive to meet you. You should have called me when you arrived," Sammy said. He took her hand in his and led her to his bedroom. Not wasting time today, Ida thought. After she got over what had happened the night before last, she'd missed him last night. More than once she'd wanted to call him but changed her mind. She didn't want to appear too eager. Let him come to her.

"I was worried when you didn't answer my calls this morning." He motioned for her to sit down on the bed.

"We were outside having our morning coffee. I couldn't hear the phone." She didn't need to lie, but for some reason she felt compelled to make an excuse for not answering her phone.

"Wonderful, I know how much you enjoy your time with your friends," Sammy said. He hesitated for a few seconds, then continued. "I am so ashamed of myself for the way I acted the night before last. Can you accept an old man's apology?"

Ida really wished he would stop with the "old man" business. She should tell him, but didn't want to remind him that she was only two years younger than he. "You have nothing to apologize for. I offered to lend you money for the clinic. There is no shame in accepting help, Sammy. I want to help you. As a matter of fact, my banker in New York is waiting for me to call him with your banking information. I called him on the ride over." She was so proud of herself, she beamed. For once she'd taken the initiative, grabbed the bull by the horns, whatever one called it, and she'd made a decision on her own concerning a man. Sammy hadn't begged or bribed her. This was simply the right thing to do. If not for the Center for Mind and Body she wouldn't be sitting here right now. The way she figured it, she owed Sammy and the clinic her life. If not for his medical knowledge and kind, caring ways, she would still be holed up in a room somewhere scrubbing her hands and worrying about dying from some unknown germ.

He appeared to be genuinely shocked by her generous offer. "I still don't know what to say . . . you don't have to do this, Ida. How can I ever repay you? This is such a large sum of money, it could take years before I am able to pay this back to you."

Ida almost wished he had declined her offer, though she wasn't sure why. It didn't matter anyway. Now all she had to do was write down his banking information, and it was as good as done.

"Consider this a gift, a donation to the clinic if you will. I'll have my accountant take care of all the necessary forms. All you have to do is accept this and give me your banking information."

He shook his head. "Bless you, Ida. You're a true angel, you know that? I will make sure your generosity is known to my patients. Here."

He reached inside his pocket and removed a slip of paper. "This has everything you should need to wire the funds to the account."

That was fast, Ida thought. He must have known she was going to give him the money. Why else would he have the information ready to give her? Maybe she'd hinted at it on the phone? She couldn't remember, and it didn't matter. She'd made an offer to help with the center's finances, and now she would follow through on that commitment.

She took the paper from him. "This may take a few minutes."

"Of course, I'll leave you to make your phone call. When you're finished, maybe we will have lunch, then we can . . . visit." Sammy gazed at the bed when he said they could "visit." Ida smiled; she wouldn't mind a "visit" either.

"I'll just need a few minutes," she said.

Sammy took her hand in his, kissing her wrist, then the palm. Yes, she was definitely ready for a "visit" with Sammy. She'd gotten used to having a fulfilling sex life with him over the past few months. He was a very skilled and patient lover. There was no need to stop now simply because they were business partners.

"I'll leave you to make your call," Sammy said.

Ida dialed Russ's private number at the bank in Manhattan. When he answered, she skipped the niceties and got straight down to business. "These are the numbers," she said, then rattled off the bank's routing number, the account number, and a tax identification number. "Is there anything else?"

"This seems to be everything; if not, may I call you back?" Russ asked.

Ida must have scared him with her threat to take her business to another bank. "Of course. Now how long will this take before the money can be withdrawn?"

"No more than forty-eight hours."

"Good. Thank you, Russ." Ida punched the END button on her cell phone. She couldn't wait to tell Sammy that the money would be the clinic's in forty-eight hours. She waited for ten minutes, allowing him time to return. When twenty minutes passed, Ida went in search of him. She peered out into a small, well-lit hallway. There were three other bedrooms in the house, one of them belonging to Amala, though Ida had never been inside the young woman's room.

Ida had spent most of her time in Sammy's bed. That was fine with her; it was precisely where she wanted to be. She peered inside the two other bedrooms. The first one had a computer desk, a chair, and a laptop. There wasn't a bed or a night table, nothing to indicate that the room was used for anything other than a home office. Ida closed the door. Across from the office was another bedroom. She tapped on the door before opening it, then when there was no answer she peeked inside the room hoping to find Sammy. The room had an air mattress on the floor, an inexpensive lamp placed on a stack of what looked like thick medical books. Odd, she thought. Why wouldn't Sammy have a bed in what she assumed to be a guest room? She stepped fully inside the room, more out of curiosity than anything. A canvas bag lay open on top of the blue mattress. Ida wanted to look inside, but that wasn't her style. She'd already nosed around in areas that were obviously off-limits, or the doors would have been open. She left the guest room, again being careful to close the door behind her quietly.

Around the corner and to the left of the office and guest room, Ida spied the door to Amala's room. It was open. Sure that Sammy was inside, she started to step inside, then stopped dead in her tracks. She closed her eyes for a minute, then opened them again. Ida was sure she wasn't seeing things, but this?

Sammy held several pairs of women's panties in his hands. Pale blue, a lacy white G-string, and a red-and-black pair. The red-and-black pair that she'd thought she'd misplaced months ago!

Oh my God! Ida was rooted to the floor, shocked, as she watched Sammy bring each pair of sexy underwear to his nose, inhaling each pair as though he were smelling a fine wine. When he brought her red-and-black pair up to his nose, he kissed the crotch, then took a big whiff of the same area.

Ida turned away so fast she became instantly dizzy. She raced back to Sammy's bedroom, unsure of what to do.

She sat on the bed and took several deep, calming breaths. She swallowed several times. Her mouth was as dry as a bone. Ida was in the bathroom getting a drink of water when she heard Sammy enter the bedroom.

"Ida, dear, are you in here?"

God almighty!

What to do? Act, Ida, you stupid ass. Act like you've never acted before.

She cleared her throat and took a sip of water before calling out to Sammy. "In here. I'll just be a minute."

"Wonderful. I'll be waiting for you."

Ida was screwed, or as Sophie and Toots would say, she was fucked. Yes, she liked the sound of that. She was fucked. Big-time. Now, if she could manage to get through the next few minutes without alerting Sammy that she knew his dirty little secret, then she might start a new career as an actress. At least a grade-B one. She opened the door and stepped back into the bedroom, where Sammy lay on top of the bed completely nude touching himself in places that she'd touched him.

Oh God, this was much worse than she thought!

"Sammy," Ida said loudly. He yanked his hand away from his privates.

"My dear, as you can see, I can hardly hold myself back. I want to make love to you right now. Take off your clothes, Ida."

She wasn't sure what to do! Part of her was turned on by the sudden turn of events, another part of her was mortified. What the hell, she thought. She might as well go for broke.

She stripped off her navy blouse, kicked her shoes aside, and removed her capris. Down to her pale pink bra and panties, Ida suddenly had a flash of Sammy as he'd stuck his nose on the silky undergarments, inhaling deeply as though he were on oxygen. She kept her bra and panties on. She couldn't go through with this knowing what she knew.

"Sammy, I am not feeling well. Would you mind if we didn't make love? I've been feeling . . . dizzy." That was an understatement.

"You would leave me like this?" He nodded downward.

"I'm sorry. Can't you just relieve yourself? You seemed to have no trouble doing so a few minutes ago." Ida felt her face flame with embarrassment. Never, ever in her sixty-five years had she been so humiliated!

With a wicked grin, Sammy said, "I suppose, but only if you will watch me."

Eyes widened in horror, Ida raced out of the room, not bothering to stop for her clothes. She ran outside to the deck, where Amala and Mohammed were in a heated conversation.

They stopped when they saw her. To say that both of them appeared surprised would be putting it mildly. Shocked, maybe. Ida didn't know what to say, so she didn't say anything. She just stood there in her silky pink bra and panties while Mohammed ogled her. "Stop staring at me like that, you . . . pervert!"

"Amala, do you have a robe or something I can use to cover myself?" Ida asked.

"Sure." She stood up. "I'll be right back."

Ida held her head high as Mohammed continued to rake his gaze over her nearly naked body. "Not bad, old woman, not bad at all. No wonder the good doctor likes fucking you." He smiled at her, a depraved look on his olive-skinned face. She wanted to run and hide, cover herself, but Ida was sophisticated enough to know that doing so was exactly what he would expect her reaction to be, so she stood there, letting him gaze at her.

Feeling more brazen than she should, Ida spoke up. "Do

you like what you see?" God, she was going to hell in a handbasket for sure!

"As I said, not bad for an old broad," Mohammed stated.

Amala reappeared with a robe. Grinning, she said, "This should help."

Ida took the robe from her, thankful to have something to cover herself. She wrapped herself up in a short yellow terry-cloth robe that smelled of incense and cigarettes.

"Not that it is any of my business, but why don't you just go inside and put your clothes back on?" Amala asked.

Ida didn't know what to say, so she said the first thing that popped into her head. "You're right, it isn't any of your business." There was no way she would tell them that she was waiting for Sammy to . . . finish up.

God, she had made a real mess of things! No, Sammy was the one responsible for this mess, quite literally if he finished off what the panty smelling had started.

Not caring what they thought of her actions, Ida raced inside and headed to the bedroom. If Sammy wanted to . . . fondle himself, that was his business. She would die and burn in hell before she ever came back to this house of horrors again. Sophie and Toots were right. She let men rule her.

That's when she remembered the $3 million she had just arranged to transfer into Sammy's bank account! Ida stopped so quickly her brain jostled the inside of her skull. What had she done? What kind of man borrowed $3 million from a woman, then played . . . pocket pool afterward?

Ida was shocked at herself and shocked that she'd been so stupid not to see what was right in front of her face all along. Sammy had simply been using her for sex while preparing to bilk her out of a small fortune. *Stupid* and *ashamed* didn't begin to describe the way she felt.

She figured she'd waited long enough for Sammy to take care of business. She zipped back to his room and found her clothes where she'd left them. She dressed, spotting her purse next to her cell phone. She looked around the room, making sure she hadn't left anything behind. That's when she remembered her black-and-red panties in the other room. Brazen beyond her wildest dreams, Ida hurried back to Amala's room, saw the pile of silken underclothes on the bed. She spotted her missing drawers, snapped them up, and put them in her purse. Not caring if she ran into Sammy or not, she hurried outside and literally ran all the way to the end of the road. When she stopped long enough to catch her breath, she called a cab.

"How long?" she asked.

"Fifteen minutes," they replied.

"Thanks."

Ida sat down on the curb to wait for her ride. Crushed and hurt, Ida paid no attention to the cars cruising by, and no one seemed to notice an old woman crying her eyes out. With her nose running and her eyes saturated with tears, she opened her purse to search for a tissue. When she couldn't find one, she thought, "Fuck it," and blew her nose on the panties Sammy had just sniffed.

Chapter 21

"George has asked me to go away for the weekend," Mavis told them. "I don't know what to do."

They were all gathered around the kitchen table discussing the day's events while Mavis cooked another healthy meal for all of them. Tonight's menu consisted of poached salmon, steamed asparagus, and an arugula salad with lemon juice.

Toots set the table with her new royal-blue dishes. Sophie made a fresh pot of coffee, but Ida hadn't volunteered to do anything but sit and stare out at the ocean. At the mention of George, she perked up. "Tell him no, whatever you do," Ida said.

"Don't listen to her, Mavis. She's just jealous because you've met a rich man, and she hasn't," Sophie said.

Toots put paper napkins beside each plate. "If you two start up again, I swear I'm going to drag both of you out to the beach and hold you under until you're gasping for air."

"Damn, you're a cruel bitch. Last night she threatened to throw me down the staircase. Today you want to drown me. If you weren't postmenopausal, I'd swear you had a massive case of PMS. Or maybe you just need to get laid.

Yes, I'm sure that's what it is," Sophie said, offering up her usual two cents' worth.

Toots finished setting the table, turned around so she could look at Sophie. "Do you have to talk about sex now? We're getting ready to eat."

Sophie cackled. "I won't say what I'm really thinking, but yes, I like to talk about sex. And yes, Ida, I know you're getting laid on a regular basis, but I still like talking about sex, and, no, I don't give a hoot if I ever have it again. I simply like to see the expressions on your faces when I talk about it. Ida, you might want to start taking pictures, them being worth a thousand words and all."

"Girls, I am serious. I need your advice. George has invited me to his place in La Jolla. I didn't ask, but I am sure he'll want to get . . . romantic." Mavis placed the bowl of arugula in the center of the table.

"Screw what he wants, what do you want?" Sophie asked. "Men never give a good rat's ass about what we want. It's always about them and what they want. Right, Toots?"

"Why are you asking me?" Toots said.

Sophie rolled her eyes upward. "You're the most experienced woman among the four of us. I'm sure you can help Mavis."

"Yes, Toots, not that I think you're a . . . well, you know, I don't think you're a tramp or anything, but you do have a lot of experience with men." Mavis lifted the lid on the steamer, poked the asparagus with a fork, then put the lid back on.

"Okay, since you all seem to think I'm the resident expert on the male species, what do you want to know, Mavis?"

Mavis washed her hands, dried them on a kitchen towel, then faced Toots. "He said he'd recently been measured for a VCD. I have no idea what that is, but I think it might be some sex toy or something." Mavis's faced turned ten shades of red. "I guess what I want to know is if any of you girls know what that is."

The kitchen was silent except for the hiss of the steamer and the bubbling of simmering water where four thick slices of salmon were poaching. All eyes were on Toots.

Toots held up her hand. "I'll be right back."

Mavis, Ida, and Sophie watched as she raced up the stairs. Less than a minute later she was back with her laptop.

"What are you doing with that?" Ida asked.

"Patience, Ida." Toots quickly booted up the computer and on to her Internet service provider. "I can find out anything you want to know. I'll Google it. Now I'm ready." Toots sat at the head of the table, waiting for Mavis. "Okay, Mavis. Shoot."

"I'm sure he said VCD."

Toots ran her hands along the keyboard, stopped while waiting for her search results to appear on the screen. "Oh."

"What? Is it something bad?" Mavis asked. Her face was white, and her now-slender hands gripped the dishcloth like a life preserver. Coco, sensing something was wrong with her mistress, ran from her corner in the kitchen, sliding to a stop at Mavis's feet.

"Grrr." Coco made herself known.

"I don't think 'bad' is the proper word." Toots glanced up at Mavis, who looked like she was ready to faint. "It's not bad, it's just . . . well, let me read what it says."

"Okay," Mavis said.

Toots found her reading glasses tucked in her skirt pocket. "'VCD, a Vacuum Constriction Device, is an external pump with a band on it that a man with erectile dysfunction can use to get and maintain an erection . . .'"

Toots looked up. She had never seen her three friends so . . . entranced. She continued reading. "'The VCD consists of an acrylic cylinder with a pump that may be attached directly to the end of the . . . man part.' And before you ask, Sophie, no, that is not the word they used. 'A constriction band is placed on the cylinder at the other end, which is applied to the body. The cylinder and pump are used to create a vacuum to help the . . . man part become erect while the band ring is used to maintain the erection . . .'"

Toots removed her glasses. "Well, ladies, I think that gives us a pretty good idea of what VCD stands for."

The room was deathly quiet, then exploded with laughter when Sophie removed her hand from her mouth. Toots laughed, then looked at Ida, whose shoulders shook like a hula dancer's while she struggled not to laugh too loudly. Mavis was catatonic. Her mouth moved, but nothing came out. She reminded Toots of the spirits upstairs.

"Mavis." Sophie snapped her fingers in front of Mavis's face. When she didn't get a reaction, Sophie filled a small cup with water, tossing it directly in Mavis's face.

Mavis spit and sputtered back to life. "That was a mean thing to do, Sophie! Why did you do that?" Mavis wiped her face with the kitchen towel she still held in a death grip.

"You left us for a minute. I was helping you return. I think you should sit down," Sophie said, pulling out a chair, helping Mavis sit down.

"So is that VCD thing what I think it is?" Mavis asked Toots.

"What do you think it is?" Sophie couldn't keep quiet if her life depended on it.

"It sounds like something vulgar."

Toots, Ida, and Sophie couldn't restrain themselves any longer. They burst out laughing even louder than they had before.

Sophie said, "Let me explain it in terms you can understand. It's like a . . . bicycle pump, only instead of pumping up a flat tire, you're pumping up a . . . limp noodle."

Once again, they cackled with laughter, hooting and hollering until their sides were aching. Ida laughed so hard, she snorted. Toots managed to use all the napkins on the table to dry the tears of laughter streaming down her face, and Sophie wore an evil grin a mile wide. Mavis, poor naive Mavis, just sat there while the salmon burned.

Suddenly, Mavis jumped out of her chair, "I'm ruining our dinner. I hope you girls don't mind overcooked salmon. Maybe 'overcooked' isn't the proper word. Burned salmon."

Toots replaced the napkins, Sophie poured each of them a cup of coffee, while Ida helped Mavis scrape the salmon off the bottom of the pan. Toots put the asparagus in a serving dish and placed it next to the salad in the center of the table.

"Let's eat; I for one am starving. Mavis, this looks divine," Toots lied, then forked an asparagus spear.

For the next ten minutes or so, no one spoke. The only sounds were those of silverware clinking against the glass dinner plates and Sophie slurping coffee like a pig. Toots cast her a dirty look. Sophie slurped even louder. Ida glanced at Toots as though silently asking her to tell Sophie to mind her manners. Coco sat in Mavis's lap, stretching her skinny neck just high enough so she could swipe her little pink tongue over the edge of Mavis's plate and snatch bits of salmon and asparagus.

"I don't think I will go to La Jolla with George after all," Mavis said out of the blue.

"Do you really want to?" Toots asked. "Don't let a bunch of crazy old sex-starved women like us make your decision for you. If you want to go, I think you should."

"I do, I mean I did, but now that I know about that . . . thing, I'm not sure. I haven't been with another man since Herbert. He is the only man I've been with and—"

"—Don't choke, Ida. Sorry, Mavis, go on," Sophie said.

"Shut up, Sophie!" Toots admonished. She turned her attention back to Mavis. "You were talking about Herbert being the only man you've been with."

Mavis rubbed the top of Coco's tiny brown head. "Yes, well, I'm not sure if I can have a romantic relationship with George."

Ida finally chimed in. "Can I ask if you were considering a romantic relationship with him before Toots enlightened you?"

Sophie had remained silent much too long. "Romantic relationship? Enlightened? Give me a frigging break. I swear you two act like virgins. Mavis, were you planning to screw George before you knew he needed a penis pump to get it up?"

"Sophie Manchester, you're a crude old woman. Now shut up and let Mavis speak." Toots turned to Mavis. "I'll kick her if she interrupts you again."

"And I'll shove my foot so far up your ripe old ass, you'll wish you'd been slapped," Sophie said, her eyes full of mischief.

Mavis picked up where she'd left off. "I may have been. We haven't known one another very long; I still can't believe he's interested in me. He's handsome, wealthy. He has a Porsche."

"That alone is reason enough to sleep with him?" Sophie interrupted.

"I don't care about all those material things. We do have a lot in common, though. He has all those dry cleaners. I love to sew. George said he would take me to a fabric show someday. He goes to learn about the new fabrics and how to care for them."

Toots thought Mavis looked happy, really happy. Her eyes sparkled, her peach-colored hair had grown out a bit and now, because she was spending so much time on the beach, she'd gained a few blond streaks. Her creamy skin was now a warm gold color. On top of all that, she'd lost another twenty pounds. She was a miracle makeover. Toots thought Mavis was beautiful. Her skill with a needle still amazed them. All the clothes Toots had purchased for her at Catherine's in Charleston had been remade into simple and elegant designs. Toots often wondered why Mavis had never chosen a career in fashion. She had no doubt she would've been a roaring success.

"I think you should go. If you don't want to have a sexual relationship, just tell him. I remember when I was married to . . . I think it was . . . I can't remember which husband, but one of them had the same problem as George. We had a sexless marriage, but we were the best of friends. Sex isn't everything. Love, respect, and friendship do make for a happy, satisfying life. As you all keep reminding me, I've been around the block a few times, so I should know."

"This salmon is starting to smell," Sophie said to no one in particular. "Let's clean up and go sit on the deck. I want to smoke so bad I could die."

"Me, too. I'll make a pitcher of frozen strawberry daiquiris. We can get rip-roaring drunk if we want," Toots said.

Thirty minutes later, the kitchen was so clean it sparkled, the dishes were in the dishwasher, the fishy smell long gone. Toots carried a pitcher of strawberry daiquiris and four glasses outside to the deck. This is the life, she thought, but it would never be Charleston. That was home.

Ida, Sophie, and Mavis looked comfortable as they re-laxed in the bright blue-and-green-striped lounge chairs she had shelled out a small fortune for. Nothing was too good for friends and family. Now if Abby and Chris were here, this night would be close to perfect. She looked at her watch. It was too late to call either of them, as they both had to be up early for their jobs.

Toots put the tray on the patio table. "Okay, I'll pour

the first round. Raise your hand if you're ready to get smashed." Three hands rose high in the air. Toots filled the glasses with the sweet frozen concoction. She'd put in enough rum and strawberry schnapps to knock a 500-pound gorilla on his ass.

Tonight, Toots and her dearest friends were going to get snookered.

She'd worry about the killer hangover tomorrow.

Chapter 22

"Dear Ida found out about your nasty little fetish, didn't she?" Mohammed asked Patel. His dark eyes were like two angry slits in his face. His angular jaws were clenched, his wide nostrils flaring with fury. "You make me sick, old man! If she goes to the police, our asses are as good as dead. You couldn't wait, could you? No, you just had to . . . I can't even say what you do, it is so disgusting. Did it ever occur to you that she can stop that wire transfer? You are stupid, Patel, goddamn you!"

When Patel spoke, his voice was cold and full of contempt for the arrogant punk who stood before him, the man he had treated like a son. "It is none of your concern. You and Amala may continue with your scheme to rip off the doctor. If you are smart, you will leave now and no one will be the wiser, no one gets hurt. When Dr. Sameer comes back from his sabbatical, he will discover his secretary found employment elsewhere. Amala volunteered to stay and oversee the center, remember? It was not expected by the doctor. I am sure he will find another woman or possibly a man to work for him as soon as he returns. She is not indispensable. She is trouble, I have always told you this. You laugh at me now. Someday you will wish you had listened to me, taken my advice."

Mohammed raked a hand through his thick black hair. He hadn't told Patel of his plan to take the redhead. Now, with Dear Ida out of the picture, Mohammed had to rethink his idea. Without the old woman, there was no reason for him to go to the beach house. Without the old woman, he had no decoy. He paced the length of the deck, jammed his hands in his pocket. "You have ruined more than you know, old man! I should kill you, feed you to the sharks. Dangerous creatures, but smart. They would spit you out and give you to the bottom feeders." To emphasize his point, he spit on Patel's shoes.

Mohammed turned toward the railing that encircled the deck. Before he had time to react, Patel shoved him against the wooden ledge and used his left hand to hold Mohammed down. The younger man tried to free himself, but Patel was too quick. The old man elbowed him in the throat, making it almost impossible for him to breathe. Mohammed tried to escape from his death grip, but Patel had the advantage as he towered above him. With his free hand, he slammed Mohammed's head against the wooden ledge. Once, then again and again, he bashed the younger man's head against the hard wood as blood spewed forth like a fountain and soaked the wood of the deck.

"Stop it! You will kill him!" Amala screamed. She ran up behind Patel and jumped on his back, wrapping her arms around his eyes so he couldn't see. He tossed her aside like a limp rag doll. She hit the deck hard, but not hard enough to stop her from inching her way across the floor of the deck and sneaking behind him.

"Do not move, or I will break his neck!" Patel shouted. His senses heightened by the rush of adrenaline, he was aware of Amala as she crawled toward him. "I mean it, Amala!" To prove his point, Patel raised his right leg and thrust it out behind him. In one swift motion, using the heel of his boot, he crushed the delicate cartilage in Amala's nose. He heard her quick intake of breath, then a thud as her limp body dropped against the wooden deck.

"Are you getting my point, Mohammed?" Patel asked, raising his knee, catching Mohammed in the kidney. "I told you never to betray me! You did not listen. This is what I do to people who betray me!" Patel was so enraged, he continued to smash Mohammed's head against the wood, stopping himself when he felt a chunk of flesh hit his face.

He tossed Mohammed's motionless body next to Amala's. He reached down to feel for a pulse and found that both were still alive. He would not kill them, as that was not his way.

Patel's style was to make them *wish* he had killed them.

It was after midnight, and Abby wasn't the least bit tired. She watched two Lifetime movies, both sappy love stories that left her with tears streaming down her face. Like her mother, Abby loved happily ever after. Chester was curled up next to her, his heavy body warming her feet, which were tucked beneath his belly. Not wanting to wake him, but knowing if she didn't move soon her legs would fall asleep, she slowly pulled her feet out from under the big pooch one inch at a time. When she had both feet out, she tiptoed quietly to the kitchen. She'd left her laptop on the table when she'd come home earlier, and now she was glad that she had. She hit the ON switch, and while she waited for the computer to boot up, filled the teakettle with water, twisted the knob on the stove to the highest setting, and took a mug out of the cupboard. She grabbed a chamomile tea bag from the box on the counter and dropped it into the mug.

While she was waiting for the water to heat, she logged on to her e-mail account. She had several e-mails from her staff, but one in particular caught her attention. She'd sent the e-mail out earlier that morning, and was surprised she'd received an answer so quickly. She skimmed the e-mail, then opened the attachment. Using Word to convert the file from Mac, Abby jumped when she heard the teakettle whistle. "Shit. I know what that means."

Chester was terrified of the teakettle's high-pitched whistle. Abby always tried to remove it from the burner before it whistled, but sometimes she missed. When that happened, poor Chester always howled like a wolf, just as he was doing now. She stooped down to rub his belly, then between his ears. When he'd calmed down enough for her to step away, she filled her mug with hot water, careful not to trip over Chester as he rolled over, apparently deciding to sprawl out in the middle of the floor of her small kitchen. She grabbed a doggie treat from the canister. "Just so you know, this isn't a reward for good behavior."

Abby crab-walked over Chester, careful not to spill her tea. She pulled out her chair and sat down to read the file she'd received. She skimmed the information, impressed with what she read, though it was no surprise to her, because Dr. Pauley had recommended Dr. Sameer, praised his success in curing patients afflicted with obsessive-compulsive disorder. She ran down the lengthy list of his credentials. A Harvard man, graduated in the top tenth of his class. Very impressive. No wonder Dr. Pauley gave him his gold star seal of approval. She perused the rest of the lengthy document, finding nothing even remotely negative. He had no police record. His driving history was perfect, not even a parking ticket. She continued to read through a laundry list of awards he'd received throughout his career, then stopped. Wait a minute, this can't be right, she thought. Abby scrolled through the document to the beginning. The dates had to be wrong. Squinting, Abby leaned in close to the laptop monitor, reading the dates again. If the dates were right, and she was sure they weren't, Dr. Sameer was only forty-two years old.

Abby minimized the screen with the document, then maximized her server's front page. She clicked on the Google link. As soon as the search engine appeared, she typed in Dr. Sameer's name, then hit search. There were over a million hits. Damn, this guy must be good. Abby clicked on the blue hyperlink. The home page for the Center for Mind and Body appeared. Nice, easy to navigate. Abby clicked on the link that read MEET DR. SAMEER AND HIS STAFF.

This wasn't right, it couldn't be. Abby clicked on the link that read INSIDE THE CENTER FOR MIND AND BODY. Yes, this is where Ida was treated. Abby clicked back to MEET DR. SAMEER AND HIS STAFF. Three nurses, one physician assistant, two office aides, one office manager.

Two and two was not adding up to four. She glanced at the clock on the stove. Almost one in the morning. She debated calling her mother. It was late, and Abby was sure her mother and the godmothers were fast asleep.

She clicked through every link on the center's home page. The last link read, A NOTE FROM DR. SAMEER. Abby moved her cursor over the blue letters, then clicked on the link. A small picture of Dr. Sameer wearing a white lab coat smiled down at her from the upper left corner of the page. This was not good. No. Something was definitely awry. Before she had second thoughts, Abby grabbed her cell phone from the charger, punching in Chris's home number. He was a night owl like her, so she didn't care about calling at such a late hour. A brief thought flashed through her mind; what if a female answered? She would hang up, of course. Three rings. Hell, for all she knew Chris was out with some two-bit actress.

"Chris Clay."

Abby was so relieved she was momentarily stunned when she heard his voice.

"Chris, you're home," she said, then wished she could yank back the words. She did not want him to suspect that she was suspicious of his whereabouts. Lame, Abby, lame.

"Where else would I be at one o'clock in the morning?"

"I haven't a clue. Listen, I have something I want you to see. Are you near your computer?"

"I can be in 1.2 seconds. I'm there now."

God, she loved this man's sense of humor.

"Go to Google and type in Dr. Benjamin Sameer."

"Okay."

Abby heard the keys clicking as he typed. "When your results show, click on the link for the home page for the Center for Mind and Body." More computer clicks.

"I'm there, now what?"

"Go to the links on the right side of the page. Click the hyperlink that says 'Meet Dr. Sameer and his staff.' I'll wait while you read through it."

"Hmm, give me a minute," Chris said.

"When you're finished, find the link at the very bottom of the page that says 'A Note from Dr. Sameer.' I'll wait."

"Good, because I'm a slow reader."

"Sure you are," she teased.

"Wait until you really get to know me. I'm not only a slow reader, but I'm very slow in other areas, too."

She heard his soft chuckle. Damn, if this wasn't a form of phone sex, she didn't know what was. She was not going to dignify that comment with an answer, no matter how sexy she thought it was.

"This isn't the same doctor Ida is seeing, is it?" Chris asked, all traces of humor gone.

"No, but she goes to the Center for Mind and Body. I looked at the address and the picture. It's definitely where she's been going the past couple of months."

"Then who has been treating Ida? It doesn't say anything about another doctor taking over while he's on sabbatical. Of course that doesn't mean there isn't one. Maybe he referred his patients to this doctor treating Ida, and he just didn't post this to the Web site."

Abby twirled her hair in a knot. "I suppose it's possible, but with the same name?"

"Abs, they're probably related. I bet the older Dr. Sameer is his father."

"True, but what about the rest of the staff? Where are they? I distinctly remember mom telling me that Dr. Sameer's daughter worked at the center. She's the receptionist or secretary. Neither Ida nor Mom has ever mentioned any other employees."

"Are you really worried about this, Abs?"

"Right now I'm more concerned than worried."

"This just hit me. Why were you doing Google searches on Dr. Sameer?"

"I've had too much tea. Mom took me aside and asked me if I or someone at the paper could check into Dr. Sameer's past. She said there was something about him that didn't ring true. She didn't have anything specific to add, just that she was suspicious. I put one of my second-stringers on this earlier today. I was ready to call it a night, then I decided I'd better check my e-mail, just in case. I saw I'd received a response. And you know the rest."

"Are you up for taking a ride to the beach?"

Hell yes! She'd go anywhere with Chris. The moon. End of the earth. Pink's.

"Mom will kill me if this turns out to be nothing."

"And if it isn't?"

"Then Ida will kill me. She's been dating him ever since he cured her OCD."

"Can you be ready in half an hour?"

"Shit, in half an hour I can be decked out ready to attend the presidential inauguration."

"That's impressive, Abs."

"What can I say? I'm a no-frills kind of girl. Very low-maintenance."

"I just bet you are," Chris said. "There's no traffic this late, so I'll pick you up in fifteen minutes."

"I'll be waiting," Abby said. She pushed the END button, then looked down at her clothes. Gray sweats, orange T-shirt. Red socks with a hole in the left heel. She contemplated going as she was but decided against it.

In her room she pulled on a pair of faded Levi's with a black sleeveless turtleneck. She stuffed her feet in a pair of black Uggs, relishing how warm and soft the boots were. Just like fuzzy slippers. In the bathroom, she brushed her teeth, pulled her wild curls back in a low ponytail. She wasn't about to add blush, lip gloss, or mascara. She'd showered earlier, when she came home. Not that she cared what Chris thought she looked like. Yes, she did care, but she still wasn't putting makeup on at this ungodly hour. She'd have to remove it anyway.

Exactly fifteen minutes later, Abby heard a knock. "Be right there." She glanced in the mirror, figuring this was as good as it gets. Almost. She could jazz herself up when she wanted. She hurried to the front door, stopping to move samples of granite for the new kitchen countertops she planned to install.

Abby fumbled with the deadbolt, then had trouble grasping the chain lock.

"Are you expecting a serial killer?" Chris said.

Abby finally managed to unlock the door. "No, Chris, I'm not. But in case you haven't noticed, I am a single woman living alone in a city with a relatively high crime rate. While Brentwood is an upscale neighborhood, I never take my safety for granted. Does that answer your question?"

"I think I like you better when we talk on the phone.

You're not such a smart-ass." Chris took the keys from her and locked the front door.

"Wait! Chester is in there. I can't leave him."

Abby reached for her keys and managed to unlock the door without dropping them. She went to the kitchen, only to find Chester curled beneath the kitchen table, sound asleep. She decided to let him sleep.

Chris walked around to the passenger side and opened her door. "What happened to Chester?"

"He was sleeping under the table in the kitchen. I didn't have the heart to wake him."

"And I thought you were heartless."

Abby slid across the seat, still amazed that Chris didn't drive a BMW or something that denoted wealth. A Toyota Camry. She liked that about him. Chris was Chris.

"You're a jerk, you know that?" Abby teased.

"I've been called worse."

"Like what?" Abby asked, not really wanting to know, but she liked this light, silly banter between them. It was comfortable, like her Uggs. She laughed.

"You don't need to know." Chris reached across the console, searching for her hand. He found it and held it.

Abby didn't say a word. No way was she going to screw this up. She was way too comfortable.

Chapter 23

Loud banging on the front door sent Toots bolting upright in her bed. She fumbled around in the dark, searching for the switch to the lamp on her nightstand. She looked at the alarm clock. Almost three o'clock, the witching hour. More banging. Damn, someone was knocking—no, beating—on her front door. Not having a clue who would be paying a visit at this ungodly hour, Toots instantly thought of Abby. She practically levitated down the stairs.

"I'm coming, just a minute." Toots hurried to the front door, hoping and praying it wasn't Abby or someone coming to tell her Abby had been in an accident. She flicked the outside light on, then pushed the door aside.

"Hey, Mom. Did I wake you?" Abby said.

Toots stood aside, allowing her to enter. "Are you drunk?"

Abby called out to someone. "No, I'm not drunk, and if I were, I wouldn't be driving, and I sure as hell wouldn't be knocking on your door this time of night."

"Did you bring a friend?"

Chris appeared in the doorway.

"I'm not sure I even want to know why both of you are here. Neither of you look sick, so I guess we can rule that out. Mental illness, now there's a possibility. Let's go into the kitchen. I'll make a pot of coffee while you tell me what in the name of Pete you're doing here."

"Dang, Mom don't act so happy to see us," Abby said before poking her mother in the ribs.

"Stop it! You know how I hate when you do that." Toots yanked Abby's ponytail.

Chris pulled Toots next to him, gave her a kiss on the cheek. "I could use a cup of coffee. How about you, Abs?"

"I'd rather have tea, but coffee will do. Mom, would you stop staring at me like I'm some kind of psycho or something?"

"I'm sorry, Abby. I had a flashback of your father. He was a tea drinker, too. When you said that, it just reminds me of how much I miss him."

"Oh, Mom, I'm sorry. I didn't know."

"Doesn't matter. Now let me start a pot of coffee. I have a feeling I'm not going to like what you have come all this way at this insane hour to tell me." Toots scooped coffee into the paper filter, filled the back of the machine with water, then flipped on the switch.

The smell of coffee made Abby realize she was hungry. As usual, she'd made a bag of microwave popcorn for dinner. That had been hours ago. "Have anything good to munch on?" Abby asked as she opened the refrigerator.

"All we have are good things to munch on. With Mavis doing the cooking, all we get to eat is health food. I haven't had a good sugary bowl of Froot Loops in ages."

"Step aside, Abs, let me have a look-see. I'm starving. I had ice cream for dinner again."

"I ate popcorn. Again," Abby offered.

"You two are going to wither away if you don't eat right," Toots said. She was one to talk. When the coffee finished brewing, Toots poured three mugs and brought them to the table. "Abby, grab the cream and sugar while you're up. And bring that bottle of aspirin next to the coffee-maker with you. I have a killer headache."

Abby did as instructed. She had a plate of sliced cheese, strawberries, and a sliced orange. "This is a feast. Mavis needs to come and stay with me for a while. I'll let her cook for me anytime."

"She is one of the good ones, no doubt about it," Toots said affectionately.

Once they were settled at the table, Toots was the first to speak. "Now I want you to tell me why you both drove all the way out here." Toots eyed the two, then a bomb-shell thought almost knocked her brain loose. "Are you two seeing one another? Is that why you're here? You have an announcement to make? I've seen the way you look at each other."

Had there been a large sinkhole close by, Abby would have gladly taken a nosedive right into its center. Chris just laughed, but he didn't correct her.

"Mother, let's talk about the real reason we're here, okay?"

"I've pissed you off. You never call me 'Mother' unless you're mad."

Abby forged ahead, ignoring her mother's comment. "Remember when you asked me to check into Dr. Sameer's background in that e-mail you sent this morning?"

Toots nodded. "Of course, I'm not that far gone. At least not yet."

"You were right to be suspicious. Is your laptop handy?"

"It's upstairs, I'll get it." Toots left the room, returning minutes later with the computer. She turned it on, tapped a few keys to log on to the Internet. She turned the screen around so Abby could do whatever she needed to.

Abby pulled up the e-mail she'd received from her second-stringer and downloaded the attached file. When it was finished, she scrolled through the document until she found what she was looking for. "Here, look at this and tell me your thoughts." Abby positioned the computer so her mother could read it.

Toots had known there was something wrong with that weirdo! "I don't think this is the same man we know as Dr. Sameer. Ida needs to see this. She's having sex with him. This is not good. No, not good at all."

Toots raced up the stairs, leaving Abby and Chris to discuss Ida's sex life.

When Toots reached Ida's bedroom, she stopped outside the door. This was going to tear Ida up, but better now than later. She rapped on the door before pushing it open. Ida lay sprawled across the bed like a two-dollar drunk. They'd all had too many daiquiris that evening. Toots walked over to the bed, where Ida was cutting some major logs. She hated to disturb her, especially when she was snoring. She'd heard somewhere that waking people who snored was dangerous because they were in such a deep sleep, and it frightened them when they were startled awake. Toots didn't have a clue where she'd heard that, but thought it was another crock. She nudged Ida on her shoulder. She rolled over onto her side. Her mouth hung open like a treasure chest. "Ida, wake up."

She rolled over on her back, legs and arms spread out in the shape of an X. Toots nudged her again. "Ida, this is important. I need you to wake up."

"What the hell are you doing in here, Toots? Did Bing come back? What's wrong?" Sophie, who had heard the banging on the door and finally decided to investigate what was going on, was standing in the doorway.

Toots poked Ida again. "Ida, wake up. I know you can hear me. Your mouth hangs open when you're asleep, and you snore like the town drunk. And you're talking to me. I need you up on your feet. Your armpit hair is gray."

Sophie cackled. "And you're a drunk."

Toots laughed, whispering to Sophie, "She's gonna pay you back someday, and when she does, you better watch your ass." In a loud voice, Toots said, "Ida, we have some news concerning Dr. Sameer. If you don't open your eyes and get your skinny rear end out of bed, I'm going to send Sophie downstairs for a pitcher of ice water. Abby and Chris are downstairs waiting for you."

Ida sat up in the bed immediately. "Why didn't you tell me that when you came stomping into my room?"

"I didn't stomp. Now toss something over that see-through nightgown you're wearing and come downstairs. I'll make another pot of coffee."

"Brush your teeth, too," Sophie shot back.

"Sophie, don't you ever have anything nice to say?" Ida asked.

Sophie stopped in the doorway, considering Ida's words. After giving a whole two seconds of thought to the question, she replied, "No."

"We'll be waiting for you," Toots said.

When they got back to the kitchen, Toots made another pot of coffee while Abby and Chris gave Sophie the highlights of what they'd read.

"I told your mother I thought he was strange. Too nice. I always felt like he was undressing me with those beady eyes of his," Sophie said.

Ida chose that moment to make her grand entrance. She'd cleaned up fast and looked damned good, Toots thought.

"He wasn't undressing you, Sophie, most likely he just wanted your underwear." Ida stopped cold in her tracks when she realized what she had said. "I . . . I am joking of course. Abby, dear, why are you up so early? Chris?"

"Sit down, Ida. The kids have uncovered some information. I think you need to hear it."

Ida sat down as she had been told. "Listen, if this is about the $3 million, I've already contacted the bank. They said they would stop the transfer from going through, so I'm not out any money."

Toots, Sophie, Abby, and Chris stared at her for at least ten seconds.

"What? Why are you looking at me like that?" Ida glanced over her shoulder. "Is this what you wanted to tell me?"

Abby came around the other side of the table to sit next to Ida. "None of us knew about the money. That's not what we came to tell you, but knowing that just confirms our suspicions. Did Dr. Sameer ask you for money, or did you just give it to him?"

Ida started to cry, her shoulders shaking as she wept. Abby grabbed a napkin from the holder on the table. "Here. Now go ahead and cry, it'll be good for you. When you're ready, you can tell us what happened. We'll tell you what we know. If we have to, we'll take this to the police. Right, Chris?"

"If a crime has been committed, absolutely."

"He asked. Well, not really, I guess I offered it to him."

Abby smoothed the hair back from Ida's face. "Tell me exactly what you said when you 'offered' Dr. Sameer the money. Think you can remember the details?"

Ida blew her nose and nodded. "Sammy . . . I mean Dr. Sameer, whatever his name is, we were just talking one morning a few days ago. He seemed sad. He said the clinic was in trouble. Patients weren't as plentiful. He feared he would have to close. I didn't want to see all of his work go down the drain just because of his finances. I think I said I could help him, that I almost felt as though I owed my life to him after he cured me of that terrible germ disorder. He said he couldn't take my money, that he would go to a bank. I told him the offer was there if he wanted. Nothing was mentioned again until two nights ago." Ida blotted her eyes with the napkin.

"Go on, "Abby encouraged.

"I don't know if I can. I feel like such a fool." Ida closed her eyes, her hands trembled. "This is so embarrassing."

"Ida, look, you're not the first woman to be blindsided by a man," Sophie explained. "Walter was a royal jerk who drank his career away, and when that wasn't enough, he started using me for a punching bag. Right, Toots?"

"Yes, the old bastard, may he rot in hell."

Ida looked at Sophie, "I'm sorry. I never knew. Sophie, you could have told me. I would've helped you."

"I know you would, but I was too embarrassed. I was taken in by Walter the same as you were taken in by that so-called doctor. Different situations, but I was just as easily fooled. Don't be too hard on yourself."

"Thanks, Sophie. That means a lot coming from you. So do you want to hear the rest?"

Everyone nodded.

"Looking back, I can't believe how gullible I was. Sophie, Toots, you are right when you say I can't live without a man in my life. I don't know why, and it's something I am going to take the time to discover when all is said and done. I know that sounds childish, but it's the truth. So, Sammy, that was my pet name for him, would send his limousine driver Mohammed to pick me up late at night, then he'd bring me back in the morning. I've been sneaking out for months. When I asked you all to let me sleep late in the mornings, it wasn't because I wanted to enjoy wallowing in bed. I slipped out at night and needed the extra time in the mornings to recover from my nightly adventures, if you will.

"The day of our first public date, Sammy had said he wanted to ask me something. Being the silly, needy old woman that I am, I assumed he was going to ask me to marry him. When he came with Mohammed to pick me up, I thought we were going to a fancy restaurant, he would propose, and we would live happily ever after. We never made it to dinner. Sammy had arranged for Amala, the 'daughter' or whoever she is, to make dinner at his beach house. It was all very romantic. He'd set up a table on the deck, white linen tablecloth, a rose on each dinner plate. There was a bottle of Dom Pérignon chilling. I remember when I saw that, I felt disappointed because it was so . . . common. Isn't that tacky? Don't answer that. I know it is. One thing led to another. I wasn't in the greatest mood after seeing the champagne, but Sammy didn't seem to realize that, or if he did, he chose to ignore it. Now, I'm sure that's what he was doing. Then he smiled and said he had something to ask me. I perked up, thinking I still had what it takes to attract an accomplished man, someone at the top of his profession. I know, I know. So, instead of him proposing, he asked if my offer for the loan was still open. Not in those exact words, but close enough. I felt like a balloon that had lost all of its air. Of course, I had made the offer, and wanting to be a woman who kept her word, when he asked, I said of course. Three million dollars, he said. I felt used, I guess, so I ran out. Sammy found me and brought me back here.

"The next day was the day that Abby came over. Then, yesterday, he called me to apologize. I let him sweet-talk me into coming over to his place. I told him I would take a taxi. On the ride over, I called Russ, my personal account manager at the bank, and asked him to wire $3 million to an account. I didn't have all the banking information, but I assured Russ I would have it soon. Poor guy. I practically bit his head off when he asked why I needed such a large amount of money. I'll have to call him and apologize.

"When I arrived at his house, Sammy was waiting for me in the bedroom. I told him I had called the bank and made arrangements for the transfer. I asked him for his banking numbers. This is when the alarm bells should have gone off. He whipped a slip of paper out of his pocket so fast, I was a bit surprised, but I had said I would give him the money. The paper had all the information the bank would require. I called the bank, rattled off the numbers, no, no wait, that's not the exact way it happened. I told Sammy I would call the bank, and he stepped out of the room. I made the arrangements. Russ said it would take forty-eight hours for the transfer to go through.

"This is so humiliating."

"We don't need you to go into all the sordid details, Ida."

"You need to hear this. Abby, forgive me, but you are an adult. If I didn't think it appropriate, I wouldn't tell this. Part of me wants to scream with shame, and another part of me wants to laugh like a wild hyena. If this Sammy were an actor, this story would be wonderful for *The Informer.*

"Sammy left the room while I called the bank. After a bit of time had passed, I went through the house searching for him. There are four bedrooms in the house, but only two of them are being used. While I was searching I peeked in the two empty rooms. The first one was a small office. The second one had one of those blow-up mattresses with a cheap lamp sitting on a pile of stacked books. I thought it odd that a man of Sammy's caliber wouldn't have a better guest room. I closed the door and saw that the door to Amala's room was open. I was sure Sammy was in there, so I went to the room. Before I called out, or knocked, I peered inside the room." Ida took a deep breath. "Sammy was unaware that I was there watching him. I was horrified when I saw a pile of women's panties on the bed. He held a pair in his hand, and he . . . he was sniffing them."

Chapter 24

Sophie was dumbstruck. Toots looked like she'd been sucker punched in the gut. Abby's blue eyes were wide with shock. Chris shook his head in apparent disgust. Ida just sat there with tears running down her face.

"Can you believe how stupid I am? There's a bit more than that. Maybe someday when we're all bored with nothing to do, I'll finish that part of the story. So there you have it. Abby, what is it you want to tell me? It can't be as bad as what I've just told all of you."

"Maybe, not. Though I guess it depends on whom you ask. Mom, can I tell her what you asked me to do?"

"Of course," Toots said.

Abby still sat next to Ida, hoping just being near would offer her some comfort. "Mom asked me to check out Dr. Sameer. She said there was something about him that bothered her, but she didn't know exactly what it was. I had one of my second-stringers check his background. Dr. Sameer's credentials are impeccable. He's never even had so much as a speeding ticket. The man is close to sainthood if you ask me. As I was reading through his achievements, I saw the date he graduated from Harvard Medical School. The Dr. Sameer I received information on would be about forty-two years old. I Googled his name, got over a million hits. The Center for Mind and Body has a Web site, I started searching, and this is what I found. Mom, slide your computer down here."

Abby pulled up all the Web pages for the Center for Mind and Body. She showed Ida his picture and his staff. Then she scrolled down to the note to his patients. Abby read it, then let Ida read it.

Dr. Benjamin Sameer had been on sabbatical in India for the past five months.

Ida appeared to be in a daze, stunned. "How? And who is Sammy?"

"That's what we're going to find out," Chris said. "Do you think you can take the police or an investigator to his house without arousing any suspicion?"

"Heavens no! When I left there, I raced out of the house in tears. As I said, there is a bit more to the story, and I won't tell you all the nasty business, but, no, I can't go back to that house ever again. I can tell you the address, but that's it."

Chris went out on the deck and made a few phone calls, then came back inside. "I've called the police and gave them the gist of the story. They're going to try to locate Dr. Sameer. This could be worse than we know. If we can't locate the real doctor and his staff, your Sammy might be involved in something much more sinister than sniffing women's underwear and ripping off wealthy women."

"I think I'm going to go lie down. These past three days have taken their toll on me. Toots, if you need me, just knock on the door. I'm going to take another shower. I feel very dirty right now."

"Ida, whatever you do, don't you start washing your hands and all that other business. Sammy did help you overcome your OCD, remember that," Sophie said.

"It's not that kind of dirtiness that I feel, so don't worry.

Chris, if the police need to speak with me, tell them I will do whatever I can to help find that . . . that man."

"Before you go to bed, write down the address. If the police need anything else, I'll contact you myself."

Ida scribbled down the address of Sammy's beach house and gave it to Chris, then hugged Abby good-bye.

Upstairs, in the privacy of her own room, Ida broke down. What a complete and utter fool she was! Sixty-five years old, and she still hadn't learned anything where men were concerned. She could run a minimansion with a large staff, make wise investment decisions, and at one time she'd been a well-known photographer with her work on the cover of *Life* magazine. While her accomplishments weren't off the scale, they weren't anything to sneer at either.

As she'd told Toots, she felt dirty, but not in the germ sense. Dirty right down to her core. She turned the tap on and sprinkled something sweet-smelling in the water. She stripped off her clothes and took a long look in the mirror. Ida did not admire or like what she saw. There was a callousness to her face. Hard angles, cold and sharp, not soft and warm like Mavis. Her hatefulness and self-centered ways were starting to manifest themselves on her face, in her eyes, even her carriage. Ida turned away from the mirror, not liking what she saw on the outside and not liking how it made her feel on the inside.

She slid down into the warm, velvety water and leaned her head against the back of the tub. If Mavis could change, Ida figured she could, too. Mavis embraced life with such vigor that Ida wondered if she hurt. She was going to take her friends' advice and kick her "man habit." She would be nice instead of hateful, maybe a bit more cranky and ornery like Sophie.

Ida hoped the authorities found Sammy and that sleazy driver, Mohammed. They were connected, of that she had no doubt at all. Amala, too. And if the police didn't find them, she would hire the best private detectives in the country to do so.

Resolved to make some much-needed changes in her life, Ida closed her eyes and relaxed.

When Mavis heard all the commotion coming from the kitchen, she'd immediately thought of their "spiritual house-guests," as she privately thought of them. Hurrying down-stairs to check out the noise, her heart filled with love when she saw Abby. She raced over and wrapped her arms around her, kissed her on top of those wild blond curls, then the lateness, or earliness, of the hour dawned on her. "Abby, is something wrong?" Mavis looked around for Chester. When she didn't see him, she thought the worst. "Is Chester all right?"

Abby returned her dearest, sweetest godmother's hug. "Chester is fine. He was sleeping so peacefully under the kitchen table, I didn't want to disturb him."

"That's wonderful. Chris, you and Abby must be starv-ing. You both look a little wan. Can I make you something for breakfast?" Mavis asked pleasantly.

"Nothing for me, thanks. Chris and I sort of raided the refrigerator when we arrived. Mom, I think we need to tell Mavis why we're here."

Toots stepped up to the plate. "Of course we do. Mavis, this has been the most insane night. I never thought I'd say it, but poor Ida."

She went into detail about her suspicions and how she had asked Abby to check Dr. Sameer's background. It took her ten minutes to bring her up to date on where things stood.

"So there really isn't anything we can do until we hear from the police."

"This is almost as scary as the ghosts! No, I believe it's

worse. At least our ghosts seem . . . friendly. Where is Ida now?" Mavis asked.

Chris took Mavis aside before anyone could give her an answer as to Ida's whereabouts. "Did you say ghost? Ghosts?"

"Yes, of course. Abby hasn't told you?"

Chris looked at Abby and Toots. They each smiled at him, but it was a nervous, forced smile. He smiled back, even offered a little half wave.

"No, Abby forgot to mention the ghosts. Why don't you tell me more over a cup of coffee? I'm just dying to hear this story." As Chris led Mavis around the kitchen, he never once took his eye off Abby and Toots. He even mouthed "ghosts?" to them. They just sat there like two peas in a pod and smiled.

What a night, rather day, this was turning into. Chris couldn't wait to hear their explanation. Mavis poured him a cup of coffee as he continued to stare at Toots and Abby.

"Ghosts?" he mouthed again.

Mother and daughter nodded and continued to smile.

Chapter 25

Six weeks later . . .

Abby raced home as fast as traffic would allow. Tonight was the big night, as she'd dubbed it a few weeks ago. Tonight Abby would drive to Malibu to her mother's beach house, where Sophie would—she hated to use the word *perform*—but that's exactly what she would be doing, the first séance since Ida had confessed she'd been seeing a crotch-licking panty sniffer.

Abby laughed about it now, but at the time it hadn't been the least bit funny.

She whipped her bright yellow MINI Cooper through a right turn, then made a sharp left that led to her house in Brentwood. Chester stuck his head out of the partially opened window on the passenger side.

"Almost home, boy. But you already know that, don't you?" Abby reached over with her right hand and scratched his favorite spot, right above his tail.

"Woof! Woof!"

"You're welcome," Abby said. She and Chester communicated quite nicely, she thought, as she pulled into her carport. She cut the engine and reached over to the passenger seat, where she unhooked Chester's seat belt. Abby slid out of the driver's seat just in time to avoid being knocked over as the big German shepherd leaped out of the car and raced to the backyard, where he would sit for hours and watch the squirrels darting up and down tree trunks, in and out of the high grass. But he never chased them, never became aggressive toward them as most other dogs would have. Nope, not Chester. He just liked to watch them play.

Knowing it would be a while before it was time to leave for Malibu, Abby left Chester alone in the backyard to enjoy the squirrels. He was fenced in, so she didn't have to worry about his taking off, or anyone coming in. Inside the house, she stooped over to pick up her mail the postman pushed through the slot in her front door. She thumbed through four white envelopes, two pizza ads, and a wedding invitation from one of her best friends in Charleston. She used her fingernail to open the invitation. She looked at the date and made a mental note to mark it on her calendar.

In the kitchen, Abby admired the new granite countertops that she'd installed all by herself. It hadn't been easy, but she hadn't had to rush. It had taken two weeks of hard work, late nights, and lots of takeout. But the results were well worth it. She felt a sense of pride every time she looked at them, not only because they were spectacular to look at, even if she said so herself, but also because she hadn't hired outside help. She'd spent three Saturdays at a local hardware store learning exactly what she needed to do the job herself. Soon she was going to have her mother, the godmothers, and Chris over for dinner to reveal her new kitchen.

Tonight's event—no, *event* was her mother's word for a funeral—tonight's affair had been postponed several times for one reason or another. She'd called her mother that afternoon just to make sure they were still on. Abby felt giddy, but she was also a bit frightened. She'd never attended a séance, so it would be her first. Sophie told her what to expect or not. If, and Abby knew this was a very big if, something or someone were to show themselves, Abby planned to ask questions that only they would know the answer to. If she were lucky, she would have headlines for "News From Beyond," the new column she'd started two weeks ago. The response had been overwhelming. Her mysterious employer had sent her an e-mail telling her sales were up by 30 percent. This is what she liked to hear. And with this jump in sales, readership had increased, and Abby felt for the first time since she'd been at the helm that *The Informer* was giving the other two tabloids some healthy competition.

Life was good.

With plenty of time before the night's performance—she liked that word—Abby went into the master bathroom and turned the water on as hot as she could stand it in her new sunken tub. That was her favorite place to relax. She made sure to unplug the phone and turn off her cell phone before she slid into the hot, bubbly water. She left the back door open for Chester so she wouldn't have to jump out and let him in. She sank into the heavenly warmth, allowing the jets to massage her sore muscles. Had she not been driving, she would have had a glass of wine, maybe even lit a few of the scented candles she'd placed around the giant tub's perimeter. Tonight was just to relax for a short while before she left the house. Her mother had invited Chris, but she'd said he wasn't sure he would attend. He was extremely skeptical on the subject of ghosts, haunting, or anything paranormal. Abby understood. She felt that way about the law. She'd told him that over a romantic dinner two weeks ago. Things with Chris were nice right now. He called her when he could, and she sent him silly e-mails. For now this was enough for both of them. This was the calm before the storm. The spark, the electrical magnetism between them, was almost scary. He'd kissed her on the cheek after dinner, but that had been enough to send bolts of hot desire straight to her center. Just thinking about him turned her on. She wasn't ready to take their relationship to that level, but it was nice to fantasize. Abby always thought the anticipation was half the fun.

She soaked in the tub for another half hour before she washed her hair and shaved her legs. She wanted to look nice just in case Chris showed up, and for whatever spirit decided to make its presence known.

Abby wrapped a thick bath sheet around her body and a smaller one around her head to soak up the dampness in her thick hair, which took forever to blow-dry. She flicked her CD player on. Norah Jones crooned from the speakers. Abby went to her closet, not sure what to wear. She was just going to her mother's, so she didn't have to dress up, but still she wanted to look a little special. Just in case. She chose a pair of dark denim jeans and a white blouse with billowing sleeves. She'd wear a pair of flats just in case Chris showed up and he invited her for a stroll down the beach. Flats could be kicked off easily. She was way ahead of herself, but that was all the fun. Anticipation, she thought as she removed the towel from her head. With a wide-tooth comb, she attacked the mass of heavy curls. Thirty minutes later she'd tamed her hair into soft waves. She decided to wear a little bit of makeup, but not too much. She didn't want to appear overly done up, as Sophie called it. Pink blush, a light brown eyeliner, black mascara, and a touch of clear gloss on her lips. She looked in the mirror, studied her handiwork. Not too bad, she thought.

She put her towels in the clothes hamper and rinsed out the tub before going out back to bring Chester inside. "Dinnertime," she called out into the backyard. She heard Chester's paws as they smacked against the ground. It still amazed her that a single word had the power to bring him running. He bounded through the back door, heading straight for the kitchen. Abby scooped a hearty amount of kibble in his bowl, then added some leftover meat loaf to the mixture. She knew she shouldn't give him table food, but he liked it, and the vet said he was healthy as ever, so there!

While Chester crunched down his dinner, Abby went through the house locking doors, making sure the timers for the inside and outside lights were set to come on precisely at nine o'clock. When Chester finished, she rinsed out his bowl and dried it with paper towels. She took a handful of treats from his canister and stuffed them inside a plastic bag for later. She carried a bag full in the trunk of her car, but those were trunk treats only to be given in case of an emergency. With nothing left to do, she grabbed her purse, cell phone, and Chester's leash. "Come on, boy, we're going to a séance."

Chester looked at her and howled.

Chris debated whether or not he should show up for Toots's big séance. He didn't believe in the supernatural, whatever they were calling it these days, but he knew Abby would be there, and it wouldn't hurt to at least pretend to suspend his disbelief for one night.

So it looked like he was going to Malibu after all. He checked his watch. Toots said they would start the séance promptly at nine o'clock. It was already half past eight. He'd been on the beach and smelled like salt, wind, and sand. Ten minutes later he was showered, shaved, teeth brushed, and he'd even taken the time to comb his hair. Jeans, a navy polo shirt, and deck shoes. Pretty spiffy, he thought. He'd like to see someone get spiffed up as fast as he could, then he remembered Abby said she could get ready for the inauguration in thirty minutes or less. A no-frills girl, she'd said. He didn't care if it took her a week to decide what to wear; Chris was smitten and knew it and loved it. For the first time in forever, he was ass-kicking happy. He still had to take his floozy female clients out on the town, and he wanted to talk to Abby about that. He never knew when his face and that of the latest starlet would be splashed across the pages of movie magazines. He wanted to tell her that those were business dates, they weren't even dates. He knew she didn't like seeing women wrapped around him. Maybe it was time to switch gears, do something different. Something to think on, that was for sure. He had no great love for entertainment law. He'd wanted to be a farmer when he was a kid. Maybe he'd move, buy a bit of land, and try working it himself. That he had the option was enough to make him smile.

Yep, Chris old buddy, life is lookin' good.

Chapter 26

Sophie added two extra chairs around the old wooden table just in case Abby and Chris showed up for the séance. She was pretty confident Abby would, but she wasn't sure about Chris. He'd acted like they were crazy when she'd told him what they were doing and who had made their ghostly presences known.

Sophie didn't want to change too many things for fear it would scare their ghosts away. Was that weird or what? Scaring the ghosts away. It was usually the other way around. But not in this house. She'd kept the purple silk sheet as her tablecloth, and she still used the same glass. She'd purchased more candles, but other than that and adding the two chairs, Sophie was prepared to talk to dead people. If they would talk to her. She hoped like hell that something would show itself and, even better, that something would show on her new camera equipment. Then Abby could use the photos for *The Informer*. She wasn't sure if the grainy images she'd seen were of good enough quality to reproduce, let alone to enlarge and put on the front page.

"So are we all ready and set to go?" Toots asked as she entered the dark dining room. She hadn't touched a thing in the room since remodeling the rest of the house and didn't think she would. They were having too much fun.

"Yep, all that's missing are the ghosts. Toots, you imagine Abby and Chris think we're a bunch of crazy old women with too much time and money on their hands?"

Toots considered Sophie's question. "I don't think they do. Chris is very, very skeptical about the whole ghost thing. Abby likes this as much as we do. With her new column at the paper, I think we'll be having more séances than ever. This ghost thing has really been a hit with the readers. I would bet anything before all is said and done that *The Enquirer* and *The Globe* follow in our footsteps. I know Abby is excited when 'her boss' sends her e-mails telling her how well the paper is doing. I think Abby likes being the editor in chief. I haven't heard her complaining about not being out on the streets chasing stars. I think this is her niche. What about it, Sophie, what do you think?"

"You don't want to know. I have crazy thoughts about everything these days. Nothing that would scare anyone. Seriously, I think this new twist with the ghosts is going to be an even bigger hit. There are so many new television programs now, I can't keep up with them. This happened at just the right time for Abby. She walks around with a glow on her face lately, have you noticed?"

"Yes, of course I've noticed, I'm her mother, for God's sake."

"Well I am her godmother!" Sophie shot back.

"That glow you're talking about isn't from writing stories about ghostly encounters. I think she and Chris are in love with one another."

Sophie shot a big, toothy grin. "I think so, too, and I think it's fantastic! What about you, Toots? Are you okay with Abby and Chris if something were to come of their attraction, whatever you want to call it? I know you loved Chris's father, and I also know that you are a wonderful mom to Abby, and Chris thinks you're the cream of the crop, too. I've heard him refer to you as his mom when he's talking on the phone. I guess what I want to know is if you're okay if Abby decided to marry your stepson?"

"That's always been one of the things I admire about you, Soph. You're so damn honest, cut straight through the flesh and dive right to the bone. To answer your question, yes. I would like nothing more than to see them become a couple. Garland, Chris's father, and I talked about it on more than one occasion before he died. He would've liked seeing them together, too. Chris is as handsome as his father, don't you think?" Toots asked. She sometimes got all teary-eyed when she talked about the husbands she'd actually loved. Garland had been second-best, right behind Abby's father, John Simpson.

"I agree. Both are fine-looking specimens. Sure as hell looked better than that old warthead Walter. Toots, can I ask you a question?"

"You will anyway, so why would you ask if you can ask a question?"

"You're an old whining bitch, Toots, but I love you anyway. Today."

"Ask the question, Sophie," Toots insisted.

"Did you ever suspect Walter was using me as a punching bag before you came to New York and saw it firsthand?"

Toots drew a deep breath. "Let's go out on the deck and have a cigarette before we get started."

"I'm game," Sophie said before charging out to the deck.

They smoked so much Toots had installed a small freezer where she kept at least twenty cartons of cigarettes on hand at all times. They sat in their favorite chairs, getting comfy before lighting up. After they'd sucked in a few good doses of the deadly toxins, Toots spoke up. "I had my suspicions, but I'd never seen him hit you. I always thought you would leave him if he got too rough. What about that doctor you worked for? Did you two have something going on?"

Sophie took a puff off her cig, blew the smoke out the corner of her mouth. "No, but I wish I had. He was good to me. He knew what an asshole Walter was, but, like you, he figured that if I was getting the daylights beat out of me, I would leave. I took my marriage vows seriously. It was the Catholic thing beaten into me by my parents. So I stuck it out till death did us part! The old son of a bitch. I hope Satan is torching his ass every day. Let's stop talking about Walter. It will ruin my night. Toss me another cigarette."

"It's almost nine o'clock; we'd better get Ida and Mavis and get started," Toots said.

"All right. I guess I can live without another cigarette for a few hours."

Sophie and Toots went inside, where they found Ida and Mavis in the kitchen. Ida was making coffee, and Mavis was slicing a tray of raw vegetables and, of course, fruit.

"You two about ready to get this séance started?" Sophie asked. "I am going to check one more time to make sure I didn't forget anything." She flew out of the kitchen like a witch on her broom.

A loud knock on the front door, then, "Mom, you guys didn't start without me, did you?"

"Abby, come on back, we're in the kitchen. We were waiting for you and Chris."

"He didn't come with me," Abby said.

Toots looked around. "He isn't with you? I thought for sure the two of you would ride together."

"No, I haven't mentioned this to him. I think he's a little on the unbelievers' side."

"This isn't for everyone," Toots said to Abby, though she could clearly see the disappointment in her daughter's face.

"That's cool. I don't care. So what are we waiting for? I've been hoping I would make contact with a major star from way back when. I would love to have something mind-blowing to put on the front page of *The Informer*."

"Never say never," her mother said.

"Ida and Mavis, whenever you are ready, just meet us in the séance room," Toots said

"The séance room?"

"That's what Sophie and I are calling it now. That is what we do in there."

A loud knock on the front door startled both Abby and her mother. Abby hurried to the front door. "Chris! Hi. Mom and I didn't think you'd make it," Abby said.

Toots heard the joy in Abby's voice at the sight of Chris.

"I debated, but I couldn't convince myself to pass up an opportunity to spend an evening with my two favorite ladies in the world. So if I have to hang out with a ghost or two, I'm willing to do that."

"Well, then what are we waiting for?" Toots said.

Abby, Chris, and Toots entered the old dining room, where Sophie was lighting candles. Ida and Mavis were placing them around the room so they wouldn't be in total darkness. Once that was complete, Sophie asked everyone to take their usual places around the table.

"Chris, Abby, you can sit here." Sophie pointed to two chairs side by side and to her right. "Because neither of you have attended a séance before, I'd like to take a minute to explain a few things, but you both must promise not to laugh."

"Cross my heart," Abby said.

Chris gave the Boy Scout sign. "I swear on the Boy Scout handbook."

"That's good enough. Everybody get seated while I explain the procedure."

Abby and Chris found their seats. Ida and Mavis took their usual chairs. Toots was the last to be seated.

Sophie took her seat center stage, or rather, center table. "First, I want to explain exactly what a séance is. A séance is the coming together of a number of people for the purpose of seeking to communicate with those who are no longer of this world. People who attend séances should as far as possible be of opposite temperaments. I think we can agree we meet that criterion. Of course, we must all have an open mind so that a phenomenon can occur. Successful séances require never fewer than three people and no more than twelve. Is everyone following me? In my studies the past few days, I've learned that it's best to go through what the proper conditions are for a successful séance. If I bore you, just bear with me.

"Subdued lighting is best, hence the candles. Abby, Chris, if either of you plans to attend another séance, we always use the same seats. We should all lay our hands on the table with our palms down. They say that wood when charged becomes a conductor, so it's not really necessary to hold hands. I like to think the spirits see us united with the same goal, so I think it's good to hold one another's hands."

"Hey, I like that idea, too," Chris said, then reached for Abby's hand.

They all laughed.

"They say it's best not to have any fruits or flowers in the room unless the flowers are fresh. I personally don't think this matters one way or the other."

"Chris, Abby, do either one of you have any questions so far?" Sophie asked.

"Nothing yet," Abby said. Chris nodded.

"I usually open the séance with a prayer of sorts, then we ask if there is anyone who would like to make contact with us. That's about it, so you kids still game?" Sophie asked, grinning. "If you think you won't be frightened, you may want to rethink that. Right, girls?"

"Absolutely," Toots said.

"Well, I hope we can make contact with someone. I'm more excited than afraid. So I'm ready when you all are," Abby said, then looked at Chris. "You're okay with this?"

"I wouldn't be here if I wasn't, so I say let's get this show on the road."

"One more thing. I take this seriously, try not to crack too many smart-ass comments."

"Well, I think that's almost a miracle," Ida said.

"Kiss my ass," Sophie said. "Now let's get started. Let's all join hands."

They all joined hands, forming a circle around the table. "Everyone relax. Think of a person you would like to make contact with. It doesn't have to be anyone you knew personally."

Sophie allowed the room to capture the silence and tranquillity, the wishes and desires, of the others. Well, maybe not Chris's and Abby's desires.

"Everyone take a deep breath and relax, open your minds and hearts to the possibilities of another dimension, another plane where lost souls are trapped. If there is a spirit in this room that would like to make its presence known, we are here to help you. Let's all place the tips of our fingers against the water glass in the center of the table. This is our means of communicating with the spirits."

They all unlocked their hands and each touched the glass with the tips of their fingers.

"If there is someone in this room that would like to communicate with us, move the glass to my right for yes and to my left for no."

Their eyes were glued to the glass. When nothing happened, Sophie repeated her words. "No one in the room means any harm. We want to help you, to understand you.

If you understand this message, move the glass to the right for yes and to the left for no."

Again, they waited. After several seconds had passed, the water glass moved ever so slowly to the right. Sophie heard several intakes of breath. "You understand us. Are you a male or female? Move the glass to my right if you are female, to my left if you are a male."

Sophie cast a glance at Chris and Abby. They were mesmerized.

The glass slowly moved to the left. "You are male."

"Is there someone in the room that you have a message for? To the right if your answer is yes, and to the left if your answer is no." The glass slowly moved to the right.

Everyone took a deep breath when they saw the answer.

"Can you move the glass in front of the person you wish to give a message to?"

They waited for a few minutes and nothing. Sophie was about to ask another question when the glass glided over to rest in front of Toots.

"Oh," Toots whispered.

Sophie continued with her questions. "Were you married to this woman? If so, roll the glass side to side. If you were not married to her, do not move the glass."

All eyes were focused on the glass. When several minutes passed, and there was no movement, Toots's relief was palpable.

"You were not married to this woman." Sophie liked to confirm the message for those in the room and for those not in the room.

"Do you have a message for anyone in this room? Move the glass to the right if your answer is yes and to the left if your answer is no."

The glass rolled so fast to the right but stopped as quickly as it started.

"You are angry with someone?"

Again the glass rolled to the right.

"Is the person you are angry with in this room with us now as a living, breathing human being?"

The glass rolled to the left.

Sophie was so into this, she didn't have the least bit of fear. She couldn't speak for the others, but they didn't look as though they were ready to jump up and leave.

"Can you materialize so we can identify you?"

The glass rolled to the right.

They all let out loud gasps.

"Shhh, it's nothing to be frightened of. Let's put our hands palm down on the table."

"Show yourself."

The dining room suddenly became icy cold, the candles flickered. A cloud of fog appeared. It drifted close to the table. A man's face began to form. Pale features, the fog whirled around like a small tornado, then stopped as fast as it started. The cloud hovered above the table, where all eyes were directed on the face of none other than Bing Crosby.

Sophie was so excited, she almost allowed herself to lose control.

"You are Bing Crosby."

The face actually smiled.

No one said a word. This was a true phenomenon. A paranormal masterpiece.

"Do you have a message for anyone in the room?" Sophie said.

The cloud floated over to Toots, stopping. Sophie was at a loss. What did Bing Crosby want to tell Toots? The chill in the room was so sharp, it was hurting Sophie's skin. She wasn't sure what to do but knew if she didn't gain control, she would lose the spirit.

"Sophie, I think I might know the connection," Toots whispered.

"What?"

The cloud continued to hover above Toots.

"Aaron Spelling's house. The land it was built on was the former home of Bing. Spelling demolished the Crosby estate to build his mansion."

Suddenly the cloud began to whirl around the room. The flames on the candles blew out, then they crashed to the floor. Sophie's hands were shaking so badly, she had to sit on them. As fast as it started, it stopped.

No one moved or said a word. They had all just witnessed an event which, had they not seen it with their own eyes, none of them would have believed possible.

Sophie was about to tell them to relax and vacate the room when another mistlike cloud began its foggy manifestation. The room became even colder if that were possible.

The mist floated around the room as though it had a mind of its own. Sophie didn't speak, as she didn't want to risk losing it.

Just as before, the cloud floated around the room, stopping in front of Abby. She drew in a deep breath, then slowly released it. She stared into the mist as a face began to form, again, just as before, only this time it was the face of a female. Pale skin and bloodred lips formed inside the fog. Blond hair in a style suited to the sixties materialized.

All eyes in the room were focused on the image in the foggy mist hovering above Abby's head. There was no mistaking the woman's face as she slowly smiled, a smile unlike any other.

It was the face of Marilyn Monroe.

No one made a sound. Breathing was barely heard. This was out of Sophie's league.

The face turned to Abby, as though she knew her. Abby looked into the face of one of the most famous Hollywood actresses of all time. No one moved a muscle. Abby gazed back at the famous movie star, whose death remained a mystery to that very day.

Abby gazed at the red lips as they slowly moved. It was impossible not to believe that the spirit wanted to give her a message from beyond the grave.

Abby's hands shook, but she never took her eyes off the mysterious movie star.

The room got even colder as the mist with Marilyn Monroe's face moved closer to Abby.

Abby gazed into the eyes of the dead star. The red lips mouthed slowly as though she wanted to make sure her message was understood.

"My death was an accident."

The room became so cold, Sophie feared it would ice over.

The cloudlike mist began to whirl around, just as before, but nothing fell or moved. As though swept up in a vacuum, the mist disappeared as fast as it had come.

No one moved. No one spoke. There were no words to convey what they had just witnessed. There was one possible reason for this supernatural event, and they all knew what it was, though none had put it into words.

Abby Simpson had just been given the exclusive of her—or anyone else's—lifetime.

Chapter 27

An hour later, they all gathered around the kitchen table. They weren't very chatty, as none of them could quite believe what they had just witnessed. A paranormal phenomenon.

"Toots, make a pot of coffee. No, scratch that. We all need a stiff drink. Agreed?"

"I'll blow my diet for whatever is the strongest drink in the liquor cabinet," Ida said.

"I can't drink anything. I have to drive home. I want to keep a clear head so I can recall everything that just happened. Sophie, can you let me look at those tapes before I leave?" Abby asked.

"Yes, I was going to suggest we do that. Let me get the equipment. Toots, we'll need your laptop to view the recordings. I'll only be a minute," Sophie said.

"Chris, you haven't said much. Are you okay? I mean, none of us are *okay* okay. We've witnessed something pretty scary." Abby was concerned about Chris, since he'd been too quiet since they left the séance room.

"Yeah, I'm okay. I'm just having a tough time with this because it defies everything I've ever believed in. My belief system just . . . I don't know, got a dose of reality? Another dimension? I'm an attorney. We deal in facts. And I can tell you what happened in that room was anything but factual."

"Ida, you haven't said much," Abby observed. "What are your thoughts?"

"I have had to deal with so much in the past few weeks, this is just one more thing I have to cope with. I can't fathom this actually happening in my everyday life, yet I know it did because I saw it with my very own eyes. I guess we're all still shocked. I'm not sure what I think."

"I agree with Ida," Mavis said. "This is just too strange for me. I'm just an old Maine girl. Ghosts and spirits don't scare me, and I do believe they exist. If I didn't before, I certainly do now."

Toots returned to the room with the laptop and a bottle of scotch tucked under her arm at the precise moment that Sophie returned with the equipment. Sophie made fast work of setting up the laptop so they all could view the tapes. When she finished, she placed the computers at the end of the kitchen table.

"Let's move our chairs around so we can all see this together. This is some of the same equipment they use on *Ghost Trackers*. so it's top-of-the-line. I'll sit next to the computer in case there are any glitches."

Toots poured six shots of scotch. "Anyone need a drink, help yourself."

Toots tossed back the scotch like a pro.

"I'll have one of those," Ida said. "Mavis, too."

Toots slid two glasses across the table like she'd seen them do in the old Westerns. "Sophie, you want one?"

"Not yet, let me watch this first. I do want a cigarette, though."

Toots stepped out to the deck and grabbed a pack of smokes and a lighter. One of her house rules, and she didn't have many, was no smoking in the house. She was about to break her own rule. If ever there was a time to do it, this had to be it. She lit two cigarettes and brought them into the house.

"Sophie, this is a one-time deal, okay?"

"Sure." Sophie took the cigarette and drew on the filter-tipped end so hard that her cheeks looked like someone had squeezed them together. She did this two more times, then gave the cigarette back to Toots. "That'll hold me for a while, I want to watch this. Can everyone see the screen?"

They all nodded. Toots stood behind her so as not to blow cigarette smoke at the others at the end of the table.

Sophie made a few quick strokes across the keyboard, then the séance room filled the screen. Each of them leaned as close to the screen as possible, hoping that what they'd witnessed in that room had been captured by Sophie's high-tech gizmo.

The images on the screen were of them seated around the table. The expressions on their faces were somber. Sophie's voice filled the room as she'd explained to Abby and Chris a few rules and things that might or might not happen. This was all caught on tape as the angle of the camera's lens was focused directly on the table. Like a surveillance camera, Sophie had set hers to scan the table in three-minute increments. This happened three times. They watched the glass roll to the right, then to the left, then roll across the table in front of Toots.

When it should've shown the puffs of mist with the face of Bing Crosby, the camera caught nothing except the look of shock and surprise on their faces. Sophie looked crestfallen when they all sighed in disappointment. Now they knew the mist with the face of Marilyn Monroe wasn't likely to appear on the screen either. Sophie continued to monitor the computer. All eyes were fixed on the screen, hoping against hope for an image to appear, but nothing happened.

Abby's facial expression went from apprehension to shock.

That must have been when the image of Marilyn Monroe appeared. They continued to stare at the computer screen, but other than their shocked expressions and the glass rolling across the purple sheet, nothing else appeared on-screen.

"Shit," Sophie said, as her fingers started dancing across the keyboard. "I'll save this, but we're going to have a hard time convincing anyone that glass moved on its own." She was about to cut the image when Abby saw something on the screen. "Stop! Can you rewind that a millimeter? I think I saw something."

"Sure," Sophie said. She used her finger as the mouse controller. She reversed the images on the screen by running her hand along the touch pad. When she was close to the clip where Abby asked her to stop, she touched a few keys, and they waited.

"There! Stop, go back two seconds," Abby said.

Again Sophie did as Abby asked. She hit the keys to continue playing when she saw it, too. "I'll be a son of a gun, look at this. All of you come closer."

They all gathered around the monitor as close as they could without bumping heads. Sophie did her keyboard dance for the third time, but this time she knew approximately where to stop, as she'd seen something, too.

"There, look."

One by one they took turns leaning as close to the monitor as possible. When they saw what Abby had pointed out, they observed the image, then stepped back for the next one to see. When they'd all viewed the image, they returned to their chairs.

As Sophie was the resident séance guru with the knowledge to set up, monitor, and operate the high-tech gadgets, she was officially in charge of the evening's discovery.

"One by one I want you all to tell me what you saw. I want to make sure we're all on the same page. Abby, since you were the first to see this, I want you to wait until the others tell us what they saw."

"Sure," Abby said.

"I'm sure I saw an image of Marilyn Monroe's lips moving when she said, 'It was an accident,' " Toots said.

"The same here," Ida said.

"As much as I hate to admit it, I saw that, too," Chris said.

"Same for me," Mavis said.

"Is this what you saw, Abby?" Sophie asked.

"Yes."

"Well, I saw it, too," Sophie said. "I can cut out that scene, and take snapshots, too. A program I have allows you to do that. I'll need a high-tech computer."

"We have them at the paper. The new owners haven't skimped. I've got the best that money can buy. Sophie, how soon can we have this?"

"How soon do you want it?"

"Yesterday, but tomorrow is fine. I've got an idea; I'm not sure it will work, but if it does, *The Informer* has just been given the mother of all interviews."

"You mean to say you're going to use this in the paper?" Chris asked incredulously.

"That's exactly what I'm going to do. Doesn't it strike you as odd that this Marilyn Monroe apparition stopped right in front of me? Who better to tell than a tabloid reporter? She had to know this. Don't ask me how; I'll leave that to the Big Man Upstairs. I think she wants this told. All the unanswered questions about her death will be resolved."

"Abs, this is stuff for the sleaziest of tabloids. Do you really believe your readers will believe this? Won't they put a story like this against, 'Hey, I saw Elvis eating at Dunkin' Donuts'?" Chris asked.

"Oh, sure they will. Don't you see? You've just clarified

the concept of tabloid reporting. People are intrigued. They buy the paper. They don't have to believe, but there's a chance they will," Abby said, excitement shining in her clear blue eyes, then her eyes changed from clear blue to stormy dark as the sea when she realized what Chris had said.

"I still don't get it. Why do you want to write about something that most people won't believe, or will laugh at? I can't tell you how many times I've been standing in line at Ralph's watching people's reactions as they stand in line reading the headlines on those silly papers. They laugh, make some crude comment, and most don't bother to buy the paper because they've already seen the headlines and they're so far-fetched, they don't waste their money."

"Chris Clay, you are an ass. You have just insulted me, my profession, and my mother's and my godmothers' choice of reading material. You're a real know-it-all. Damn, I wish I knew as much as you did. It must be hard work dragging those third-rate actresses out to all the hot spots you take them to in hopes that they'll be spotted by *Entertainment Weekly*, *Us*, or any other magazine that considers what some two-bit wannabe has for dinner as news! Seems to me we're pushing the same envelope, just in different colors."

"I'm sorry, Abby. I was out of line," Chris said, his voice full of regret.

"Tough, I don't accept your apology. Leave before I decide to scratch your eyes out. That won't look good in all those magazines that you spend so much time trying to get your clients' photographs in. Go home." Abby stepped outside to the deck. She didn't want to look at Chris Clay, let alone stay in the same room with him. Once an ass always an ass. She should've known better.

She heard his footsteps as he walked across the deck. "I know you don't want to hear this again, but I really am sorry, Abs. I'm very good at sticking my foot in my mouth."

"Yeah, well I'm real good at sticking my foot up some-one's ass. Go home, Chris."

"You're right, it's time to call it a night. See you around, Abby."

Abby stayed on the deck until she heard Chris's car drive away, then she stepped inside, where her mother and god-mothers were all seated at the kitchen table staring at her like she had a third eye in the center of her head.

"Don't say anything. I don't want to hear it. I'm ex-hausted after tonight."

"I wasn't going to say anything, Abby. I am in complete agreement with you. I think your idea to publish what we all know was asked of you is the right decision. I do think you shouldn't be so hard on Chris. You know how lawyers are? They say the first thing that comes to mind without regard for anyone's feelings. You should call him and ask him to dinner."

"Thanks, Mom. I feel this was almost a divine experi-ence. It's going to put *The Informer* on top. What about the Bing Crosby and Aaron Spelling story? And I am going to ignore what you said about inviting Chris to dinner."

Toots nodded. "Whatever you say, dear."

"Well, I would put that in next week's edition, don't know if it's front-page news, but this is what you do, Abby. And I for one am damn proud of you." Sophie gave her a kiss and a quick hug. "I'll come to the paper first thing in the morn-ing so we can work on that photograph. You know what I'm thinking, Abby, we might need to bring Ida along. We could use her expertise."

"I think it's a grand idea," Abby said. "Would you come with us, Ida?"

"I'd consider it an honor. But you all have to make me a promise first." Ida cleared her throat. "All that stuff that happened with that imposter Dr. Sameer, Patel, a.k.a. panty sniffer, and Mohammed, the drug king who got beaten to within an inch of his life, is going to be in the news, since the real Dr. Sameer pressed charges against them. I can't forget Amala, the hooker, either. I know I will have to testify against them. Toots, Sophie, Mavis, and you, too, Abby, let's all take a vacation after my face is splashed all over the country. I have a feeling this is going to be one of those trials that Nancy Grace will cover, and I don't think I can bear to be the object of her sly innuendo as she 'sympathizes' with me as one of the aggrieved victims of their plot to steal millions of dollars. Would you all do that for me? Mavis, you can ask George to come along if you're still seeing him. What do you say? Oh and the trip is on me. I've got an extra $3 million burning a hole in my pocket. Deal?"

One by one they placed their hands one on top of the other. Ida, then Sophie and Mavis, then Toots.

"Come on, Abby, it's time you learned about our secret handshake."

"What secret handshake?"

"Toots, you mean to tell me you haven't told Abby about our secret handshake?"

"Why don't you tell her, Sophie?"

"I'll do better than tell her, I will show her. Join us, Abby, in your first official secret handshake."

Abby placed her hands atop those of four of the most fantastic women she would ever know.

"On the count of three," Toots said. "One . . . two . . . three . . ."

Just like they had in seventh grade all those years ago, the four best friends, now five, tossed their hands high in the air.

Together, four of them shouted, "Damn, when you're good, you're good!" Abby's echoing shout was a beat behind.

Epilogue

Ghostly Encounters
Abby Simpson

When it comes to the ghost of Marilyn Monroe, she's been around. It is believed that her ghost travels through Hollywood, haunting many locations, places she once felt quite comfortable visiting while she lived.

Many believe she haunts the site of her burial at the Westwood Memorial Cemetery here in Los Angeles. Her ghost has been seen floating around her tomb, waving at other Hollywood stars whose ghosts live among us.

After her tragic death in August 1962, many speculated her death was a suicide, but there are those who believe there was a conspiracy against her. Some even believe that one or more former members of the Kennedy family might have contributed to her untimely death.

The Informer attended a private séance, where Marilyn herself appeared, smiling her famous smile . . . but she had a message she has asked me to share with the world. . . . I am honored that she chose me to deliver her message through *The Informer*. . . . We are proud to share the ghost of Marilyn Monroe's words over her untimely death. . . . And I quote, "My death was an accident."

See photos below.